'There is never a dull moment . . .'
THE GUARDIAN ONLINE

Anyone looking for 'the next *Hunger Games*' would
do well to get lost in Dashner's maze.
THE TELEGRAPH

[A] mysterious survival saga that passionate fans describe as a
fusion of *Lord of the Flies*, *The Hunger Games* and *Lost*.
EW.COM

. . . gripping and fast-paced . . . I found myself holding my
breath . . . If you are looking for a new dystopian world to enter,
then this book is definitely for you.
SERENDIPITY REVIEWS

This is simply one of the best books I've read so far this
year – in fact scrap that – ever and is highly recommended to
dystopian fans . . . an action-packed brilliant book.
JESS HEARTS BOOKS

. . . it really is genius and definitely makes you
want to pick up the sequel.
BOOKS, BISCUITS & TEA

Dashner has created a terrifying and claustrophobic
little world . . . fast-paced and full of twists and turns that
are bound to keep you guessing.
REFLECTIONS OF A BOOKWORM

. . . fast-paced and has plenty of action . . .
kept me guessing until the end.
FANTASY BOOK REVIEW

. . . thrilling beyond belief and full of twists and turns that will
keep you gripped from start to finish.
BLOGS OF A BOOKAHOLIC

The Maze Runner will certainly be a hit with fans of the
dystopian genre . . . this book is a winner!
THE BOOKETTE

A MESSAGE FROM CHICKEN HOUSE

I've always been fascinated by 'origin stories' – HOW the heroes got to where they were, and what happened along the way. So when James announced that THE FEVER CODE was to tell the story of how the Maze came to be, I couldn't wait to find out how it all began. Long-since-dead characters are back and even better than we remembered – and so are the thrills, shocks and nail-biting twists. As usual, Mr Dashner had me reading well into the night . . .

BARRY CUNNINGHAM
Publisher
Chicken House

MAZE RUNNER
——— THE ———

FEVER CODE

JAMES DASHNER

2 Palmer Street, Frome, Somerset BA11 1DS
chickenhousebooks.com

Text © James Dashner 2016

First published in the United States by Delacorte Press, an imprint of Random House Children's Books, a division of Penguin Random House LLC, New York.

First published in Great Britain in 2016
Chicken House
2 Palmer Street
Frome, Somerset BA11 1DS
United Kingdom
www.chickenhousebooks.com

Cover design by Helen Crawford-White
Cover illustration by Paul Young
Interior design by Scholastic UK
Typeset by Dorchester Typesetting Group Ltd
Printed and bound in Great Britain by CPI Group (UK) Ltd, Croydon CR0 4YY

The paper used in this Chicken House book is made from wood grown in sustainable forests.

1 3 5 7 9 10 8 6 4 2

British Library Cataloguing in Publication data available.

HB ISBN 978-1-910655-16-0
Waterstones edition ISBN 978-1-911077-70-1

For all the die-hard *Maze Runner* fans.
You're crazy and full of passion and I love you.

BOOKS BY JAMES DASHNER

The Maze Runner Series
The Maze Runner
The Scorch Trials
The Death Cure
The Kill Order
The Fever Code

The Mortality Doctrine Series
The Eye of Minds
The Rule of Thoughts
The Game of Lives

The 13th Reality Series
The Journal of Curious Letters
The Hunt for Dark Infinity
The Blade of Shattered Hope
The Void of Mist and Thunder

PROLOGUE

NEWT

It snowed the day they killed the boy's parents.

An accident, they said much later, but he was there when it happened and knew it was no accident.

The snow came before they did, almost like a cold white omen, falling from the grey sky.

He could remember how confusing it was. The sweltering heat had brutalized their city for months that stretched into years, an infinite line of days filled with sweat and pain and hunger. He and his family survived. Hopeful mornings devolved into afternoons of scavenging for food, of loud fights and terrifying noises. Then evenings of numbness from the long hot days. He would sit with his family and watch the light fade from the sky and the world slowly disappear before his eyes, wondering if it would reappear with the dawn.

Sometimes the crazies came, indifferent to day or night. But his family didn't speak of them. Not his mother, not his father; certainly not him. It felt as if admitting their existence aloud might summon them, like an incantation calling forth devils.

Only Lizzy, two years younger but twice as brave, had the guts to talk about the crazies, as if she were the only one smart enough to see superstition for nonsense.

And she was just a little kid.

The boy knew he should be the one with courage; he should be the one comforting his little sister. *Don't you worry, Lizzy. The basement is locked up tight; the lights are off. The bad people won't even know we're here.* But he always found himself speechless. He'd hug her hard, squeezing her like his own personal teddy bear for comfort. And every time, *she'd* pat *him* on the back. He loved her so much it made his heart hurt. He'd squeeze her tighter, silently swearing he'd never let the crazies hurt her, looking forward to feeling the flat of her palm thumping him between his shoulder blades.

Often, they fell asleep that way, curled up in the corner of the basement, on top of the old mattress his dad had dragged down the stairs. Their mother always put a blanket over them, despite the heat – her own rebellious act against the Flare, which had ruined everything.

That morning, they awoke to a sight of wonder. 'Kids!'

It was his mother's voice. He'd been dreaming, something about a football match, the ball spinning across the green grass of the pitch, heading for an open goal in an empty stadium.

'Kids! Wake up! Come see!'

He opened his eyes, saw his mother looking out the small window, the only one in the basement room. She'd removed the board his dad had nailed there the night before, like he did every evening at sunset. A soft grey light shone down on his mother's face, revealing eyes full of bright awe. And a smile like he hadn't seen in a very long time lit her even brighter.

'What's going on?' he mumbled, climbing to his feet. Lizzy rubbed her eyes, yawned, then followed him to where Mum gazed into the daylight.

He could remember several things about that moment. As

he looked out, squinting as his eyes adjusted, his father still snored like a beast. The street was empty of crazies, and clouds covered the sky, a rarity these days. He froze when he saw the white flakes. They fell from the greyness, swirling and dancing, defying gravity and flitting up before floating back down again.

Snow.

Snow.

'What the bloody hell?' he mumbled under his breath, a phrase he'd learned from his father.

'How can it snow, Mummy?' Lizzy asked, her eyes drained of sleep and filled with a joy that pinched his heart. He reached down and tugged on her braid, hoping she knew just how much she made his miserable life worth living.

'Oh, you know,' Mum replied, 'all those things the people say. The whole weather system of the world is shot to bits, thanks to the Flares. Let's just enjoy it, shall we? It's quite extraordinary, don't you think?'

Lizzy responded with a happy sigh.

He watched, wondering if he'd ever see such a thing again. The flakes drifted, eventually touching down and melting as soon as they met the pavement. Wet freckles dotted the windowpane.

They stood like that, watching the world outside, until shadows crossed the space at the top of the window. They were gone as soon as they appeared. The boy craned his neck to catch a glimpse of who or what had passed, but looked too late. A few seconds later, a heavy pounding came on the front door above. His father was on his feet before the sound ended, suddenly wide-awake and alert.

'Did you see anyone?' Dad asked, his voice a bit croaky. Mum's face had lost the glee from moments earlier, replaced with the more familiar creases of concern and worry.

'Just a shadow. Do we answer?'

'No,' Dad responded. 'We most certainly do not. Pray they go away, whoever it is.'

'They might break in,' Mum whispered. 'I know I would. They might think it's abandoned, maybe a bit of canned food left behind.'

Dad looked at her for a long time, his mind working as the silence ticked by. Then, *boom, boom, boom*. The hard cracks on the door shook the entire house, as if their visitors had brought along a battering ram.

'Stay here,' Dad said carefully. 'Stay with the children.'

Mum started to speak but stopped, looking down at her daughter and son, her priorities obvious. She pulled them into a hug, as if her arms could protect them, and the boy let the warmth of her body soothe him. He held her tight as Dad quietly made his way up the stairs, the floor above creaking as he moved towards the front door. Then silence.

The air grew heavy, pressing down. Lizzy reached over and took her brother's hand. Finally he found words of comfort and poured them out to her.

'Don't worry,' he whispered, barely more than a breath. 'It's probably just some people hungry for food. Dad will share a bit, and then they'll be on their way. You'll see.' He squeezed her fingers with all the love he knew, not believing a word he'd said.

Next came a rush of noises. The door slammed open. Loud, angry voices.

A crash, then a thump that rattled the floorboards. Heavy, dreadful footsteps.

And then the strangers were pounding down the stairs. Two men, three, a woman – four people in total. The arrivals were dressed sharply for the times, and they looked neither kind nor menacing. Merely solemn to the core.

'You've ignored every message we've sent,' one of the men stated as he examined the room. 'I'm sorry, but we need the girl. Elizabeth. I'm very sorry, but we've got no choice.'

And just like that, the boy's world ended. A world already filled with more sad things than a kid could count. The strangers approached, cutting through the tense air. They reached for Lizzy, grabbed her by the shirt, pushed at Mum – frantic, wild, screaming – who clutched at her little girl. The boy ran forwards, beat at the back of a man's shoulders. Useless. A mosquito attacking an elephant.

The look on Lizzy's face during the sudden madness. Something cold and hard shattered within the boy's chest, the pieces falling with jagged edges, tearing at him. It was unbearable. He let out an enormous scream of his own and threw himself harder at the intruders, swinging wildly.

'Enough!' the woman yelled. A hand whipped through the air, slapped the boy in the face, a snakebite sting. Someone punched his mother right in the head. She collapsed. And then a sound like the crack of thunder, close and everywhere at once. His ears chimed with a deafening buzz. He fell back against the wall and took in the horrors.

One of the men, shot in the leg.

His dad standing in the doorway, gun in hand.

His mum screeching as she scrambled off the floor, reaching for the woman, who had pulled out her own weapon.

Dad firing off two more shots. A ping of metal and the crunch of a bullet hitting concrete. Misses, both.

Mum yanking at the lady's shoulder.

Then the woman threw an elbow, fired, spun, fired three more times. In the chaos, the air thickened, all sound retreating, time a foreign concept. The boy watched, emptiness opening below him, as both of his parents fell. A long moment passed when no one moved, most of all Mum and Dad. They'd never move again.

All eyes went to the two orphaned children.

'Grab them *both*, dammit,' one of the men finally said. 'They can use the other one as a control subject.'

The way the man pointed at him, so casually, like he was finally settling on a random can of soup in the pantry. He would never forget it. He scrambled for Lizzy, pulled her into his arms. And the strangers took them away.

1

Stephen, Stephen, Stephen. My name is Stephen.

He'd been chanting it over and over to himself for the last two days – since they'd taken him from his mom. He remembered every second of his last moments with her, every tear that ran down her face, every word, her warm touch. He was young, but he understood that it was for the best. He'd seen his dad plummet into complete madness, all anger and stink and danger. He couldn't take seeing it happen to his mom.

Still, the pain of their separation swallowed him. An ocean that had sucked him under, its coldness and depth never-ending. He lay on the bed in his small room, legs tucked up to his chest and eyes squeezed shut, curled into a ball, as if that would bring sleep down on him. But since he'd been taken, slumber had come only in fits, snatches full of dark clouds and screaming beasts. He focused.

Stephen, Stephen, Stephen. My name is Stephen.

He figured he had two things to hold on to: his memories and his name. Surely they couldn't take the first away from him, but they were trying to steal the second. For two days they'd pressed him to accept his new name: Thomas. He'd refused, clinging desperately to the seven letters his own flesh and blood had chosen for him. When the people in the white coats called him Thomas, he thought they were talking to someone else. It wasn't easy when only two people stood in the room, which was usually the case.

Stephen wasn't even five years old, yet his only glimpse of the world had been full of darkness and pain. And then these people took him. They seemed intent on making sure he realized that things could only get worse, every lesson learned harder than the one before it.

His door buzzed, then immediately popped open. A man strode in, dressed in a green one-piece suit that looked like pyjamas for grown-ups. Stephen wanted to tell him he looked ridiculous, but based on the last few encounters he'd had with these people, he decided to keep his opinion to himself. Their patience was beginning to wear thin.

'Thomas, come with me,' the man said.

Stephen, Stephen, Stephen. My name is Stephen.

He didn't move. He kept his eyes squeezed shut, hoping the stranger hadn't noticed that he'd taken a peek when the man had first entered. A different person had come each time. None of them had been hostile, but then, none had been very nice either. They all seemed distant, their thoughts elsewhere, removed from the boy alone in the bed.

The man spoke again, not even trying to conceal the impatience in his voice. 'Thomas, get up. I don't have time for games, okay? They're running us ragged to get things set up, and I've heard that you're one of the last ones resisting your new name. Give me a break, son. This is seriously something you want to fight about? After we saved you from what's happening out there?'

Stephen willed himself not to move, the result only a stiffness that couldn't possibly look like someone sleeping. He held his breath until he finally had to suck in a huge gulp of air. Giving up, he rolled onto his back and glared at the stranger dead in the eye.

'You look stupid,' he said.

The man tried to hide his surprise but failed; amusement crossed his face. 'Excuse me?'

Anger flared inside Stephen. 'I said, you look stupid. That ridiculous green jumpsuit. And give up the act. I'm not going to just do whatever you want me to do. And I'm definitely not putting on anything that looks like those man-jammies you're wearing. And don't call me Thomas. My name is Stephen!'

It all came out in one breath, and Stephen had to suck in another huge gulp of air, hoping it didn't ruin his moment. Make him look weak.

The man laughed, and he sounded more amused than con-descending. It still made Stephen want to throw something across the room.

'They told me you had . . .' the man paused, looked down at an electronic notepad he carried, '. . . "an endearing, child-like quality" about you. Guess I'm not seeing it.'

'That was before they told me I had to change my name,' Stephen countered. 'The name my mom and dad gave me. The one you took from me.'

'Would that be the dad who went crazy?' the man asked. 'The one who just about beat your mom to death he was so sick? And the mom who asked us to take you away? Who's getting sicker every day? *Those* parents?'

Stephen smouldered in his bed but said nothing.

His green-clothed visitor came closer to the bed, crouched down. 'Look, you're just a kid. And you're obviously bright. Really bright. Also immune to the Flare. You have a lot going for you.'

Stephen heard the warning in the man's voice. Whatever came next was *not* going to be good.

'You're going to have to accept the loss of certain things and think of something bigger than yourself,' he continued. 'If we don't find a cure within a few years, humans are done. So here's what's going to happen, *Thomas.* You're going to get up. You're going to walk with me out that door. And I'm not going to tell you again.'

The man waited for a moment, his gaze unwavering; then he stood and turned to leave.

Stephen got up. He followed the man out of the door.

2

When they entered the hallway, Stephen got his first glimpse of another kid since he'd arrived. A girl. She had brown hair and looked like she might be a little older than him. It was hard to tell, though; he only got a brief look at her as a woman escorted her into the room right next to his. The door thumped closed just as he and his escort walked by, and he noticed the plaque on the front of its white surface: 31K.

'Teresa hasn't had any problem taking her new name,' the man in green said as they moved down the long, dimly lit hallway. 'Of course, that might be because she wanted to forget her given one.'

'What was it?' Stephen asked, his tone approaching something like politeness. He genuinely wanted to know. If the girl had really given up so easily, maybe he could hold on to her name as well – a favour to a potential friend.

'It'll be hard enough for you to forget your own,' came the response. 'I wouldn't want to burden you with another.'

I'll never forget, Stephen told himself. *Never.*

Somewhere at the edge of his mind, he realized that he'd already changed his stance, ever so slightly. Instead of insisting on calling himself Stephen, he'd begun to merely promise not to *forget* Stephen. Had he already given in? *No!* He almost shouted it.

'What's *your* name?' he asked, needing a distraction.

'Randall Spilker,' the man said without breaking his stride. They turned a corner and came to a bank of lifts. 'Once upon a time, I wasn't such a jerk, trust me. The world, the people I work for' – he gestured to nothing in particular all around him – 'it's all turned my heart into a small lump of black coal. Too bad for you.' Stephen had no response, as he was busy wondering where they were going. They stepped onto the lift when it chimed and the doors opened.

Stephen sat in a strange chair, its various built-in instruments pressing into his legs and back. Wireless sensors, each barely the size of a fingernail, were attached to his temples, his neck, his wrists, the crooks of his elbows and his chest. He watched the console next to him as it collected data, chirping and beeping. The man in the grown-up jammies sat in another chair to observe, his knees only a couple of inches from Stephen's.

'I'm sorry, Thomas. We'd usually wait longer before it came to this,' Randall said. He sounded nicer than he had back in the hallway and in Stephen's room. 'We'd give you some more time to choose to take your new name voluntarily, like Teresa did. But time isn't a luxury we have any more.'

He held up a tiny piece of shiny silver, one end rounded, the other tapered to a razor-sharp point.

'Don't move,' Randall said, leaning forwards as if he were going to whisper something into Stephen's ear. Before he could question the man, Stephen felt a sharp pain in his neck, right below his chin, then the unsettling sensation of something burrowing into his throat. He yelped, but it was over as fast as it had begun, and he felt nothing more than the panic that filled his chest.

'Wh–what was that?' he stammered. He tried to get up from the chair despite all the things attached to him.

Randall pushed him back into his seat. Easy to do when he was twice Stephen's size.

'It's a pain stimulator. Don't worry, it'll dissolve and get flushed out of your system. Eventually. By then you probably won't need it any more.' He shrugged. *What can you do?* 'But we can always insert another one if you make it necessary. Now calm down.'

Stephen had a hard time catching his breath. 'What's it going to do to me?'

'Well, that depends . . . *Thomas*. We have a long road ahead of us, you and me. All of us. But for today, right now, at this moment, we can take a shortcut. A little path through the woods. All you need to do is tell me your name.'

'That's easy. Stephen.'

Randall let his head fall into his hands. 'Do it,' he said, his voice little more than a tired whisper.

Until this moment, Stephen hadn't known pain outside of the scrapes and bruises of childhood. And so it was that when the fiery tempest exploded throughout his body, when the agony erupted in his veins and muscles, he had no words for it, no capacity to understand. There were only the screams that barely reached his own ears before his mind shut down and saved him.

Stephen came to, breathing heavily and soaked in sweat. He was still in the strange chair, but at some point, he'd been secured to it with straps of soft leather. Every nerve in his body buzzed with the lingering effects of the pain inflicted by Randall and the implanted device.

'What . . . ?' Stephen whispered, a hoarse croak. His throat burned, telling him all he needed to know about how much he'd screamed in the time he'd lost. 'What?' he repeated, his mind struggling to connect the pieces.

'I tried to tell you, Thomas,' Randall said, with perhaps, *perhaps,* some compassion in his voice. Possibly regret. 'We don't have time to mess around. I'm sorry. I really am. But we're going to have to try this again. I think you understand now that none of this is a bluff. It's important to everyone here that you accept your new name.' The man looked away and paused a long time, staring at the floor.

'How could you hurt me?' Stephen asked through his raw throat. 'I'm just a little kid.' Young or not, he understood how pathetic he sounded.

Stephen also knew that adults seemed to react to *pathetic* in one of two ways: either their hearts would melt a little and they'd backtrack, or the guilt would burn like a furnace within them and they'd harden into rock to put the fire out. Randall chose the latter, his face reddening as he shouted back.

'All you have to do is accept a name! Now – I'm not playing around any more. What's your name?'

Stephen wasn't stupid – he'd just pretend for now. 'Thomas. My name is Thomas.'

'I don't believe you,' Randall responded, his eyes pools of darkness. 'Again.'

Stephen opened his mouth to answer, but Randall hadn't been speaking to him. The pain came back, harder and faster. He barely had time to register the agony before he passed out.

'What's your name?'

Stephen could barely speak. 'Thomas.'

'I don't believe you.'

'No.' He whimpered.

The pain was no longer a surprise, nor was the darkness that came after.

'What's your name?'

'Thomas.'

'I don't want you to forget.'
'No.' He cried, trembling with sobs.

'What's your name?'
'Thomas.'
'Do you have any other name?'
'No. Only Thomas.'
'Has anyone ever called you anything else?'
'No. Only Thomas.'
'Will you ever forget your name? Will you ever use another?'
'No.'
'Okay. Then I'll give you one last reminder.'

Later, he lay on his bed, once again curled up into himself. The world outside felt far away, silent. He'd run out of tears, his body numb except that unpleasant tingle. It was as if his entire being had fallen asleep. He pictured Randall across from him, guilt and anger mixed into a potent, lethal form of rage that turned his face into a grotesque mask as he inflicted the pain.

I'll never forget, he told himself. *I must never, never forget.*

And so, inside his mind, he chanted a familiar phrase, over and over and over. Though he couldn't quite put a finger on it, something *did* seem different.

Thomas, Thomas, Thomas. My name is Thomas.

3

222.2.28 | 9:36 A.M.

'Please hold still.'

The doctor wasn't mean, but he wasn't kind either. He was just kind of there, stoic and professional. Also forgettable: middle-aged, average height, medium build, short dark hair. Thomas closed his eyes and felt the needle slide into his vein after that quick pinprick of pain. It was funny how he dreaded it every week, but then it lasted less than a second, followed by the flood of cold inside his body.

'See, now?' the doctor said. 'That didn't hurt.'

Thomas shook his head but didn't speak. He had a hard time speaking ever since the incident with Randall. He had a hard time sleeping, eating, and just about everything else, too. Only in the last few days had he started to get over it, little by little. Whenever a trace memory of his real name came forward in his mind, he pushed it away, not ever wanting to go through that torture again. *Thomas* worked just fine. It'd have to do.

Blood, so dark it looked almost black, glided up the narrow tube from his arm and into the vial. He didn't know what they tested him for, but this was just one of many, many pokes and prods – some daily, some weekly.

The doctor stopped the flow and sealed off the vial. 'All right, then, that does it for the blood work.' He pulled out the needle. 'Now let's get you into the scanning machine and capture another look at that brain of yours.'

Thomas froze, anxiety trickling in, tightening his chest. The anxiety always came when they mentioned his brain.

'Now, now,' the doctor chided, noticing Thomas's body tense. 'We do this every week. It's just routine – nothing to fret over. We need to capture regular images of your activity up there. Okay?'

Thomas nodded, squeezing his eyes shut for a moment. He wanted to cry. He sucked in a breath and fought the urge.

He stood and followed the doctor to another room, where a massive machine sat like a giant elephant, a tube-shaped chamber at its centre, a flat bed extended, waiting for him to be slid inside.

'Up you go.'

This was the fourth or fifth time Thomas had done this, and there was no point fighting it. He jumped up onto the bed and lay flat on his back, staring up at the bright lights on the ceiling.

'Remember,' the doctor said, 'don't worry about those knocking sounds. It's all normal. All part of the game.'

There was a click and then a groan of machinery, and Thomas's bed glided into the yawning tube.

Thomas sat at a desk, all by himself. In front of him, standing by a writing board, was his teacher, Mr Glanville – a gruff, grey-toned man with barely any hair. Unless you counted his eyebrows. Those bushy things looked like they'd commandeered every follicle from the rest of his body. It was the second hour after lunch now, and Thomas would've given at least three of his toes to lie down, right there on the floor, and take a nap.

Just a five-minute nap.

'Do you remember what we talked about yesterday?' Mr Glanville asked him.

Thomas nodded. 'FIRE.'

'Yes, that's right. And what does it stand for?'

'Flares Information Recovery Endeavour.'

His teacher smiled with obvious satisfaction. 'Very good. Now.' He turned back to his board and wrote the letters *PFC*. 'P . . . F . . . C. That stands for Post Flares Coalition, which was a direct result of FIRE. Once they'd heard from as many countries as possible, gathered representatives and so forth, they could start dealing with the spectacular disaster caused by the sun flares. While FIRE figured out the full ramifications of the sun flares and who had been affected, the PFC tried to start fixing things. Am I *boring* you, son?'

Thomas jerked upright, completely unaware that his head had dipped. He might've even nodded off for a moment.

'Sorry,' he said, rubbing his eyes. 'Sorry. FIRE, PFC, got it.'

'Look, son,' Mr Glanville said. He took a few steps, closing the distance between them. 'I'm sure you find your other subjects more interesting. Science, maths, physical fitness.' He leaned down to look directly into Thomas's eyes. 'But you need to understand your history. What got us here, why we're in this mess. You'll never figure out where you're going until you understand from where you came.'

'Yes, sir,' Thomas said meekly.

Mr Glanville straightened, glaring down his nose. Searching Thomas's face for any sign of sarcasm. 'All right, then. Know your past. Back to the PFC. There's a lot to discuss.'

As his teacher returned to the front of the room, Thomas pinched himself as hard as he could, hoping that would keep him awake.

'Do you need me to go over it again?'

Thomas looked up at Ms Denton. She had dark hair and

dark skin, and she was beautiful. Kind eyes. Smart eyes. She was probably the smartest person Thomas had met so far, as made evident by the puzzles she constantly challenged him with in his critical thinking class.

'I think I've got it,' he said.

'Then repeat it back to me. Remember—'

He cut her off, quoting back what she'd said a thousand times. '"One must know the problem better than the solution, or the solution becomes the problem."' He was pretty sure it meant absolutely nothing.

'Very good!' she said with mockingly exaggerated praise, as if shocked that he'd memorized her words. 'Then go ahead and repeat the problem. Visualize it in your mind.'

'There's a man in a train station who's lost his ticket. One hundred and twenty-six people stand on the platform with him. There are nine separate tracks, five going south, four going north. Over the next forty-five minutes, twenty-four trains will arrive and depart. Another eighty-five people will enter the station during that time. At least seven people board each train when it arrives, and never more than twenty-two. Also, at least ten passengers disembark with each arrival, and never more than eighteen . . .'

This went on for another five minutes. Detail after detail. Memorizing the parameters was challenging enough – he couldn't believe she actually expected him to solve the stupid thing.

'. . . how many people are left standing on the platform?' he finished.

'Very good,' Ms Denton said. 'Third time's the charm, I guess. You got every detail right, which is the first step to finding any solution. Now, can you solve it?'

Thomas closed his eyes and worked through the numbers. In this class, everything was done in his head – no devices, no writing. It strained his mind like nothing else, and he actually loved it.

He opened his eyes. 'Seventy-eight.'

'Wrong.'

He took a couple of minutes then tried again. 'Eighty-one.'

'Wrong.' He flinched in disappointment.

It took another few tries, but he finally realized the answer might not be a number at all. 'I don't know if the man who lost his ticket got on a train or not. Or if some of the others on the platform were travelling with him, and if so, how many.'

Ms Denton smiled.

'Now we're getting somewhere.'

4

223.12.25 | 10:00 A.M.

In the two years since they'd stolen Thomas's name, he'd been busy. Classes and tests filled his days – maths, science, chemistry, critical thinking and more mental and physical challenges than he would have thought existed. He'd had teachers and been studied by scientists of all sorts, yet he hadn't seen Randall again or heard any mention of him, even once. Thomas wasn't sure what that meant. Had the man's job been completed, and then he'd been let go? Had he got sick – caught the Flare? Had he left the service of Thomas's caretakers, racked with guilt for doing such things to a boy hardly old enough to start school?

Thomas was just as happy to forget Randall for ever, though he still couldn't help that spike of panic whenever a man in green scrubs turned a corner. Always, for just an instant, he thought it might be Randall again.

Two years. Two years of blood samples, physical diagnostics and constant monitoring, class after class after class, and the puzzles. So many puzzles. But no real information.

Until now. He hoped.

Thomas woke up feeling good after an excellent night's sleep. Shortly after he'd dressed and eaten, a woman he'd never seen before interrupted his normal schedule. He was being summoned to 'a very important meeting.' Thomas didn't bother asking for any details. He was already seven or so, old enough to not go along with everything grown-ups wanted him to do, but after two years of dealing with these people, he'd realized that he never got any answers. He'd realized also that there were other ways to learn things if he was patient and used his eyes and ears.

Thomas had lived at the facility for so long at this point that he'd almost forgotten what the outside world looked like. All he knew were white walls, the paintings he passed in the hallways, the various monitor screens flashing information in the labs, the fluorescent lights, the soft grey of his bedclothes, the white tile of his bedroom and bathroom. And in all that time, he'd only interacted with adults – he hadn't once, not even in a brief chance encounter, been able to speak with anyone approaching his own age.

He knew he wasn't the only kid there. Every once in a while, he caught a glimpse of the girl who bunked in the room next to his. Always only a mere second or two, eyes meeting just as his or her door closed. The placard on that door read TERESA. He desperately wanted to talk to her.

His life was one of immeasurable boredom, his scant free time filled with old vids and books. A lot of books. That was the one thing they allowed him to peruse freely. The huge collection to which they allowed him access was the lifeline that probably saved him from insanity. The last month or so he'd been on a Mario Di Sanza kick, relishing every page of the classics, all set within a world he hardly understood but loved to imagine.

'It's right here,' his guide said as they entered a small lobby, two male guards with weapons posted at the doors. The woman's tone made him think of a computer simulation. 'Chancellor Anderson will be right with you.' She turned abruptly, and without meeting his eyes, she left him with the men.

Thomas took in his new companions. They both wore official-looking black uniforms over bulging armour, and their guns were huge. There was something different about them from the guards he'd grown used to. Across their chests, in capital letters, was the word *WICKED*. Thomas had never seen that before.

'What does that mean?' he asked, pointing to the word. But the only response he got was a quick wink and the barest trace of a smile, then a hard stare. Two hard stares. After so long interacting with only adults, Thomas had grown much braver, sometimes even bold in the things he said, but it was clear these two had no intention of conversing, so he sat down in the chair next to the door.

WICKED. He pondered the word. It had to be . . . what? Why would someone, a guard, have such a word printed across his very official uniform? It had Thomas at a loss.

The sound of the door opening behind him cut off his train of thought. Thomas turned to see a middle-aged man, his dark hair turning to grey and storm-cloud-coloured bags underneath his tired brown eyes. Something about him made Thomas think he was younger than he looked, though.

'You must be Thomas,' the man said, trying but failing to sound cheerful. 'I'm Kevin Anderson, chancellor of this fine institution.' He smiled, but his eyes stayed dark.

Thomas stood, feeling awkward. 'Uh, nice to meet you.' He didn't know what else to say to the man. Though he'd mostly been treated well the last couple of years, visions of Randall haunted his mind, and there was the loneliness in his heart. He didn't really know what he was doing standing there, or why he was meeting this man now.

'Come on into my office,' the chancellor said. Stepping to one side, he swept an arm in front of him as if revealing a prize.

'Take one of the seats in front of my desk. We have a lot to talk about.'

Thomas looked down and walked into the chancellor's office, a tiny part of him expecting the man to hurt him as he passed. He went straight for the closest chair and sat down before taking a quick look around. He sat in front of a large desk that looked like wood but most definitely wasn't, with a few frames scattered along its front edge, the pictures within them facing away from Thomas. He desperately wanted to see what parts of Mr Anderson's life were flashing by in that instant. Besides a few gadgets and chairs and a workstation built into the desk, the room was pretty much empty.

The chancellor swooped into the room and took his seat on the other side of the desk. He touched a few things on the workstation's screen, seemed satisfied about something, and then leaned back in his chair, steepling his fingers under his chin. A long silence filled the room as the man studied Thomas, making him even more uncomfortable.

'Do you know what today is?' Chancellor Anderson finally asked.

Thomas had tried all morning not to think about it, which had only made the memories of the one good Christmas he'd known all the more crisp in his mind. It filled him with a sadness so sharp that every breath actually hurt like a spiky rock laid atop his chest.

'It's the beginning of holiday week,' Thomas answered, hoping he could hide just how sad that made him. For a split second, he thought he smelled pine, tasted spiced apple juice on the back of his tongue.

'That's right,' the chancellor said, folding his arms as if proud of the answer. 'And today's the best of all, right? Religious or not, everyone celebrates Christmas in one way or another. And hey, let's face it, who's been religious the last ten years? Except the Apocalyptics, anyway.'

The man fell silent for a moment, staring into space.

Thomas had no idea what point the guy was trying to make, other than to depress the poor kid sitting in front of him.

Anderson suddenly sprang to life again, leaning forwards on his desk with hands folded in front of him. 'Christmas, Thomas. Family. Food. Warmth. And presents! We can't forget the presents! What's the best gift you ever received on Christmas morning?'

Thomas had to look away, trying to shift his eyes in just the right way so no tears tumbled out and trickled down his cheek. He refused to answer such a mean question, whether it had been intended that way or not.

'One time,' Anderson continued, 'when I was a little younger than you, I got a bike. Shiny and green. The lights from the tree sparkled in the new paint. Magic, Thomas. That's pure magic. Nothing like that can ever be duplicated for the rest of your life, especially when you get to be a crotchety old man like me.'

Thomas had recovered himself and looked at the chancellor, trying to throw as much fierceness into his gaze as possible. 'My parents are probably dead. And yeah, I *did* get a bike, but I had to leave it when you took me. I'll never have another Christmas, thanks to the Flare. Why are we talking about this? Are you trying to rub it in?' The rush of angry words made him feel better.

Anderson's face had gone pale, any trace of happy Christmas memories wiped clean. He put his hands flat on the desk, and a shadow descended over his eyes.

'Exactly, Thomas,' he said. 'That's *exactly* what I'm doing. So you'll understand just how important it is that we do whatever it takes to make WICKED a success. To find a cure for this sickness, no matter the cost. No matter . . . the cost.'

He sat back in his chair, swivelled a quarter turn, and stared at the wall.

'I want Christmas back.'

5

The silence that stretched out from that moment was a long one, so awkward that Thomas wondered more than once if he should get up and leave. At one point he even worried that maybe Chancellor Anderson had died – that he was sitting frozen in death, eyes open, glazed over.

But the man's chest rose and fell with each of his breaths as he sat staring, staring at that wall.

Thomas actually found himself feeling sorry for him. And he couldn't take the stillness any more.

'I want it back, too,' Thomas said. It was simple, and true – and, he knew, impossible.

It was as if the chancellor had forgotten that Thomas was sitting there. He snapped his head around at the boy's voice. 'I . . . I'm sorry,' he stammered, adjusting his chair to face the desk again. 'What did you say?'

'That I want everything back to normal again, too,' Thomas answered. 'The way it was before I even existed. But I don't think that's going to happen, is it?'

'But it *can,* Thomas.' A light had somehow found its way into the man's eyes. 'I know the world is in horrible shape, but if we can find a cure . . . The weather will normalize eventually – it's already starting. The Cranks can die off; all of our simulations tell us they'll wipe each other out. There are plenty of us who are still healthy – who can rebuild our world if we can only ensure that they don't catch that damn disease.'

He stared at Thomas as if Thomas should know what to say next. He didn't.

'Do you know what our . . . institution is called, Thomas?' the chancellor asked.

Thomas shrugged. 'Well, you said WICKED a few minutes ago – and those guards had it on their uniforms. Is that *really* the name of this place?'

Chancellor Anderson nodded. 'Some people didn't like it, but it really makes perfect sense. It explains exactly what we're here to do.'

'At any cost,' Thomas said, repeating what the chancellor had said earlier, making sure he realized that Thomas had understood what that implied, though he wasn't quite sure he did.

'At any cost.' The man nodded. 'That's right.' His eyes were bright now. 'WICKED stands for World In Catastrophe, Killzone Experiment Department. We want our name to remind people of *why* we exist, what we plan to accomplish, and how we intend to do it.' He paused, seeming to rethink something. 'To be fair, I think the world will fix itself eventually. Our objective is to save humanity. Otherwise, what's the point?'

Chancellor Anderson watched Thomas carefully, awaiting his answer, but Thomas's head hurt too much by then to figure out half of what the man had said. And he was really creeped out by the word *killzone*. What could it possibly mean? It seemed even worse than the word right before it, *catastrophe*.

He'd always thought that given the chance, he'd ask these

people a million questions. And here he was, with even more questions.

At some point they didn't seem to matter any more, though. He was tired, angry and confused – all he wanted was to go back to his room and be alone.

'Things are going to get very busy over the next several years,' Chancellor Anderson continued. 'We've brought several young survivors here – just like you – and we've finally determined that we're ready to get to work. Complete more and more testing to see which of our sub— which of our students will rise to the top. Take my advice when I say that you'll want to do your best. Being immune to the Flare holds power, but it will take more than simple biology to succeed here. And we have such magnificent structures to build, biomechanical labs to construct . . . *wonders* of life to create. And all of this will ultimately lead to mapping out the killzone. We'll identify the differences that cause immunity and then design a cure. I am sure of it.'

He paused, his face alight with excitement. Thomas sat still, doing his best to remain calm. Anderson was getting a little scary.

The chancellor seemed to realize he'd got carried away with himself and let out a sigh. 'Well, I suppose that's enough of a pep talk for one day. You're getting older, Thomas, and doing better than almost anyone in the testing programme. We think very highly of you, and I felt it was time that we meet face to face. Expect a lot more of this in the future – more freedom, and a bigger role to play here at WICKED. Does that sound good to you?'

Thomas nodded before he could stop himself. Because, well, it did sound good. He sometimes felt like he lived in a prison, and he wanted out. Plain and simple. Maybe the path had just been laid before him.

'Can I just ask another question?' he said, unable to get that one horrible word out of his head. *Killzone.*

'Sure.'

'What does . . . *killzone* mean?'

Anderson actually smiled at that. 'Ah, I'm sorry. I guess I assumed you knew. It's what we call the brain – the place where the Flare does the most damage. Where it eventually, well, ends the life of those who are infected. And that's what we're battling. I guess you could say it's *the* battleground for us here at WICKED. The killzone.'

Thomas was a long way from understanding, but for some reason this explanation made him feel better.

'So we're set, then?' Chancellor Anderson asked. 'You're ready to play a role in the important things we're doing here?'

Thomas nodded.

The chancellor tapped a finger on the desk a couple of times. 'Fantastic. Then go on back to your room and get some rest. Big times ahead.'

Thomas felt a little rush of excitement, followed immediately by a shame he didn't even understand.

Thomas couldn't help himself after the same lady had escorted him back to his room. Right before she closed the door, he stuck his hand in the gap to stop it.

'Uh, sorry,' he said quickly, 'but can I just ask you one question?'

A flash of doubt crossed her face. 'That's probably not a good idea. This . . . all of this . . . it's a really controlled environment. I'm sorry.' Her face flushed red.

'But . . .' Thomas searched for the right words, the right question. 'That guy . . . Chancellor Anderson, he said something about big times ahead. Are there many others like me? Are they all kids? Will I finally get to meet some of them?' He hated how much he dared to hope. 'Like the girl next to me . . . Teresa . . . will I actually get to *meet* her?'

The woman sighed, sincere pity in her eyes. She nodded.

'There are lots of others, but what's important now is that you're doing great in the testing, and meeting the others won't be too far away. I know you must be lonely. I'm really sorry. But maybe it helps to know that everyone is in the same boat. Things will get better soon, though. I promise.' She started to close the door, but Thomas stopped it again.

'How long?' he asked, embarrassed at how desperate he sounded. 'How much longer will I be alone?'

'Just . . .' She sighed. 'Like I said. Not much longer. Maybe a year.'

Thomas had to whip his hand away before she slammed the door on it. He ran over and crumpled onto the bed, trying to hold in his tears.

A year.

6

224.3.12 | 7:30 A.M.

A knock on his door, early morning. It had become as routine as clockwork. Same time, but not always the same face. Yet he knew who he hoped it to be – the nicest doctor he'd met so far. By a long shot. The same one who'd taken him to see the chancellor two months earlier. Unfortunately, it usually *wasn't* her.

But when he opened the door today, there she stood.

'Dr Paige,' he said. He didn't know why he liked her so much – she just put him at ease. 'Hi.'

'Hi, Thomas. Guess what?'

'What?'

She gave him a warm smile. 'You're going to be seeing a lot more of me from here on out. I've been assigned to you. And to you only. What do you think of that?'

He was thrilled – he already felt comfortable with her, even though they'd only met a few times. But all that came out to show his excitement was, 'Cool.'

'Cool indeed.' Another grin that seemed as genuine as Ms

Denton's. 'There are a lot of good things on your horizon. *Our* horizon.'

He barely stopped himself from saying 'Cool' again.

She motioned towards the rolling tray at her hip. 'Now, how about some breakfast?'

He didn't know how she did it, but when Dr Paige took Thomas's blood, he didn't even feel the prick of the needle piercing his skin. Usually one of her assistants did the deed, but every once in a while she took care of it herself. Like today.

As he watched the blood slide down its tube, he asked, 'So, what're you learning about me?'

Dr Paige looked up. 'Pardon?'

'With all these tests you run. What're you learning? You never tell me anything. Am I still immune? Is my information helping you? Am I healthy?'

The doctor sealed off the vial and took the needle out of Thomas's arm. 'Well, yes, you're helping us a lot. The more we can learn about how your body, your health . . . just by studying you and the others, we're discovering *what* to study. Where to focus our efforts on finding a cure. You're as valuable as they say you are. Every one of you.'

Thomas beamed a little.

'Are you just telling me this to make me feel good?' he asked.

'Absolutely not. If we're going to stop this virus, it'll be because of you and the others. You should be proud.'

'Okay.'

'Now, let's get you on the treadmill. See how quickly we can get your heart rate over one-fifty.'

'This drastically changed people's everyday lives, connecting society in a way that had never . . .'

Ms Landon – a small, mousy lady with perfect teeth – was describing the cultural impact of cellular technology when Thomas raised his hand to get her attention. He was desperately bored. Everyone knew the cultural impact of cellular technology.

'Uh, yes?' she asked, stopping mid-sentence.

'I thought we were going to talk about the invention of the Flat Trans soon.'

'Did I say that?'

'I think you did. Anyway, it just seems a little more interesting than . . . this stuff.' Thomas smiled to take away the sting of his words.

Ms Landon folded her arms. 'Who's the teacher here?'

'You are.'

'And who knows best what we should talk about each day?'

Thomas smiled again; for what reason, he had no idea. He liked this lady, no matter how boring she got. 'You do.'

'Very good. Now, as I was *saying,* you can imagine how much the world changed when suddenly every person in the world was connected by . . .'

Ms Denton had the patience of a snail. Thomas had been analyzing the forty odd-shaped blocks on the table in front of him for over thirty minutes. He'd yet to actually touch one. Instead, he gazed at each separate piece in turn, trying to build a blueprint in his mind. Trying to approach the puzzle the way his teacher had taught him.

'Would you like to take a break?' she finally asked. 'You need to go to your next class anyway.'

Even her patience could run thin, he supposed. 'I can be late. Mr Glanville won't mind.'

Ms Denton shook her head. 'Not a good idea. Once you run out of time, you'll start rushing things. You're not ready to rush things. For now, it's okay to take as much time as you need. Even over several days. Give your brain a solid workout, visualize what you've been analyzing while you lie in bed at night.'

Thomas forced himself to look away from the blocks and leaned back in his chair. 'Why do we do so many puzzles anyway? Aren't they just games?'

'Is that what *you* think?'

'Not really, I guess. Seems like it works my brain more than any of my other classes.'

Ms Denton smiled as if he'd just told her she was the smartest teacher in the school. 'That's exactly right, Thomas. Now, off to Mr Glanville. You shouldn't make him wait.'

Thomas stood up. 'Okay. See you later.' He started for the door, then turned back to face her. 'By the way, there are seven extra pieces – they don't belong.'

Impossibly, her smile grew even wider.

Sample after sample.
Class after class.
Puzzle after puzzle.
Day after day.
Month after month.

7

224.9.2 | 7:30 A.M.

The knock on the door came precisely at the correct time, maybe a few seconds off. Thomas opened it to find a stranger staring at him. A bald man who didn't seem very happy to be there. Maybe not very happy to be alive. He had puffy red eyes and a frown that seemed to be reflected in every wrinkle on his wilting face.

'Where's Dr Paige?' Thomas asked, a little crestfallen. As much as he sometimes hated the routine, disrupting it made him uncomfortable. 'Is she okay?'

'May I *please* come in?' the man replied, nodding down at the tray of food he'd brought. His voice had none of the warmth of Dr Paige's.

'Um, yeah.' Thomas stepped aside, opening the door wider. The stranger rolled the food cart past him and up to the small desk. 'Make sure you eat it all,' the man said. 'You're going to need a lot of strength today.'

Thomas really didn't like his tone. 'Why? And you didn't answer my question – what's wrong with Dr Paige?'

The man straightened, as if trying to make himself taller, and folded his arms. 'Why would anything be wrong with Dr Paige? She's perfectly fine. Make sure to speak with kindness and respect to your elders at all times.'

Thomas had his response on the tip of his tongue – the sharp words that always felt as though they came easy – but he stayed quiet and willed the man to just go away.

'You've got half an hour,' the stranger said. His eyes never left Thomas, a dark, unnatural gaze. 'I'll be back for you at eight o'clock sharp. You can call me Dr Leavitt. I'm one of the Psychs.' He finally broke eye contact and left, gently closing the door behind him.

I'm one of the Psychs.

Thomas had no idea what that meant, though he'd heard the term *Psych* before. He had zero appetite. He sat down and ate anyway.

It seemed as though Dr Leavitt banged on the door far harder than he needed to, right on schedule. Thomas had finished his breakfast in plenty of time, only wishing he could have another hour. Another half a day. He might as well wish for a month. But he didn't want to go anywhere with this new guy. If Dr Paige was gone for some reason, he'd be devastated.

When he opened the door, Leavitt was just as bald and just as droopy as he'd been half an hour earlier.

'Let's go,' he said curtly.

They walked down the hallway in silence; Thomas gave Teresa's door a wistful glance as he passed it. 31K. How many times had he seen that plaque on the door, wishing he could open it and meet the girl on the other side? What possible reason did these people have for keeping everyone separate? Surely it wasn't mere cruelty? How could Dr Paige be a part of such a thing?

'Look,' Dr Leavitt said, snapping Thomas's attention back to the white walls of the hallway, the fluorescent lights above. 'I know I've been a little unfriendly this morning. I'm sorry. Today's project has been quite an undertaking, and we have a lot riding on it.' He let out a strangled laugh that sounded like a frog being electrocuted. 'You could say I'm under a pretty fair amount of stress.'

'It's okay,' Thomas replied, not knowing what else to say. 'We all have our bad days,' he added nervously. What could possibly have this guy so stressed out? He wasn't the one taking all the tests.

'Yeah,' Dr Leavitt grunted more than said.

They got in the lift and the doctor pressed the button for a floor Thomas had never visited before. Nine. For some reason, that had an ominous feel to it. The ninth floor. Would it have felt so haunting if Dr Paige were standing next to him? He had no idea.

The doors opened with a cheerful chime, and Dr Leavitt exited to the left. Thomas followed, quickly taking in a desk in front of glass partitions. Beyond that he could see the blinking lights of monitors and instruments. This floor was some kind of hospital unit, by the looks of it.

Maybe something *had* happened to Dr Paige – maybe they were going to visit her.

Thomas tried to sound as nice and as at ease as possible. 'So, can you tell me what's going on today?'

'No,' Leavitt replied. Then added a 'Sorry, son' as an after-thought.

Thomas followed Leavitt past the front desk and beyond the glass. They continued down the hallway, passing door after door, but aside from the medical monitors outside each room, none gave up any clues. The doors were all numbered, but they were closed, and the walls of frosted glass were obscured with floor-to-ceiling curtains, firmly drawn. Thomas could swear he heard voices coming from inside one room, and jumped at a sharp cry that left no doubt. He kept walking until an echoing scream came bouncing down the hall behind them. Thomas stopped and spun around to take a look.

'Keep walking,' Dr Leavitt directed. 'There's nothing to worry about.'

'What's going on?' Thomas asked again. 'What's wrong with that—'

Leavitt grabbed Thomas's arm – not hard enough to hurt, but not exactly gently, either. 'Everything's going to be okay. You have to trust me. Just keep walking – we're almost there.'

Thomas obeyed.

They stopped in front of a door identical to all the others, an electronic chart next to it with a bunch of information too small for Thomas to see from where he stood. Dr Leavitt studied it for a moment, then reached to open the door. He'd just turned the knob when a commotion down the hall erupted in the silence.

Thomas turned to see a door open, and a boy dressed in a hospital gown, his head bandaged, stumbled out, two nurses supporting him. He was staggering as if heavily drugged, and he fell to the ground. He then struggled back to his feet, fighting off the two people who had been helping him moments before. Thomas was frozen, staring at the boy as he fell again, then drunkenly clambered to his feet and attempted to run away, swerving from side to side as he headed straight for Thomas.

'Don't go in there,' the boy slurred. He had dark hair, Asian features, was maybe a year older than Thomas. The boy's face was flushed and sweaty; a tiny red spot blossomed on the bandage wrapped around his head, just above his ears.

Thomas watched in stunned disbelief. Then suddenly Dr Leavitt was standing between Thomas and the oncoming boy. One of the two pursuing nurses shouted, 'Minho! Stop! You're in no condition . . .' But the words faded to nothing.

Minho. The boy's name was Minho. Now Thomas knew at least two other names.

The boy slammed into Dr Leavitt, almost as if he hadn't seen him standing there. Minho's eyes were completely focused on Thomas, bright with dazed fear.

'Don't let them do it to you!' he yelled, now struggling with Leavitt, who'd wrapped his arms around him. Minho was way too small to break free from the man, but that didn't stop him from trying.

'What . . .' Thomas said, too quietly. He spoke louder. 'What's going on?'

'They're putting things in our heads!' Minho called out to him, eyes still wild, boring into Thomas. 'They said it wouldn't hurt, but it does. It does! They're a bunch of lying . . .'

That last word died in the boy's mouth as one of the nurses injected something into his neck that made him go slack, his body slumping to the floor. Within seconds they were dragging him down the hallway towards the room he'd exited, his feet trailing along behind him.

Thomas turned to Leavitt. 'What did they do to him?'

The doctor, his demeanour wrapped in a surprising calmness, simply said, 'Don't worry, he's just having a reaction to the anaesthesia. Nothing to worry about.'

He seemed to like that phrase.

Thomas thought about running. He thought about it the whole time he watched Leavitt open the door, as he followed him inside the room, as he heard the door close behind him.

I'm a coward, he thought. *I've got nothing on that Minho kid.*

It definitely looked like a hospital room. There were two beds, both with privacy curtains. The one to the left was open, revealing a newly made bed. The one to the right had the curtains drawn, hiding whoever lay there – Thomas could see the shadowy figure of a body through the thin material. Medical equipment filled the room, as state-of-the-art as any of the equipment he'd seen in the labs during his tests. Leavitt already stood at one of the displays, perusing a screen of charts and entering information.

Thomas returned his attention to the closed curtain, the bed behind it. Leavitt was a good six or seven feet away from him, consumed by what he was reading on the charts.

I have to see who's behind that curtain, Thomas thought. He couldn't remember the last time an urge had struck him so powerfully.

To his left, Leavitt leaned closer to the screen, reading something in small print. Thomas went for it. He crept towards the closed curtain to the right and pulled it to the side, stepped around it, rushed to the bed. Another boy lay there, blond hair cropped short, eyes closed, covers pulled up to his chin. Leavitt was across the room in a second, fumbling with the curtain. He grabbed Thomas by the arm, yanking him away from the bed. Thomas had seen the boy, though. And he'd got a good look at two things.

First, just like the boy named Minho, this kid had a bandage above his ears, a bright red spot of blood seeping through on one side.

And second, he saw the name on the monitors.

Newt.

Three now.

He knew three names.

8

224.9.2 | 8:42 A.M.

'What were you thinking?' Leavitt asked. He guided Thomas across the room to the empty bed. 'We need to follow medical protocols, honour our safety zones, take the utmost care. Aren't you aware of these things?'

Thomas almost laughed at the question. 'Uh, no,' he replied, not trying to be sarcastic. He wasn't even ten years old – of course he didn't know those things!

'That boy has been through a surgery. He's fragile. There are germs. Surely you know about germs?' Leavitt spoke with an eerie calm. 'Viruses like the Flare?'

'I'm immune,' Thomas said. 'Aren't we all immune?'

'Most of you –' Leavitt broke off, sighed, pinched the bridge of his nose. 'Never mind. Just . . . please don't go through that curtain again. Is that understood?'

Thomas nodded.

'Now. I need to start prepping you.' Leavitt held his hands out and looked around the room as if getting his bearings. 'The surgeon will be here in half an hour.'

A bubble of panic had been growing for some time in the pit of Thomas's stomach. 'So that kid . . . Minho . . . he was telling the truth? You're going to do something crazy to my head?'

'Not something crazy,' Leavitt said, the strain of forced patience clear in his voice. He opened a drawer and pulled out a linen gown. 'Something *vital*. And again, Minho was just having a reaction to the medicine we gave him – it happens only rarely. We'll take care with your dosage, I promise.' He paused, turned towards Thomas. 'Listen, you know the stakes. You know that you're immune to the Flare. You also know that the human race is in serious trouble. Am I right? Do you know all this?'

Thomas had only one answer for that. 'Yeah.'

'Then you understand why it's so important that you cooperate.' Leavitt tossed him the hospital gown. 'We're studying the killzones of the immune so we can find a cure. *You* are immune. And all we're doing today is placing a small instrument in your head that will help us understand what makes you different. I promise you'll recover quickly, and you'll be glad that we can monitor your vitals more efficiently. You won't have to get your arm pricked quite so much!' He made this last statement with forced cheerfulness. 'Now, that's not all so bad, is it?'

Thomas kind of shrugged and nodded at the same time. The man made it sound so reasonable to cut open a kid's brain. He looked down, turning the gown in his hands.

'There's a bathroom right over there.' Leavitt pointed to a door in the corner. 'Why don't you get dressed, then get in bed. I give you my word that everything will be just fine. You'll be knocked out, won't feel a thing. Maybe a headache for a couple of days. And we have pills for that. Okay?'

'Okay.' Thomas took a step towards the bathroom, when he heard a girl scream out in the hallway. He looked at Leavitt, who met his eyes. For a long moment they stood like that, waiting to see who'd act first. Thomas did.

He was at the door in an instant. He threw it open and practically jumped into the hall, feeling Leavitt right on his tail. Just a few dozen feet away, a familiar scene played out in front of him. Two nurses – a man and a woman – were dragging a girl with brown hair down the hallway, and she was kicking and screaming the whole way. It was her. The girl from room 31K. Teresa.

There was no sense in what Thomas did next. He ran after her. The anguish on her face and the fear in her eyes had finally burst that bubble of panic swelling inside him.

'Let her go!' he yelled at the same time that Leavitt shouted at him to come back.

The nurses turned to look at Thomas and stopped, curiosity crossing their faces, maybe even a hint of amusement. That just angered him all the more. He picked up speed, already realizing that the entire thing was a lost cause. At least he would show Teresa that he'd tried.

At the last second he jumped, arms outstretched, as if he'd become a superhero, ready to take down the two—

One of the nurses swung a forearm in defence, connecting with the side of Thomas's head. Sharp pain ignited along his cheek and ear as his world turned upside down and he landed forcefully on the ground; his nose banged into the wall just hard enough to stun him. He rolled over and looked up. Both nurses stared down at him as if to ask *What's* wrong *with you?* Even Teresa had stopped struggling, though her face expressed something completely different: awe. Wonder. Could that be almost a *smile?*

Thomas suddenly felt on top of the world.

Leavitt appeared, looming over him, a syringe in his hand. 'I thought we'd come to an understanding, son. I was really hoping I wouldn't have to do this.' He knelt down and stuck the needle in Thomas's neck, compressed the syringe with his thumb.

Before he passed out, Thomas looked at Teresa again, their

eyes meeting for just a few precious seconds. The world had already started to blur when they dragged her away, but he clearly heard what she called out to him.

'Someday we'll be bigger.'

He had crazy dreams.

Flying through the air with some kind of machine strapped to his back, watching the world below him, scorched and ruined and lifeless. He saw small figures running across the sand, and then they grew, getting closer to him. He saw wings, then hideous faces, then arms outstretched, monsters reaching for him.

Luckily that one ended before he got ripped apart. The next one was much more pleasant.

Thomas, his mom, his dad. A picnic. By a river. He didn't know if it was a memory or a wish, but he enjoyed it all the same. It created an ache in his chest that he thought might linger for a very long time.

At some point he dreamed about Teresa. The mysterious girl who lived so close – literally next door – and yet only one sentence had ever been spoken between them.

Someday we'll be bigger.

He clung to those words. Saw her say them over and over in his dreams. There was something so tough about them, so . . . rebellious. He liked her for saying them. In his dream, he and Teresa were both sitting in the same room – *his* room, he on the bed, she in a chair. They weren't talking, they were just . . . there. Together. He wanted a friend so desperately that he wished the surgery would go on for ever, leave him in this dream.

But then Teresa started saying his name, over and over, only it wasn't her voice. On some level, he knew what was happening, and his heart melted in sadness. The harder he tried to hold on to the counterfeit moment, the more quickly it faded. Soon there was only darkness and the repeated sound of his name.

Time to wake up.

He opened his eyes and blinked at the bright lights of the hospital room. A woman stared down at him. Dr Paige.

'Doct—' he started, but she shushed him.

'Don't say a word.' She smiled then, and everything seemed okay. Dr Paige wouldn't have done anything bad to him. No way. 'You're still under a heavy dose of drugs. You'll be woozy. Just lie there and relax, enjoy the medicine.' She laughed, a thing that didn't happen very often.

Thomas did feel floaty, peaceful. The whole incident with Teresa seemed almost funny now. He could only imagine what those nurses had thought at seeing this little kid charging down the hallway, leaping into the air like Superman. At least he'd shown Teresa that he cared. That he was brave. He sighed happily.

'Wow,' Dr Paige said, looking over from the monitor she'd been studying. 'I'd say you're taking my advice to heart.'

'What did you do to me?' Thomas mumbled, each word slurred.

'Oh, now you're ignoring my advice. I said *not* to speak.'

'What . . . did you do?' he asked again.

Dr Paige turned to face him, then sat down on the bed. The shifting of the mattress hurt something somewhere on his body. But it was a dull, distant ache.

'I think the Psych told you what we were going to do, right?' she asked. 'Dr Leavitt?' She looked around as if to make sure he hadn't come back into the room. He wasn't there.

Thomas nodded. 'But . . .'

'I know. It sounds horrible. Putting something inside you.' She smiled again. 'But you've learned to trust me a little, haven't you?'

Thomas nodded again.

'It'll be so much better for you, for everyone, in the long

run. We can measure your killzone activity so much faster and more efficiently now. Plus, you won't have to come to the lab quite as often to extract data. It'll all be instantaneous, real-time. Trust me, you'll be glad we did it.'

Thomas didn't say anything. He wouldn't have, even if he could speak normally. What she said made sense. Mostly. He just wondered why Minho and Teresa had freaked out so much. Maybe their surgeries hadn't gone as smoothly.

Dr Paige stood up from the bed, patted Thomas's arm. 'All right, young man. Time for you to let those drugs pull you back to sleep. You'll be doing a lot of that in the next couple of days. Enjoy the rest.' She started to walk away, but then turned around and came back. She leaned down and whispered something into Thomas's ear, but his eyes were already closed and he was fading fast. He caught the words *surprise* and *special*.

Then he heard footsteps and the soft thump of the door as it shut behind her.

9

224.10.07 | 12:43 P.M.

Thomas's head healed much quicker than he would've guessed. Soon he was back in his own room, attending classes as if nothing had changed. Since the day of the operation, he hadn't seen a trace of Teresa, Minho, or the boy named Newt. Or anyone else, for that matter. Sometimes, as he walked down the hall towards his classes, he heard voices. They were distant enough that he couldn't quite tell which way they were coming from, but he was sure they were kids. It made him wonder what was wrong with him that others were allowed to interact so much. When was it going to be his turn?

He wondered about it every day. At times he could explain it away as part of the experiments. Maybe some kids were together and some were alone. Maybe they'd switch it soon.

A bumpy line above his ear marked where they'd cut him open, but the hair had already grown over it and he hardly thought about it any more. He figured soon he wouldn't even be able to feel it. Sometimes he got a deep, resounding ache inside his skull, as if a magical hand had reached in there and squeezed. Whenever he asked Dr Paige or his instructors about the implant, they simply told him what they'd told him before – it was analyzing his system – and they were always quick to point out how much less frequently he had to have tests done. That was something he did appreciate.

Dr Paige constantly reassured him that there were reasons he was so isolated for now, that they wanted to take good care of him, keep him safe. The outside world was a scary, scary place, radiation and Cranks everywhere. And she said they needed to understand the disease better before Thomas interacted with others, that his was a special case – though she never went into much detail. But she brought him books and a handheld entertainment pad so often that he couldn't doubt her kindness, which reassured him that she wasn't just making things up to appease him. She always made him feel better about his strange life.

One day he woke up with a blistering headache and a weighty grogginess like he'd never felt before. It took every last ounce of his willpower to get up and slog through the morning routine. He took a nap in his room at lunchtime and felt like he'd barely closed his eyes when someone knocked on his door. It startled him, but he jumped up to answer it, worried he'd slept through his afternoon class. The movement brought another wave of pain crashing through his head.

His heart sank when he saw Dr Leavitt standing in the hallway, the lights shining off his bald head.

'Oh.' It came out of Thomas's mouth before he could stop it.

'Hey there, son,' Leavitt replied, as cheerful as he'd ever been. 'We've got a big surprise for you this afternoon, and I think you'll like it.'

Thomas stared at him, suddenly dizzy. Hearing those words had triggered such a strong moment of déjà vu that he thought he might still be sleeping.

'Okay,' he said, trying to hide his discomfort. Any change

in his daily schedule was welcome. 'What is it?'

Dr Leavitt had an odd, nervous smile. 'We – the Psychs,' the man said through a shifty grin, 'have decided it's time for you to have some interaction with others. We're, um, going to start you off with Teresa. How does that sound? Would you like to meet her and spend some time with her? Maybe things will go a little better than your first, uh, unofficial meeting.' His smile grew bigger, but it didn't touch his eyes.

It had been a long, long time since Thomas had felt anything like what burned inside him at that moment. He wanted to meet Teresa more than anything else in the world.

'Yes,' he said, 'absolutely. I think I'd like that very much.'

During the walk, that strange déjà vu came over him again, as if he'd made this exact same walk with the exact same purpose before. The man guided him into a small office on his floor, the only furniture a desk with nothing on it, a couple of chairs on either side. The girl named Teresa was already sitting in one of the chairs, and she gave Thomas a very shy smile.

The feeling hit him even stronger than before, almost making him stumble. Everything about the episode – the room, Teresa, the lighting – felt so familiar that it seemed impossible that it was happening for the first time. Confusion clouded his mind.

'Have a seat,' Leavitt said, gesturing impatiently.

Thomas tried to compose himself. He sat, and the man stepped back out into the hallway, pulling the door almost completely shut. 'We thought it was time we let you guys have a chitchat,' he said, then added with a quick smile, 'Enjoy,' and closed the door. There was another strong wave of familiarity.

Thomas couldn't stop staring at where the man had been standing moments before, too embarrassed to turn his attention to Teresa. He felt so awkward – a few minutes ago he'd been excited; now he was two seconds from getting up and running away, baffled by the strange rush of feelings. Finally he shifted in his chair, forcing his gaze to flick to her, and found that she was staring at him. Their eyes met.

'Hey.' It was the best he could do.

'Hi,' Teresa replied. She gave another shy smile. A smile Thomas could swear he'd seen at some point before today, in this very room.

But now wasn't the time to dwell on what might have happened – he had all the time in the world to think about the weirdness later. He motioned around him. 'Why did they put us in *here*?'

'I don't know. They wanted us to meet and talk, I guess.'

She hadn't got his point – he wondered if maybe that was her attempt at sarcasm. 'How long have you lived here?'

'Since I was five.'

Thomas looked at her, tried to guess her age, gave up. 'So . . .'

'So four years,' she said.

'You're only nine?'

'Yeah. Why? How old are you?'

Thomas wasn't sure he knew the answer to that question. He figured that was close enough. 'Same. You just seem older is all.'

'I'll be ten soon. Haven't you been here just as long?'

'Yeah.'

Teresa shifted in her seat, pulled one of her legs under her body and sat on it. Thomas didn't think it looked particularly comfortable but loved that she seemed a little more at ease. The same was true for him – the more they spoke, the more that disorientating pulse of déjà vu retreated to the background.

'Why do they keep some of us separate?' she asked. 'I can hear other kids screaming and laughing all the time. And I've seen the big cafeteria. It's gotta feed hundreds.'

'So they bring your food to your room, too?'

Teresa nodded. 'Three times a day. Most of it tastes like a toilet.'

'You know what a toilet tastes like?' He held his breath, hoping it wasn't too soon for a joke.

Teresa didn't miss a beat. 'Can't be worse than the food they give us.'

Thomas let out a genuine laugh that felt great. 'Heh. You're right.'

'There must be something different about us,' Teresa said, suddenly getting serious. It threw Thomas a bit. 'Don't you think?'

Thomas gave his best impression of an intelligent, thinking nod. He didn't want to give away that the idea had never occurred to him. 'I guess. There has to be a reason we're kept alone. But it's hard to guess what when we don't even know why we're here.' He frowned on the inside, hoped it didn't show on the outside. He'd said the word *guess* twice, and the whole thing had sounded stupid.

Teresa didn't seem to think so. 'I know. Is your life pretty much school stuff from the wake-up to lights-out?'

'Just about.'

Teresa nodded, then said almost absently, 'They keep telling me how smart I am.'

'Me too. It's weird.'

'I think it all has something to do with the Flare. Did your parents catch it before WICKED took you?'

All the joy Thomas had started allowing himself to feel came to a grinding halt. He suddenly saw his dad, drunk with rage, his mom saying goodbye to him when he wasn't even five years old. He tried to shut the vision out.

'I don't want to talk about that,' he said.

'Why not?' Teresa asked.

'I just don't.'

'Fine, then. Me neither.' She didn't seem mad.

'Why are we in here, anyway?' Once again, he gestured at the tiny room where they sat. 'Seriously, what're we supposed to be doing?'

Teresa folded her arms and let her leg drop back down to the floor. 'Talking. Being tested. I don't know. Sorry being around me is so boring for you.'

'Huh? Now you're mad?'

'No, I'm not mad. You just don't seem very nice. I kind of liked the idea of finally having a friend.'

Thomas wanted to slap himself. 'Sorry. That sounds kind of good to me, too.' He didn't know if this meeting could have gone any worse.

Teresa let him off the hook with another smile. 'Then maybe we passed the test. Maybe they wanted to see if we'd get along.'

'Whatever,' he said with a smile of his own. 'I quit guessing about things a long time ago.'

After a long pause, she said, 'So . . . friends?'

'Friends.'

Teresa held out her hand over the desk. 'Shake on it.'

'Okay.' He leaned forwards and they shook on it.

Teresa sat back in her chair, and her expression shifted again. 'Hey, does your brain hurt sometimes? I mean, not just like a normal headache, but deep down inside your skull?'

Thomas could only imagine the look of shock on his face. 'What? Are you serious? Yes!' He was just about to bring up his terrible morning headache – maybe even the feelings of having done this before – when she held a finger to her lips.

'Quiet, someone's coming. We'll talk about it later.'

How she'd known, Thomas had no clue. He hadn't heard anything, but someone knocked at the door a moment after she spoke. A second later it opened and Dr Leavitt popped his head through the crack.

'Hello, kids,' he said brightly. He looked from Thomas to Teresa. 'Time's up for today. Let's get you back to your rooms. We think this went well, so there'll be plenty more opportunities to get to know each other.'

Thomas exchanged a glance with Teresa. He wasn't totally

sure what her eyes said, but he really did believe he had a new friend. They got up from their chairs and moved towards Leavitt. Thomas was thankful for even the short time they'd been given, and would keep his fingers crossed that the good behaviour would truly lead to more meetings, as promised.

They were at the door when Teresa stopped and asked Dr Leavitt a question. Two, actually. And it was enough to change the man's demeanour completely.

'What's a swipe trigger? And is it true that seven kids died during the implant surgeries?'

The questions stunned Thomas. He turned to look at Teresa as the doctor fumbled for an answer.

'How . . . ,' the man began, then stopped, realizing at the same moment what Thomas did: Teresa had stumbled on something major. Something *true*. 'Where would you come up with such nonsense?'

Thomas wondered the same thing. How could she have heard something like that? He never heard anything.

Teresa shrugged. 'Sometimes you people talk when you think we can't hear.'

Leavitt was not pleased, but his voice remained steady. 'And sometimes when you overhear things, you don't hear the whole story. Let's not concentrate on what doesn't concern you, okay?'

And with that he turned and started back down the hall. He didn't seem to care whether they followed or not, but both were right on his heels.

'This is kind of fun,' Teresa whispered to Thomas. 'Walking along with my new friend.'

He looked at her in bemused disbelief. 'Really? You drop that bombshell about kids dying and now you act like it's no big deal? You're so weird.' He tried to make a joke of it to hide just how horrified he'd been by her second question. Surely it was just a rumour?

He felt better when she suddenly kissed him on the cheek, then sprinted down the hall, passing Dr Leavitt.

Thomas definitely liked having a friend. But as he watched her run, that feeling of panic came back to him. What had happened to him today? From the splitting headache to the overwhelming sense of déjà vu – it made him feel off-balance, scared to stand up for fear of tipping over. Like he wasn't in tune with the spinning of the earth.

He tried hard not to think of the worst possible answer.

He tried not to think of the Flare.

10

A week later, right after a particularly tough puzzle session with Ms Denton, Thomas found himself once again in the small room, sitting across the desk from Teresa. Thankfully, none of the strangeness of their last meeting came back to haunt him.

It had been the longest week of his life, wondering every minute of every day if he'd be able to see his new friend. The only answer he got from Dr Paige or his teachers or anyone else was that yes, they'd meet again soon. Letting a whole week go by seemed the most effective torture method he'd ever heard of. And despite considering it many times, he'd never got up the courage to ask about the powerful episode of déjà vu. He worried people might think something was wrong with him.

'Hey, good to see you again,' Teresa said to start things off. Leavitt had just left the room, refusing to answer her question as to how long they'd have together.

'Yeah, definitely,' Thomas agreed, pulling himself together. He felt too silly asking about the strange feelings he'd had last time, so he took another direction. 'Hey, I've been dying to ask you about those kids you said . . . died. Is that really true? And at times Dr Paige somehow makes it sound like they're doing us a favour by keeping us alone. I feel like I've got a million other things I want to talk about, too.'

'Whoa, not all at once,' Teresa said with a grin. Then she looked up at the corners of the ceiling – each of the four – with a worried glance. 'I wonder if we should be a little careful about what we say. I mean, they're obviously watching us. Or at least listening.'

'Probably both,' Thomas said in a loud, mocking voice. 'Hellooooooo! Hello, old people!' He waved all around as if he were in a parade, unsure where this sudden elation was coming from.

Teresa exploded with laughter, making him do the same. It went on for a good minute or two, each triggering the other to laugh again just when they were about to stop. He was smart enough to know, however, that he was trying to avoid thinking about the deaths in question.

'Let's not worry about it too much,' Teresa said when the chortling had stopped. 'This is our time, and we can talk about whatever we want. Let them get their kicks.'

'Amen.' Thomas slapped the top of the desk.

Teresa jumped in surprise, then laughed again. 'The stuff I heard about kids dying – I don't know. Probably just a rumour. I hope so. I guess I didn't hear it that clearly. They could've been talking about something that happened before we came. I was just trying to get a reaction from Leavitt.'

Thomas hoped so badly that was the case.

'So, anything new or exciting in your life?' Teresa asked.

'Can't say there is,' Thomas replied. 'Let's see, I eat. I go to school. Lots of school. Lots of medical tests. Oh, and I sleep, too. That about sums it up.'

'Sounds a lot like my life!'

'Really? Shocker.'

Smiles, a pause. Then Teresa leaned forwards and put her elbows on the desk.

'I don't know about the other kids, or any secrets or anything like that, but listen. Our heads should be totally healed, right?'

The question took him by surprise. 'Um, yeah, you'd think so.' He touched the scar hidden by the hair above his left ear. 'Seems like it, at least. I'm sure our brilliant brains are just fine.'

'You mean what WICKED calls the killzone?'

Thomas nodded. He'd heard the word here and there but didn't know much except the basics. 'Yeah. Seems like something they stole from a vid game. But Dr Paige says that's where the Flare does all its damage.'

'Isn't it so weird that we're immune? I mean, that should be the coolest thing in the world – that we don't have to worry about turning into crazy people.'

'Right.'

'But all it's done for us is landed us in this stupid place. Their name should be BORING, not WICKED. I'm seriously going insane from being locked in rooms all day.'

Thomas looked at the door, pondering for a second. 'Is it that bad outside? Is that why we're not allowed to go out there?'

'It must be bad. You always hear that the radiation is weakening but still pretty high in some places. All I remember is blinding white light outside the Berg that brought me here. I've been through a Flat Trans and ridden on a Berg – all before the age of five. Can you believe that?'

Thomas could just remember the big flying machine in which he'd also ridden. As sad as he'd been, he'd thought the thing was cool. Bergs were supposed to be for people who were crazy rich. But that was nothing compared to a Flat Trans. He'd never been through one of those, but if WICKED had them, they must have a lot of money.

'When did you go through a Flat Trans?' he asked.

Her face shifted from awe to sadness. 'I barely remember it.

I was born in the east somewhere. I lost my parents and got rescued . . .' She looked down and went silent. Maybe a topic for another time.

'Hey,' he said to change the subject, 'about that ache in our heads. I have it, too, sometimes.'

Teresa's eyes flicked up to the corners of the ceiling again. Nothing visible hung up there, but they both knew that cameras could be hidden anywhere. And microphones. WICKED could fit hundreds of microphones in a place that size. Not to mention whatever had been inserted into their brains – who knew what those things could monitor.

Teresa stood, picked up her chair, and brought it around to the other side of the desk. She placed it right next to Thomas, as close as possible. She sat down and leaned towards him, pressing their shoulders together.

She whispered in his ear, so lightly that he barely heard the words. Her breath against his skin sent tingles in all directions.

'Let's talk this way until they stop us,' she said.

Thomas nodded, then spoke into her ear. 'Sure.' He liked sitting close to her.

'That ache in my head,' she said, so quietly. 'It's actually more like an itch. Like something's in there that needs to be scratched. It just about drives me crazy sometimes. I want to dig in there with something until I can scratch the itch, you know?'

Thomas didn't know. That sounded even crazier than his déjà vu.

'I guess mine is kinda like that,' he said without much conviction.

She laughed, leaning away for a second. 'Perfect response,' she said aloud. Then she leaned in again to whisper. 'I know it's weird, but just hear me out. There's something in there that isn't being used. I heard the words "trigger switch" when I was coming out of the anaesthesia. And it *does* feel like that to me. Like a trigger that needs to be pulled, or a switch that needs to be pressed. Make sense?'

Thomas slowly nodded. Dr Paige had actually said something too, hadn't she? She'd said *special*. He vaguely remembered that word, but it could have been a dream. These implants were a complete mystery.

Teresa continued, her expression pinched. 'I feel like there's something linked with my brain. Something extra there. I've been lying in bed, concentrating until my head hurts from *that*.'

'What're you concentrating on?' Thomas asked, bursting with curiosity now.

'Using my brain as a tool. Like, conjuring up a physical thing in my thoughts, trying to use it on the implant. You know, like a hook to pull that trigger. Does any of this make even the slightest bit of sense?'

'Of course not,' Thomas said.

She pulled away, folded her arms, huffed in frustration.

He touched her arm. 'But that's why I'm interested.'

She raised her eyebrows.

He continued. 'You seem totally sane to me' – she laughed – 'and I'm pretty sure Dr Paige may have tried to say something about this to me. It's really got me thinking. Consider me curious.'

She nodded, kept nodding, her eyes filled with relief. She sat up and came in again for whispers.

'I'm going to keep working on it. Thanks for not thinking I've got the Flare after all. But I mean, come on. These people have some crazy technology. They have Flat Transes and Bergs . . .' She paused and shook her head slightly. 'My point is these things they put in our heads might be integrated somehow with our actual consciousness. Our actual thoughts. That's what I think.'

Thomas, a little overwhelmed with this fascinating barrage of things to think about, put his lips right next to her ear. 'I'll try, too. It'll be fun to have something different to work on.'

She stood, a genuine smile lighting up her face. She carried her chair back to its original position on the other side of the desk and sat back down.

'I really wish they'd let us meet more often,' she said.

'Me too. I hope they're not mad about our whispering.'

'They're just a bunch of oldies.' She laughed. 'You hear that, WICKED?' she shouted. 'We're talking about you. Wake up from your naps and come stop us!'

Thomas sniggered through the whole thing, but both of them froze when a knock sounded at the door.

'Uh-oh,' Thomas whispered.

The door cracked open and Dr Leavitt stepped inside. But any fear of punishment disappeared as soon as Thomas saw the man's face – he didn't seem the slightest bit angry.

'Another session over,' he announced. 'But before you go back to your normal schedule, we want to show something to the both of you. Something that's going to knock your socks off.'

Thomas, not knowing what to think, and more than a little suspicious, considering how their session had just went, stood up. So did Teresa, a worried look shadowing her face. Maybe they were heading straight to the chancellor's office for a reprimand.

But Dr Leavitt seemed genuinely excited. He opened the door wider. 'Okay, then! Prepare yourself for wonder.'

11

224.10.14 | 1:48 P.M.

Leavitt led Thomas and Teresa to the lift and all three of them rode it to the basement level – somewhere Thomas had never been before – then escorted them down a long hallway that ended at another bank of lifts. It was an entirely different section of the complex. Thomas and Teresa didn't say a word along the way, but they exchanged plenty of questioning looks. Finally, when the doctor pushed the call button to go down again, Thomas couldn't hold back his questions any more.

'What's this amazing thing you're going to show us?' he asked.

'Ah, now,' the man replied. 'It's not my place to ruin the surprise for you. You could say that's above my pay grade.' He barked a laugh that echoed loudly. 'Some very important people are going to show you the . . . project. I give my opinion on these matters, but I'm not involved in the actual . . . fulfilment.' He didn't seem very comfortable talking about it.

The chime of the lift saved him from further explanation,

and the doors opened.

Four people stood inside the car, and Thomas's breath caught in his throat. He recognized Chancellor Anderson and Dr Paige. There were another man and woman, each of them dressed very professionally.

'They're all yours,' Leavitt said; then, without waiting for a response, he turned and retreated down the hallway they'd come from.

Dr Paige held her arm out to keep the lift doors open. 'Come on in, Thomas. Teresa. We're really excited about what we're going to show you today.'

'Yes, we are,' Chancellor Anderson said. He shook Thomas's hand as he stepped inside the car, then Teresa's. 'We've been waiting and waiting for the Psychs to conclude that you two were ready, and here we are.'

'What's going on?' Teresa asked. 'Why all the mystery?

'The lift doors had closed, and Dr Paige pushed a button to get them moving. A soft hum filled the air. Thomas wondered how they could be going *down* instead of up – the other bank of lifts had said they'd exited at the basement. He felt a small trickle of fear.

Chancellor Anderson gave them his warmest smile. 'It's nothing you should be worried about,' he said. 'We think the best way to explain what we're planning is to show you in person. You'll see what I'm talking about soon.'

'But why us?' Teresa asked. 'We know there are lots of other kids – we can *hear* them through the walls. Why are we separate? Are you going to show them what you're showing us?'

The woman Thomas had never seen before stepped forward. She was short, with dark hair and a pale complexion. 'First, introductions, shall we? My name is Katie McVoy, and I'm an assistant vice president with special oversight of the production you're about to see. This' – she pointed at the other man, a serious-looking man with darker skin, grey hair, and stubble on his cheeks – 'is Julio Ramirez, our current chief of security.'

As hands were shaken and smiles shared all around, Thomas wondered about the word she'd used, *current*. It seemed weird that she would describe the man's job that way. Almost as if he wouldn't be holding the position much longer.

Ms McVoy continued. 'Regarding your questions, several of you have done leaps and bounds better than anyone else in the schooling and testing we've conducted here. Now, we're as pragmatic as anyone, especially in today's world, and we see the value in your skills and smarts. Today is a reward of sorts. You'll be the first subjects to see this.'

'That's right,' Anderson said with a bright smile. '*Reward* is a good word for it. You two and a few others are off the charts and perfect for what we're going to need over the next two years to finish what we've begun. And we should be arriving . . . Ah, there we go.'

The car came to a stop, having plummeted to the earth's core, for all Thomas could tell. The journey, combined with everything he'd just heard, had him feeling even more uneasy than when he'd stepped into the lift. Who were these 'others' they were talking about? Of all the new things that were apparently about to be opened to him, having other kids around excited him the most by far. The constant loneliness had begun to eat away at his heart. But it also sounded too good to be true. Could he believe it?

The doors had opened while he was lost in thought, and the others had all exited. Teresa stood across the threshold, gesturing for him to follow. She looked as if she was worried the whole thing might be cancelled if he didn't snap out of it and get moving. Thomas felt the same way. He stepped out of the car into a large room about the size of a gym, its exposed ductwork lit with blue lights. It was empty except for the hundreds of cords and tubes waiting to be connected, countless boxes and construction materials. One corner held what looked like an office – it was set up with multiple monitors and workstations, all lighting the space with their electric glow.

'Our plan,' Chancellor Anderson said, 'is for this to be the command centre for what we're calling the Maze Trials, as advanced a facility as any research institution has ever had. This should be finished within a couple of months, and then the two mazes themselves completed within two or three years. Maybe four.'

He'd been looking around the room proudly, but when he turned back to face Thomas and Teresa he froze, surprised. Thomas imagined that was because he himself must look completely confused.

Teresa asked the question for both of them. 'The Maze Trials?'

Chancellor Anderson opened his mouth to answer but seemed at a loss for words. Ms McVoy came to his rescue with a polished grin.

'Well, our esteemed chancellor has got a bit ahead of himself, but that's okay. See that door over there? Behind that door is a set of stairs that will take us to a temporary observation platform. We want to show you something, then explain what it will be used for. Are you ready?'

Thomas was. More than ready, dying of curiosity. He nodded at the same time Teresa said, 'Definitely.'

They walked as a group towards the door McVoy had indicated, the serious Ramirez taking the rear, looking around as if expecting trouble. They passed a long wall with nothing but huge power docks set far enough apart to accommodate something as big as a car.

'What're those for?' Thomas asked. They were halfway across the big room.

McVoy started to answer, but the chancellor cut her off. 'Let's just get through one thing at a time,' he said kindly, and shot McVoy a look Thomas couldn't quite make out. 'We have a few things in development that we're not quite ready to share.'

Thomas had too many butterflies in his stomach to give the

comment much thought. He figured he'd have plenty of time later, lying in his bed, to contemplate the onslaught of information being dumped on him.

He followed Anderson through the exit and the small group climbed four sets of stairs. Then they all squeezed in together on the landing directly in front of a massively fortified metal door. McVoy tapped in a security code on a screen. There was a great hissing sound, and then, with a heavy, booming clunk, the door popped open. Anderson and McVoy pushed it open all the way and then stood aside, allowing Thomas and Teresa to go through first.

Thomas had been high on anticipation but couldn't imagine what to expect. And what he saw before him almost made his heart stop from the sheer shock of it. The open door had created a conduit for air escaping the vast, open space before him. He stood frozen, the breeze washing over him as he took it all in.

He was standing on a platform facing a cavern so massive his mind could barely conceive of its size. He could tell the space had been gouged from the earth – the ceiling was uncovered, roughly cut rock dotted with enough huge, blinding lights to illuminate the entire space. That was a feat impressive on its own. But even more impressive were the steel girders that ran around the room; Thomas could only imagine they'd been put in place to reinforce the expansive ceiling, and they glittered in the reflected light of the brilliant spotlights overhead.

And they were underground.

It seemed impossible, yet they were actually *underground.* The cavern had to be at least a few miles square and as tall as a skyscraper. Building materials – wood and steel and stone – were scattered in piles across the vast floor. Far in the distance – what looked to be a mile, maybe even two – a huge wall was under construction, its skeletal frame almost reaching the ceiling.

Thomas suddenly sucked in a breath on reflex, not realizing

he'd been holding it. He just didn't understand what lay before him. It was a massive abyss under the ground, so huge it seemed to defy natural law. How could that roof *not* just cave in?

He looked over at Teresa, whose eyes were wide and glistening in awe.

'I'm sure you have many, many questions,' McVoy said. 'And we can answer them, one at a time. Things are going to be different for both of you from now on. You're going to know a lot more, and you're going to be very, very busy.'

'Busy doing what?' Teresa asked.

Chancellor Anderson chose to answer that one.

'You're going to help us build this place.'

12

224.10.14 | 2:34 P.M.

A few minutes later, they were sitting in a small conference room around a table with Ms McVoy, Dr Paige and Mr Ramirez, who had yet to say a single word. The chancellor had excused himself, but not before reiterating how excited he was to bring Thomas and Teresa to the next level. He assured them that Ms McVoy would take as long as they needed to answer their questions.

The thing was, Thomas wasn't sure he could sort out his questions. After the massive scale of the cavern he'd just stood over, the small room felt almost claustrophobic. And now, gathering his thoughts – it seemed like an incredible feat.

'Okay,' McVoy said, her hands folded gracefully on the table in front of her, 'as you can imagine, what you just saw is the culmination of several years' worth of developments. I couldn't possibly go over everything in one sitting. But let's do this: ask me your questions, and let's see where that takes us. How does that sound?'

Thomas and Teresa both nodded.

'Great. Teresa, why don't you go first?'

'What *is* that place?' she asked, the first and most obvious question.

McVoy nodded as if expecting those exact words. 'What you saw is one of two natural caverns we found in this area that we then expanded significantly to house what we plan to build inside.'

'And what's that?' Thomas asked.

'A maze. Two mazes, actually. Like I said, there are two caverns.'

'Why?' Teresa asked. 'Why in the world are you building two mazes?'

'As a testing ground. As a controlled environment to stimulate a long list of reactions, both physical and emotional, from our test subjects. We couldn't risk these locations being in the open air, and not just because of the obvious reasons like the decimated landscape and the potential for Crank invasions. The world is a dangerous, dangerous place at the moment. But just as importantly, we need a closed testing area so we can effectively control the stimuli.' Thomas heard all this but found it hard to believe. Or maybe just too much to process at once.

'Thomas?' McVoy said. 'Do you want to ask the next question?'

'I . . .' He searched for words. 'It's just so crazy. A maze? *Two* mazes? What are you going to test inside them? *Who* are you going to test?'

'It's complicated, like I said. But basically we need a large-scale environment that we can control with no outside influence. Our doctors and Psychs think this is a perfect environment to get what we need.' She leaned back and sighed. 'But I'm rambling. The simple answer is this: we'll be continuing to do what we've already begun. We'll be testing immunes, studying their brain function and biology, figuring out how they can live with the Flare virus without succumbing to its effects. In short, we're trying to find a cure, Thomas. We're trying to prevent all this unnecessary death that now surrounds us.'

'What did you mean about us helping you to build the place?' Teresa asked.

'Exactly that,' McVoy replied with a genuine smile. 'We've decided to use you and Thomas, as well as two other children your age, to assist us. Perhaps others. But the four of you are just so . . . beyond what we'd expected from people so young. We're going to utilize that. As I've said before, we're pragmatic people with limited resources. We don't plan to waste your talents. The planning, design, execution of these mazes . . . it's all going to be tricky.'

Thomas's shortage of words continued. He just sat there, stunned. Teresa was quiet as well, maybe feeling the same.

'You do *want* to help us, don't you?' McVoy asked.

Dr Paige, who had been quiet throughout the afternoon, chimed in here. 'It's an honour and a fantastic opportunity, you guys. I know things are dire in the world right now, but this project could even be fun for you. A challenge. We have a lot of faith in you both. And in the others as well. Aris and Rachel are their names.'

After a long silence, McVoy said, 'Well? What do you think?'

Thomas knew they had no choice in the matter. And that it might be a lot of hard work. But the whole idea was exciting. And something *new* to take up his days.

'Of course,' he said, barely able to contain his happiness.

'Yes,' Teresa added, sounding more serious.

McVoy stood up, then shook both Thomas's and Teresa's hands. 'This will be a fun project. You're becoming more a part of WICKED every day!' She said it as if it were the biggest compliment she could give.

As they left the conference room and headed back to their rooms, winding through the hallways, stairs and lifts of the complex, McVoy's parting words echoed through Thomas's mind. *A part of WICKED.*

He wasn't sure how he felt about that.

Dr Paige told Thomas that he had the rest of the day off to rest, relax and think about things. He lay on his bed and stared at the ceiling. What he really wanted to do, though, was hang out with Teresa, to talk through it all. His mind spun with the life-changing things he'd heard and seen that day, and he needed Teresa's help to process it all.

He looked at his door. It was closed, as always. And for as long as he could remember, it automatically locked upon closing. But he couldn't remember the last time he'd tried it. For months, maybe even a year or two, he'd just always assumed it was locked and didn't bother. Well, now he had a reason to give it a shot.

He rolled out of bed and went to the door. Slowly, he reached out, as if it might electrocute him upon touch. He grabbed the handle and turned.

The door popped open.

Thomas pushed it closed and ran back to his bed, his heart thumping in his ears. He looked around, wondered about the many, many ways they kept tabs on him. Cameras, micro-phones, sensors, who knew what else – some were in plain sight, some he couldn't see at all. The fear he suddenly felt wasn't rational – all he'd done was open the door a crack and then close it. WICKED had treated him well, for the most part. He hadn't even seen Randall in a long time. Why the sudden chill icing his bones?

They watched his every move – he was sure of it. Maybe that was why they'd stopped locking the doors. For all he knew, they wanted him to leave, to observe him, to see what hap-pened. Or it was possible that his obedience in staying put all these years was what had ensured his rise to the top along with Teresa and those other two kids. Could that be it?

It took a while, but his heart finally calmed, and the sweat that had dampened his face and arms evaporated. He stared at the door, pretending, even to himself, that what would happen next was actually up for debate. It wasn't, and he knew it. Something would have to strike him dead to prevent him from exploring.

But he had to be smart about it. He would wait until night-time.

The fear turned to pure anticipation.

The hours dragged.

He desperately wanted to sleep so that he'd be rested for his planned excursion, but it took forever to finally doze off, and then dinner came and ruined it. He ate, rested, finally fell asleep again.

He came awake with a start to a darkened room. Worried he'd wasted the entire night, he quickly checked the time – just a few minutes past midnight. He took a quick shower to wash away the grogginess, got dressed, then found himself standing in front of his door again, hesitant, full of doubts. He could ruin everything by wandering the hallways. Ruin the chance to work on WICKED's crazy, insane project to build giant mazes underground. Ruin his chance to be with Teresa and others.

He sighed, angry at the dent in his enthusiasm. Maybe there was a time mechanism and the door *would* be locked. Oh well. They weren't going to punish him for opening a stupid door, or even for venturing into the hallway. He could always take a peek and then come back if it felt wrong.

Something clicked and then the door swung several inches towards him.

At first he didn't understand what had happened – he actually looked down at his hands to see if they'd acted on their own and turned the handle. But they were at his sides, palms sweaty. No, someone had opened the door from the other side.

He leaned his head around the edge of the frame and his heart leaped when he saw a complete stranger staring back at him. A boy about his age. No, *not* a stranger. The kid just looked different because his blond hair wasn't covered with a bandage and he was a little older.

'Hey, I'm Newt,' the boy whispered. 'And I know bloody well who you are. Which is why we've decided to finally snag you. Come on, I want to show you something.'

13

Thomas had never had to think so fast in his life. A thousand things went through his mind in the two or three seconds before he answered Newt. Should he actually go with the boy or slam the door in his face? How could Newt have possibly showed up on the very night that Thomas had discovered his door unlocked and planned to go out on his own? In a place like WICKED, he didn't believe in coincidences – anything might be a test of some sort. What did this kid want to show him? Was it a trap? Should he invite him into his room and grill him about it? What if –

'Okay,' he finally said, stepping into the hallway. He closed the door behind him, then quickly checked to make sure it didn't lock on him. It didn't. He turned to Newt and asked, 'Can we take Teresa with us? She's right next to me.'

Newt huffed. 'This isn't a slumber party.' But then he grinned mischievously. 'I actually woke her up before coming to you. She's getting dressed. Nab her and let's go. We only have an hour or two.'

Thomas stepped over to 31K and opened the door, still bewildered. None of the doors were locked? Really? When he stepped inside, Teresa was sitting at her desk, fully dressed. She stood up immediately, looking battle-ready until it registered that her intruder was Thomas.

'What . . .' she started, but didn't finish. 'Do you know . . .' That didn't get completed, either.

'All I know is there's a kid named Newt in the hall,' Thomas said to Teresa, 'and he says he has something to show us. And I think we should go.' She was by his side and opening the door before he could finish the last sentence.

'Okay, then,' he said as he followed her into the hallway.

'Hello again,' she said to Newt, who responded with a friendly nod.

'We've heard about the two of you,' the new boy said, 'and those kids Aris and Rachel.' If it weren't for the kind look on his face, Thomas would have been suspicious of his direct words.

'What's going on?' Thomas asked. 'Are you sure this is okay? What if we get caught?'

'Don't be such a worrywart,' Newt replied. 'If they catch us, what're they gonna do? Lock you up in your room?'

Thomas knew exactly what they could do – take away the new opportunity with the mazes. He tried to communicate that to Teresa with his eyes. Maybe this was a terrible idea.

'Good point,' Teresa said, eyeing Thomas back with a look defying him to challenge her. 'Let's go.' She paused. 'Wait, where are we going again?'

Newt laughed through his nose. 'First things first. Let's meet Alby and Minho.'

With those words, Thomas couldn't say no.

Sweat trickled down the back of Thomas's neck as Newt led them through various halls, through doors, up and down stairwells. Who needed a maze when their very complex served as one? Thomas expected Dr Leavitt or someone worse to pop out at any minute, catching them in the act. Things had been looking up that day – he really didn't want to ruin it. But then again, he was having the time of his life. It felt good to take a risk, step out on a ledge.

They ended up in a dimly lit hall in the basement, where the last door had a sign that read MAINTENANCE.

'This is our favourite hiding spot,' Newt said, pride in his voice. He opened the door and ushered them into a large dusty room filled with wooden tables and cleaning equipment, boxes and a million other odds and ends.

'What's up, gents?'

The greeting came from Minho – the boy Thomas had met in the hallway during the crazy day of the implants. He seemed a lot happier now than he had then, screaming and yelling like the world had come to an end. Thomas wondered if he even remembered the ordeal.

'Would you stop saying *gents*?' another boy said, dark-skinned and older, with the wisest eyes Thomas had ever seen. 'It's not funny, and it's gettin' on my nerves.'

The rebuke didn't faze Minho in the least. He walked up, a huge smile on his face, and hugged Thomas, then Teresa, the last thing either of them had expected. But Thomas had to admit it felt pretty good. Dr Paige might be a nice lady, but he hadn't felt this kind of warmth in years. Maybe not since he'd said goodbye to his mom.

Teresa seemed as stunned by the situation as he did, but she also had a small grin on her face. They were having *fun*.

'You two seem cooler than I thought,' Minho said as he stepped back. 'I was expecting a couple of greasy-haired, buck-toothed weirdos quoting Shakespeare and writing out maths problems on your hands. You actually look half normal!'

'Thanks?' Thomas said it as a question.

The other boy stepped forwards and pushed Minho out of the way. 'I'm Alby,' he said. 'Good to meet you guys. Minho actually for once has a good point. With all the rumours about you highfalutin folks, we didn't know what to expect. And that's why we brought you here today. To check you out. It's nice to see you're not too bad, by the looks of it.'

It was Teresa's turn to say thanks with a question mark. That made everyone laugh and broke the ice a bit.

'So,' Thomas said, not sure where to begin, 'how long have you guys been sneaking out like this? It's obviously not the first time.'

'Nope,' Alby replied. 'It gets so boring following all their rules, doing everything they tell us to. And yeah, they might know what we're doing – we're not idiots. But hey, until they actually come out and tell us to stop, we ain't stopping.' He turned to Minho and Newt. 'Am I right, guys?'

Minho whooped a cheer and Newt gave a bored thumbs-up.

'What are all these rumours about us that you guys keep bringing up?' Teresa asked. 'And why are we isolated from you? It seems like you three have known each other for years. Thomas and I *just* met.' She looked at him, and something in her eyes said she'd almost mentioned the mazes but caught herself at the last second. That the mazes should be their secret for now.

Newt, sitting on a stool by the wall, answered her questions. 'Honestly, we don't know what's different about you and those other two. The rest of us have been sharing a cafeteria, going to the same classes, and all that for over a year. Way I see it, you're either way smarter or way dumber than us.'

'Way smarter, obviously,' Teresa said. Her sassy reply threw everyone off kilter for a beat, but then Alby clapped and laughed, and the ice broke just a little more.

'Man, I like you guys,' he said.

'Look,' Minho said, 'as much as I'd like to say we're just being nice inviting you down here, I'm guessing you know we have a reason.'

'Of course,' Teresa quickly answered.

Minho nodded, an appraising look in his eyes. 'Good. Good. We have ideas. Plans. Nothing solid. Nothing too crazy. But information is king, and we feel like we're in the dark not knowing you two. Though it'll be a while before there's complete trust. Fair enough?'

'Fair enough,' Thomas replied. 'We'll tell you what we know if you tell us what you know.'

Minho smiled. 'Nice. But let's not get ahead of ourselves. There'll be plenty of other chances to talk. First we wanna just get to know you, maybe show you around a bit. Have some fun. The serious stuff can come in a few weeks or so. When we know you better. Sound good?'

Thomas and Teresa looked at each other and shrugged. They both turned back and said yes.

Newt hopped off his stool and went to the door. 'Let's get out of here before we get cabin fever,' he said. 'I know a good place to start their tour – let's go show them Group B.'

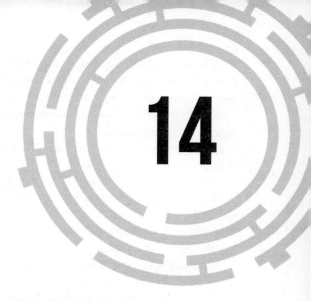

14

224.10.15 | 2:03 A.M.

Thomas had never heard the words *Group B* before, but they definitely piqued his interest. He also noticed a shadow cross over Newt's face when he said it, and a look of discomfort pass over his friends Alby and Minho.

Something was weird about it, but that only intrigued Thomas even more.

Newt led their little group of five down the basement hallway until they came to a small, unmarked door that only came up to Thomas's waist. It had a latch and padlock, but the lock had been broken long ago, its surface covered in orange rust – this area of WICKED was obviously off the beaten path. Newt bent down and opened the little door, then crawled through. Thomas gave Alby a questioning look, and Alby leaned in to whisper something in his ear.

'This is sort of like a ritual for us.' Teresa had come close so that she could hear too. 'Newt thinks up reasons to make it happen. See, they have his little sister over there, and when he says he wants to go see her . . . Well, we learned months ago that you better just go along with it or there'll be hell to pay. You got me? Family, man. It's something most of us don't have any more. Come on.'

The trip was a dusty one, involving ladders and grimy passages barely wider than Thomas's hips. Minho said something about it being a secret escape route from years ago. No one really knew what the original purpose of the building had been before WICKED took over.

They finally reached their destination, a loft of sorts dotted with dirty windows overlooking a huge barracks full of bunks. And those bunks were full of sleeping kids. Thomas strained his eyes, looking up and down the rows. As far as he could tell – based on hair length and what he could see of the faces illuminated by the scant light – there wasn't a single boy in the entire room.

Thomas didn't know what to think. It was such a contrast to the private rooms in which he and Teresa slept.

'They call us Group A,' Alby explained. 'And this is Group B. We're all boys, they're all girls. How Aris and Teresa here fit into all that, I don't get. I mean, I guess it makes sense to separate us. Who knows.'

'So you guys live in a place like this?' Teresa asked.

Minho answered. 'Yep. I think I could handle transferring to Group B, though. Someone remind me to put in a request.'

'Why are we . . .' Thomas trailed off. The question was obvious, and he suddenly had the absurd feeling that it'd come across as bragging if he asked it.

'Special?' Alby asked. 'That's what we hope to find out from you.'

'Looks like you know more than us,' Teresa said in an absent voice. Her mind was spinning, Thomas could tell. He wished he could take a peek inside her brain, see what churned there.

He looked at Newt. The boy stood silent, looking through a window a few feet down from them. Thomas walked over to him.

'What're you looking at?' Thomas asked, even though he knew.

Newt sniffed, and Thomas noticed for the first time that the boy was crying.

'You see her?' he said, the tip of his index finger touching the glass. 'Far row, third one from the left side.'

Thomas saw a girl curled up under a blanket, her arms wrapped around a pillow, dark hair spilling out. 'Yeah. That your sister?'

Newt looked at him in surprise. 'That's right. Her name's Lizzy.' A long pause, during which his head sank until it rested against the window. 'At least, it used to be. They may think they have us all brainwashed with our new names, but no way I'll ever forget hers.'

'What did they change it to?' Thomas asked.

'Sonya.' Bitterness filled his voice. 'Can you believe that? They renamed her *Sonya*.' He coughed. Or sobbed. Something. His eyes glistened in the gloom. 'And WICKED's so mean about it. They won't let me see her, and I've had to pretend that I've forgotten it all or they . . . punish me.'

Thomas was stunned. For the first time since the man named Randall had hurt him, he felt a sudden and shocking anger towards the people behind it all. Towards WICKED. Here stood a boy, a few dozen feet from his own sister, and he couldn't even pretend to know her.

'I did as they asked, I stopped using my real name,' Newt continued. 'I think I was one of the last holdouts. But hers I'll never forget. They'll have to kill me first.'

'I'm sorry,' Thomas whispered, not sure what to say. His own heart ached thinking of his mom, and just how impossibly hard it would be if she lay in a bed in the barracks below him. How could he *not* break the glass and go to her? How?

Newt stood up straight and wiped the tears from his eyes. He appeared to feel no shame whatsoever at letting anyone see him cry.

'That's the way of things, Tommy,' he said, his voice not quite steady. 'The world outside's gone to hell. Why should we expect any different in here? At least I can see her there, sleeping peacefully. How many people in this world would chop off their own arm to be able to say that about someone they love who's dead and gone? It's just the way of things.'

He said it as if they'd been friends for years.

Teresa came up behind Thomas, leaned in against his back.

'Everything okay?' she asked.

'Yeah,' he said. 'Newt was just showing me his sister down there.'

'We better not push our luck tonight,' Alby said. 'Let's go get some shut-eye until the wake-up, then do this all over again tomorrow. What do you say?'

Everyone agreed. As they walked back, a sombre silence hung over them, and the journey seemed much longer than before. Thomas had hoped they'd have time to compare what they did and didn't know, but it looked like that was going to have to wait. Goodbyes were said and ways were parted.

Thomas made it back to his room without incident, said goodnight to Teresa – quickly, worried someone might appear in the hallway – then went inside and crashed on the bed without getting undressed. He fell asleep far faster than he would have imagined after all that had happened.

Throughout his shortened night, he dreamed of Newt and Sonya.

Of Newt and Lizzy.

The next few days and nights went by in a whirlwind of discovery and exhaustion; Thomas got less than three or four hours of sleep each night. The morning alarm was like a dagger in his skull, and his head never stopped aching throughout the long, long days of schooling. He waited for Dr Paige or Dr Leavitt or one of his teachers to comment on his night-time escapades, or worse, an armed WICKED guard to whisk him away to a holding cell. But no one acted like anything was out of the ordinary.

On their second night of exploration, they discovered a huge laboratory with foul-smelling vats of steaming liquid, at least two dozen of them. Even in the deepest part of the night, workers in full hazard suits worked among the odd containers, doing all kinds of tests. A few times, Thomas and the others caught sight of what looked like large fish or tentacles moving beneath the steam, breaking the surface of whatever revolting liquid they swam in. The whole thing baffled even Newt, who said he'd been watching the place for months.

They searched the administrative offices on the third night, even catching a man and woman lingering behind after work hours for some lovey-dovey private time. Alby barely stopped Minho in time from jumping out and scaring the poor couple to death. Thomas almost wished he'd let it happen.

The fourth and fifth nights were filled with new adventures – more labs, the cafeterias, a giant sports facility that Thomas had never even heard about. They found a hospital room where complicated mask-like devices hung over each bed, tubes and wires branching out like the legs of a monstrous spider, studded with all kinds of monitoring equipment. Thomas desperately wanted to stay longer and figure out what the things were for, but Alby got them out of there quick. It was the first time Thomas had really seen him flustered, beads of sweat covering his forehead. Something had struck a nerve.

It was fun. Exciting. Terrifying. Invigorating. In all the years since WICKED had taken Thomas, he'd never felt so alive. He could feel the bonds of trust growing between them, although he still had no idea where that trust was leading. It was as if the original purpose of their summons had been lost in a burgeoning friendship.

Alby, Minho, Newt, Teresa.

Thomas had *friends*.

15

Newt had been promising them that he was saving something special, and he did that annoying zipped-lip sign every time Thomas or Teresa asked him *what* – pinched fingers swept across his tightly closed mouth. The little light in his eyes showed he enjoyed every second of their torture.

Regardless of where they were headed on any given night, they always assembled in the basement maintenance room. The dusty old room had become something of a sanctuary for their group. After their third escapade, Newt stopped coming to escort Thomas and Teresa there – they knew their own way – and the exhilaration of sneaking through the dark halls of WICKED only became more enjoyable every time Thomas did it.

He lightly tapped on Teresa's door and she opened it immediately. She poked her head out cautiously and looked up and down the hallway to make sure the coast was clear.

'Okay,' she said the fourth night, as she joined him and closed her door. She couldn't hide the smile blooming on her face. 'What do you think it is tonight?' They started making their way.

Thomas did Newt's zipped-lip gesture, and that got him a sharp poke in the ribs.

'Ow,' he said dryly, and they picked up the pace.

Minho and Alby were wrestling when they walked into the maintenance room. For a second Thomas thought it was a genuine fight, but then Alby let out a whooping laugh when he pulled a manoeuvre that flipped Minho onto his back with a grunt.

'Not this time, sucker!' Alby yelled. He pressed his forearm into Minho's chest and Newt slapped the floor three times.

Alby jumped up, arms raised in a victory dance.

Minho scrambled to his feet as well, dusting himself off. He let loose a few words Thomas used to hear his dad say, then added a very insincere 'Good job.' Alby seemed to take it all as a compliment. It meant he'd won.

'All right, then,' Newt said, stretching his arms over his head and letting out a yawn. 'Let's get on with it, shall we?'

'What's the big surprise tonight?' Thomas asked. 'Where're we going?'

Newt looked up at the ceiling. 'Well, we've pretty much been from one end of this place to the other.'

It was hard for Thomas not to look over at Teresa. The truth was, Newt and his friends had no idea what was hidden right under their feet. Trust or no trust, though, there was no way Thomas and Teresa could share the information about the maze cavern. He was just shocked that with all their exploring, the others hadn't already discovered it on their own. And there were supposed to be *two* mazes. How had Newt and his friends not stumbled upon either one of them?

'Tommy?'

Thomas realized Newt was staring straight at him, eyebrows raised.

'Sorry,' he said, embarrassed. 'Wandered off there for a second. What'd you say?'

Newt shook his head in admonishment. 'Try to keep up, Tommy. Are you ready to see the great outdoors?'

They climbed up a ladder hidden behind a cinder-block wall, its original purpose mysterious to Thomas. The building had been built way before any organization named WICKED came into being, and the ladder had a sinister feel to it, as if it had been put there without the knowledge of the original planners or owners. Put there to accomplish devious deeds.

Thomas choked on dust as they climbed rung by rung, up and up and up. Somehow he'd got stuck going last, so he had four people above him kicking loose dirt and gravel and anything else that had collected over the years. A couple of nails even dropped down, one of them almost piercing his right eyeball.

'Could you guys be a little more careful up there?' he whisper-shouted at the group more than once. The only response was a giggle, and he was pretty sure Minho was the guilty one.

Finally, after climbing what had to be ten floors, they reached a steel landing that was barely big enough to hold the five of them. A heavy metal door, curved and rusted, sat like an ugly tooth in the cement wall to their left. The only thing on the door that didn't look a hundred years old was a handle, rubbed shiny silver from usage.

'How many times have you guys done this?' Teresa asked.

'A dozen?' Alby replied. 'Maybe fifteen? I don't know. You have no idea how nice it is to get some fresh air, though. You're about to see for yourself. Oh, man, and the sound of the ocean in the distance. Can't beat it.'

'I thought the outside world was a wasteland,' Thomas said, butterflies swarming more than ever in his gut. 'Radiation and heat and all that? Little things called sun flares?'

'Not to mention Cranks,' Teresa added. 'How do you know there aren't Cranks out there?'

'Hey, people,' Minho said, holding a hand up as if to say slow down. 'You think we're morons? Would we have gone out there fifteen times if we'd lost a finger to a Crank every time or had our privates zapped by radiation? Come on, now.'

Newt waggled his fingers in front of Thomas's face. 'Still got 'em all. And I'm not too worried about down under just yet.' A laugh exploded out of Thomas's mouth that sent spray everywhere.

'Sorry,' he said, wiping his lips on his sleeve.

Alby took over the conversation with a little more sense of reason. 'Things are starting to get better out there. Plus, we're way up north, which wasn't hit as badly. A couple of times we've seen snow in the trees.'

'Snow?' Teresa repeated, sounding as shocked as if he'd said *aliens.* 'Are you serious?'

'Yep.'

'Enough chitchat,' Newt said. 'Minho, open her up.'

'Yes, sir!' Minho barked. He grabbed the handle and pushed it down with a grunt of effort. There was a loud metallic clunk; then the door opened on squealing hinges, swinging outwards.

A stiff breeze blew up the ladder chute as pressurized air escaped the complex, as if rushing to freedom. It ruffled Thomas's clothes as it crossed over him, giving him a slight chill, and the anticipation of what awaited them spiked so hard that he could barely contain himself. Minho went out first, then Alby. Newt gestured for Teresa to go next, and she did so, but not before throwing one last glance at Thomas. Her eyes said a million things, but he couldn't decipher any of them.

'You're next, Tommy,' Newt said. 'Try not bangin' your head, all right?'

Thomas ducked through the small opening and stepped onto a wide platform of concrete, the air outside crisp and cool. Every memory of the time before WICKED when he was allowed to go outside came rushing back to him, bringing with it thoughts of warmth and heat and sweat. But this outside was different. It was odd, but fantastic, to feel such a refreshing bite of fresh air – just as Alby had predicted – and to hear the ocean waves crashing on rocky cliffs in the distance.

'Whatcha think?' Minho asked.

Thomas looked around, though he couldn't see much in the darkness. Lights shone down from somewhere above, obscuring his vision even more. All he could make out was the platform, a railing around its edge, and a sea of blackness beyond. The sky showed the faintest pinpricks of stars.

'Can't see a whole lot,' Thomas answered after a moment of silence. 'But, man, it feels great.'

'Told ya,' Alby said. Thomas could hear the smile in his voice.

'There's a drainpipe over here,' Newt said, leaning over the railing at the corner of the platform. 'Has notches in it, see? Makes it easy to climb down, but it's a bit of an effort coming back up. A little sweat'll be good for you, though.'

'Let's show them the woods,' Minho said. 'Maybe we'll get lucky and see a deer. And maybe it'll let us pet it.'

Thomas had the feeling he'd never be sure whether Minho was joking or not. He used the exact same tone – his words tinged with amusement – no matter what came out of his mouth.

Alby scrambled over the railing and started his descent. Newt had Thomas go second this time. His fingers ached as he gripped the notches in the drainpipe. Luckily, the trip was nowhere near as long as the climb up the ladder inside. When Thomas's feet finally landed on the soft earth, it felt as if he'd stepped onto an alien planet.

He stood next to Alby as they waited for the others to join them. There was no snow, but a cool bite to the air hinted it might not be too far away.

'What's out there?' Thomas asked, gesturing to the wide-open space that ended in the dark wall of the forest. 'Can we really just walk away? Why would we even come back?'

'Trust me,' Alby responded, 'we've thought about it. We've talked about hoarding a bunch of food and making a run for it.

But . . . the odds, man. Who knows how long we'd last. But even more than that, we've got it pretty good on the inside. We're fed, it's warm, no Cranks. . . Still, it's something we think about.' There seemed to be more on his mind that he chose not to share.

Teresa was the last one to jump the few feet off the bottom of the drainpipe. Thomas saw Alby open his mouth to say something, but before he got a word out, blazing lights ignited from all directions, along with a series of clunks, as if giant switches were being thrown. Thomas shielded his eyes, spun in a circle, but he couldn't see a thing, blinded by light.

Squinting, he could gradually make out three dark figures piercing the brightness. They approached, hunched over some sort of handheld weapon, and as they got closer, Thomas could see they wore uniforms and helmets. A fourth man appeared behind them, and as he neared, Thomas's insides felt like they were melting into something toxic. It was a man Thomas hadn't seen since his naming day.

Randall. And it appeared he'd graduated from the green scrubs.

'You kids really shouldn't be out here,' he said. He sounded almost sad. 'But I don't think you need me to tell you that. You're smart enough to have figured it out on your own. It seems we need to teach you a lesson about the dangers of the outside world. Make you appreciate what WICKED does for you just a teeny bit more.' His speech had an odd cadence, as if he were reciting something he'd memorized and practised beforehand.

He pointed at Newt. 'That one's not immune – get him back to his room and call a doctor in to test him. Pronto!'

As one of the guards moved towards Newt, Randall sighed loudly, then waved a hand towards Thomas and the others.

'Take the rest of them to the Crank pits.'

16

224.10.20 | 2:09 A.M.

Thomas didn't know when it had started, but he and Teresa were holding hands. They were standing together, sharing their sudden fear of what was about to happen, worrying about their punishment. One of the guards, a woman, stepped up to them.

'Don't be scared,' she whispered. 'Randall just wants to teach you a quick lesson about the dangers of being out here. It's for your own good, and you'll be safe. Just do as we say and it'll be over soon. Deal?'

Thomas nodded; the words *Crank* and *pits* were still reverberating through his mind. How many times in his life had he heard about Cranks – people with the Flare who were well past the Gone? Who were nothing more than animals consumed by bloodlust?

What had Randall meant? *Where* were they being taken?

'Come on now,' the female guard said to him, reaching out and gently taking his arm. 'If you cooperate you'll be back in your room safe and sound before you know it, with enough time for a quick nap before the wake-up.'

Teresa was squeezing his hand so hard it hurt. But he nodded and then followed the guard when she started walking away from the drainpipe, leading them along a path that followed the footprint of the WICKED complex. Another guard walked with Alby and Minho, who both looked just as stunned as Thomas felt.

The third guard stayed at the building, Newt by his side, looking at the ground, his face unreadable. Thomas looked for Randall, but the man was on the phone, several yards from his friend.

Thomas lost sight of them as they turned a corner, but he couldn't shake what Randall had said about Newt – that he wasn't immune. It didn't hit Thomas until that moment just how enormous the implications of that were. And then, why was Newt here if he wasn't a Munie?

Teresa's voice tore him from his thoughts.

'Can't you tell us where we're going?' she asked. 'What *are* the Crank pits?' The little group continued walking, following the path. The lady didn't answer, nor did the guard escorting Alby and Minho, just a few steps behind. The sounds of the ocean and the smell of salt and pine filled the silence.

'Answer her,' Thomas said. 'Please. We didn't do anything wrong – we were just exploring. What are we, prisoners?'

This also was met with silence.

'Say something!' Teresa yelled.

Their guard whirled to face them. 'You think I like this?' she snapped. Then she looked around like someone caught stealing. She lowered her voice. 'I'm sorry. Really. Just do as you're told – it makes things a lot easier. All we're going to do is help you to realize why it's better to stay inside.'

After that ominous statement, she turned and continued leading them along the exterior of the building. No one said another word.

*

They came to a road. To the right, it wound through some fields, then disappeared into the forest looming in the distance. To the left, it intersected with the WICKED complex itself and turned into a steep ramp that descended beneath the building. Without hesitating, the guard stepped onto the asphalt and turned left, towards the darkness of the tunnel thirty feet in front of them.

Thomas looked up as he followed her. Saw the tall granite walls of the WICKED facility, the faint scattering of stars in the dark sky above that. He'd been hoping so badly to see the moon.

The road dipped down, and soon they were beneath the building, in a wide tunnel with no lights. Someone must have turned them off, because there was no way they'd normally keep this place unlit.

He heard a sound that made him pause midstep. It was haunting, a human sound between a cry and a moan. Maybe not so human. Goosebumps prickled across his skin, and he felt a shudder of horror go through his chest.

It was so dark he could barely see the outline of their guard when she stopped and turned to face them. She pulled out a torch and flicked it on, shone it in their faces, then to her left. It revealed a rickety iron gate, a chain and padlock wrapped around its bars to keep it closed. Without saying anything, the other guard left Alby and Minho and walked over, pulled out a key, then unlocked the padlock. The loud rattle of the chain being unwrapped echoed through the tunnel.

The man dropped the chain to the ground and opened the gate.

'In you go,' he said. 'This is only meant to give you a scare – they won't be able to actually harm you. I promise.'

'What's in there?' Thomas asked.

'Cranks,' the female guard answered in a kind tone completely incongruous with the word itself. 'Sometimes we need to remind you just how awful this disease is.'

'They won't hurt you,' the man said again. His voice was solemn. 'They'll scare the pants off you, but they won't hurt you.'

'Come on, guys,' Minho said, marching past the guard. 'Let's see what's inside this hellhole.'

Thomas didn't want to. Every nightmare he'd ever had was welling up inside him. Teresa's bravery shook him out of it. She went through the gate, then Alby. Thomas followed.

17

The darkness was the scariest part. Even though the guard continued to shine her light behind them, it seemed the beam was lost in a black fog. They walked, small step by small step, across crunchy gravel, down a narrow path lined on both sides with the iron railings of a fence. The bars, rising from the ground, were spaced about five inches apart; two long bars ran along the top and bottom. If there was anything on the other side of the fence, Thomas couldn't make it out.

'This is spooky,' Minho spoke quietly, though it seemed loud in the still darkness. 'Alby, hold my hand.'

'Dude, chill,' was Alby's response.

Their feet scraped against the gravel, causing an echo that almost sounded like whispers. Thomas felt claustrophobia edging in the farther they went. It took everything he had not to turn around and run back. They kept on.

Soon they came to a brick wall, the fence on both sides leading right up to it. A dead end. This only fanned the flames of Thomas's panic.

'What now?' he asked, hating how the whine in his voice gave away his fear. 'Go back?'

'Definitely go back,' Teresa answered. 'Maybe this was just a test to see if we'd do what we were—'

Minho shushed her, holding a finger to his lips. He looked down, listening. In the dim light coming from behind them, he looked like a phantom.

'Something's coming,' he said. He pointed at the bars to the left of the brick wall. 'From back there.'

Thomas turned to face where Minho indicated and stared into the darkness beyond the fence. He strained to hear. And there it was. Although the four of them weren't moving, barely even breathing, the scrape of footsteps echoed throughout the tunnel. Thomas thought he heard it coming from behind as well, and he spun around to look. But now the sound was everywhere, seeming to come from all directions. Getting louder.

'Cranks,' Alby whispered. 'They throw them in a creepy jail under their own building. Nice.'

Shapes were coming into view to match the scuffing of footfalls. Bodies.

'I think they must keep them somewhere else, actually,' Minho said. 'Or they would've been pressed against the bars while we walked down here. I think they just released them like wild animals to pay us a visit.'

Moans and indecipherable murmurings broke out among the crowd of oncoming Cranks, increasing rapidly. Thomas and his friends had definitely been spotted.

And then, like a switch had been flipped, the room filled with thunderous sound, deafening. Screams and cries of anguish. Roars. Slapping footsteps as they rushed towards the bars. Thomas shook with a drowning fear as all around them, Cranks crashed against the fence, bodies upon bodies pressing against those who'd made it first. Arms reached through the bars, hands clasping and unclasping as they tried in vain to grab

Thomas and the others.

Thomas stood in the very centre of the passageway, Teresa right beside him – Alby and Minho were a few feet away. Alby had his back to the brick wall, jerking his head left to right, left to right, trying to take it all in. Minho was in front of him, in a fighting stance, as if that would do any good if the bars gave way to the press of the crowd.

Thomas looked at the Cranks, all of them so far past the Gone that he felt equal parts terror and pity. The creatures' eyes emanated an emptiness like he'd never seen, and scratches and torn flesh covered their faces and arms. Their clothes were filthy, bloody, ripped. Some screamed, some sobbed, tears streaming down their faces. Others spoke, harshly and rapidly, the words impossible to make out. All of them reaching, reaching, as if Thomas and the others were their only hope to escape the horrific disease that had ruined their minds.

One woman suddenly appeared, having fought her way to the front. Her face relatively clean, she stared straight at Thomas, her lips working as if she was trying to figure out what to say. And then she was speaking, her voice hitching with tremors.

'My babies my babies my babies my babies my babies my babies.' Those two words, over and over. She wept the entire time, then abruptly attacked the bars like a rabid gorilla, throwing her body against the fence viciously until she finally fell down. It looked like she'd knocked herself out. Other Cranks stepped on the woman as they took her place. Thomas felt a crushing sadness, a black despair that filled his chest.

'I think we've learned our lesson!' Alby shouted. 'Head back, now!'

Thomas shook his head. The horror of their surroundings had hypnotized him in a way, frozen him in disbelief. And that was what it was. Even after watching his dad degenerate into an angry shell of a man, even after all the stories he'd heard over the years, nothing could have prepared him for this.

He couldn't possibly believe it until seeing it for himself right now.

'Thomas, go!' Minho shouted. They were lined up next to him, all of them standing in the centre of the path, staying well out of the way of the outstretched arms of the Cranks.

Thomas nodded, not as afraid as he'd been. Just sinking ever deeper into that black feeling. Had this happened to his mom? Had she cried for her baby over and over in her madness? His feet felt attached to the gravel under him. He couldn't move.

'Thomas,' Teresa whispered into his ear. 'It's okay. This. *This* is why we're here. We're going to help them find a cure. Save people from this.'

Her voice lit a fire in him. Made him feel something. He turned, started walking back the way they'd come. He didn't need to look to know that Teresa was right behind him. Her hand was on the small of his back as if she alone were pushing him forwards. Cranks filled the tunnel on both sides, a never-ending mass of them, the iron bars the only thing keeping them from tearing apart their next meal.

Thomas looked at the ones on the left. The ones on the right. They were all different, and he tried to focus on one thing that made each an individual: a face, hair colour, body type. Because in all other ways, they'd become one. A raving mass of lunacy, completely unaware of their own actions.

Thomas looked straight ahead and saw someone standing in his path just a few feet away. He gasped, stopped. Teresa bumped into him from behind. Fear lodged in his throat, choking him.

It was a man. He looked nothing like the Cranks behind the bars, but he also didn't appear to be well. His blond hair was dirty and uncombed, his clothes rumpled, his eyes blood-shot. But he had no wounds that Thomas could see, and he stood straight and still, calm. The strangest thing of all, though, was that he held a small chalkboard in the crook of one arm.

Without speaking, he pulled it out and used the piece of chalk in his other hand to write on it. Then he held it up for the group to read. The three words seemed to glow in the dim light:

WICKED is good

18

The stranger pointed at the chalkboard and nodded solemnly, his lips quivering as if he might cry. He brought the board back down to rest in his arm again.

Thomas was just about to speak when the man turned around and began to walk. Thomas didn't know what else to do but follow – the only other choice was to go deeper into the Crank pits again. To each side, the Cranks wailed and screamed and gnashed their teeth, arms reaching, reaching. They'd almost become background noise to Thomas, his focus was so riveted on the stranger in front of him.

Thomas followed the man, passing through the gated tunnel, until he realized the awful sounds of the infected had faded. Finally the man reached the gate leading back into the main tunnel, opened it, and stepped through. He waited for Thomas and the others to do the same, then closed it. The guards, still where they'd left them, watched the whole sequence of events transpire; then one of them stepped forwards, picked up the chain, and locked it back up. The sounds of the Cranks were now distant echoes that could have been almost anything.

Thomas and his friends stood packed closely together, an instinctive circle of protection. Alby and Minho were quieter than they'd ever been, and Teresa looked as shaken as Thomas felt. He couldn't take his eyes off the man with the weird sign. *WICKED is good.*

As Thomas pondered it, the man walked closer to his little group until he stood only a couple of feet from them. He took a second to gaze into the eyes of each of them in turn; then he spoke for the first time.

'You're probably wondering who I am,' he said. His voice was unsettling. Too . . . cheerful to fit the circumstances. 'As well you should. You've seen the burden that I must bear, the weight that I must carry around with me. Three words, my friends. Only three words. But I hope tonight has taught you that they are the most important three words in the world.'

'Who are you?' Alby asked, the question they were all thinking – certainly Thomas was. 'Do you . . . work here?'

The man nodded. 'My name is John Michael. I . . .' He paused to cough, pressing his hand to his chest. 'I was so . . . essential to this organization. Once. Once upon a time. It was me. It was . . . I . . . who gathered the survivors. The leaders. Gathered them here. I had the idea, my friends. I . . . had the . . . *idea!*' The last word came out in a shout, spit flying from his mouth.

Thomas took a step backwards, the others moving right with him.

'But then, you see,' John Michael continued, his eyes a little wilder, his demeanour a little more ruffled, 'then I caught the Flare. The . . . damned . . . Flare. I fought so hard to help our fellow humans.' His head drooped and tears trickled down his cheeks. 'It's not fair that I should be the one to catch it. Soon I'll be living with . . .' His gaze found its way past them, through them, and focused on the cages on the other side of the tunnel. The pits.

'But then . . . No,' he said. 'No, we won't allow such an undignified ending for me. Not for me. Not for the man who started the Post-Flares Coalition, fought for its survival, preached its importance. Would you throw someone like that into those pits? I ask you, now. Would you?' The man was becoming hysterical, staring straight at Thomas. 'Would . . . you?'

Thomas shook his head adamantly, finding himself more afraid now than he had been all day.

John Michael moved half a step closer to the group, a shuffle that was slightly off balance. His whole face glistened with tears.

'I'm not here to ask you any favours,' he said. 'I'm here to tell you there's no choice in the matter. It's your . . . obligation to help people like me. Help *future* people like me. *Do you understand?* He emphasized the last sentence with a heart-wrenching sadness.

The guards nearby did nothing, just stood like they'd been carved from wax. The shadows made it impossible to see their eyes.

'We . . . understand,' Teresa said in a far steadier voice than Thomas would have been able to muster. 'We're sorry you're infected. Most of our parents got sick too, so we know what it's like.'

The man's face suddenly transformed into a hideous trembling red mask. His eyes bulged as he erupted into rage and began to spew a tirade of anger.

'You have no idea what it's like!' he screamed, his voice cracking. 'How could you be trying to escape, running away from our chance to cure?'

The man was barely holding it together. Thomas didn't know how much more he could take of the meltdown. Minho stepped past Thomas and put himself directly in front of John Michael. Shockingly, the guards did nothing to interfere.

'We weren't going anywhere,' Minho said, trying poorly to steady his voice. 'And it doesn't seem right to treat us like this.'

'Who do you think you—' In mid-sentence the man sprang forwards with arms outstretched, reaching for Minho's throat. He caught him before Minho could move, both hands clasping the boy's neck as they fell to the ground. John Michael quickly scrambled on top of him, then put all his weight on Minho's throat, pressing him down.

Minho kicked, arched his back, tore at the man's hands, all the while making a strangled choking sound. Thomas had started moving to help even though he had no idea what to do, but Alby knocked him out of the way and dived, crashing shoulder-first into John Michael, knocking him off Minho, who sat up, heaving for breath.

Thomas watched as Alby and John Michael rolled over a couple of times, each struggling to be on top. Then the man was straddling Alby just as he had Minho. Thomas was unable to move before Minho was on his feet, running to rescue his friend. Minho toppled John Michael, his momentum slamming the man to the ground.

The guards broke out of their stupor and moved in to stop the sudden violence.

'All right,' the female guard said, her voice calm. 'That's enough. He's obviously not well.'

Neither Minho nor Alby made one move that suggested they'd heard a word she said.

The guard cocked her gun, then yelled in a much louder voice, 'Stop! Everyone!'

Thomas and Teresa managed to grab their friends around the chests and drag them away from the fallen man. Soon they were all standing there, working to catch their breath, looking down at the grown man who now lay on the ground weak and childlike, bleeding from the nose with a swollen lip. Then, shocking everyone once again – even the guards, by the looks of it – he pushed himself onto his knees and clasped his hands

together, held them out in front of his chest, fingers inter-
twined so tightly they shone white.

'Please,' he said in a trembling voice. 'Please don't judge me.
Please *save* me. If not me, those who come after. Please, I'm
begging you. Please, please, please.' His every word was a
whimper now, tears streaming from his face as if a tap flowed
behind his eyes. His shoulders shook, his arms and hands
shook, his chest lurched with heavy sobs.

'Please, please save us. Please find us a cure.' Almost a whisper now. His eyes slowly closed; he slumped back to sit on his
haunches. 'Please, please, please, please.' Each word came out
between sobs, tremors quaking his body.

Then, out of the darkness, Randall appeared, as if he'd been
watching the whole thing from deep in the shadows. He
walked forwards, not saying a word until he stood directly over
John Michael.

'*This* is what the world has come to,' Randall said. 'Unless
you're immune, of course, and until we have a cure. Otherwise,
there are two choices. Become one of those . . . *things* you saw
in the cages, or end it all before you reach the Gone, end your
life. Which this good man has asked me to do when the time
seems right. I hope you can appreciate the effort it must have
taken him to put together a few coherent sentences tonight.'
He jerked his head at the guards. 'Take them back in. I think
our old friend has reached his end date.'

Randall pulled a gun out of his waistband and cocked it.

'What're you going to do?' Thomas asked.

Randall didn't reply, which was answer enough.

19

224.10.20 | 4:01 A.M.

No one spoke. Not a word. They walked into the WICKED complex and got checked in. Thomas and his friends remained stone silent. The two guards accompanied them to a lift and they rode it up several floors, then walked down a few halls. Eventually they got to another lift and took that up as well. Minho and Alby were escorted off the lift first by the male guard. They exited the car with barely more than a nod of goodbye each, their eyes filled with sadness. Thomas and Teresa nodded back and waited quietly for the doors to close. Thomas rode the remaining floors consumed with his own thoughts.

Finally, after what seemed like an endlessly long journey, Thomas and Teresa stood in front of the doors to their rooms, the female guard next to them.

'Here we are,' she said, the first words spoken since the tunnel. And they were light-hearted enough to anger Thomas.

'How could he do that?' he said, cringing at how loud his voice sounded in the confines of the hallway. 'Just shoot a man in the back of the head?' *And slap a kid who's barely five years old,* he wanted to add, but didn't.

The woman sighed, out of some deep frustration that seemed too complicated to understand. 'Mr Michael himself, the man who made it possible for all of us to be here today, *asked* him to.' She opened Thomas's door. 'Come on, now. Bedtime. It might be a while before you and your friends can have another get-together, okay? Now get some shut-eye.'

'How long?' Thomas asked, surprised by that sudden announcement. In all that had happened, it hadn't occurred to him that he might not see his friends again anytime soon.

'Couple of years, they tell me,' was her response. 'There's plenty of work to do, and everyone needs a full night's sleep. Just . . . no more parties for the time being. It's for your own safety.' She turned away and left in a hurry.

Thomas went into his room and closed the door, then leaned back against it, staring at the dull interior in which he'd lived since coming to WICKED. Despite all the horrors of the night, the guard's parting words had been the toughest to bear.

Couple of years, the woman had said. Then his earlier worry came back to hit him. What if they took away his meetings with Teresa? Or the job that had been dangled in front of them, building the maze? Ms McVoy had said WICKED could use all the help available to them. Surely tonight didn't change that.

He went to his bed and lay down, but he couldn't sleep. His clock told him it would soon be time for breakfast, and his mind was churning with all he'd seen that night. He closed his eyes and thought through all the goods and evils of this place they called WICKED. Thought of the Cranks he'd been forced so close to only hours earlier – their empty eyes, their torn clothes, their hollow cries of misery. They were human, but at the same time the furthest thing from it. He thought of John Michael and the pitiful end to his life.

He thought of the Flare. The stupid Flare.

And WICKED wanted to find a cure for it. Wanted him to

help them. Shouldn't he want to? His head throbbed by the time the knock came for breakfast. It was Dr Paige.

Thomas asked her if she knew about the night's events.

She only smiled a very sad smile.

20

225.05.11 | 6:13 P.M.

A few months later, Thomas had one of the worst days ever. It started with more medical tests than he'd had in a while. Blood taken, of course, but plasma also, followed by a full forty-five minutes on the treadmill with what seemed like hundreds of sensors attached to his body. Throughout the whole experience his stomach hurt. It felt like he was being stabbed there with knives, and it only got worse as the day wore on. A headache joined in the fun shortly after, and forced him to excuse himself from Mr Glanville's class early. He didn't appreciate the disapproving glance that earned him. Then Ms Denton had sent him a note saying she'd been sorry to see him miss his session, the underlying message clear.

Ever since the supposed 'escape' attempt, his teachers and the staff members had seemed a little more distant. Even Dr Paige, who'd always been so nice to him – her smile didn't feel as genuine. And her eyes always had something behind them, like she knew a thousand things that he didn't, and that part of her wanted to share.

But Thomas would've gladly accepted stomach cramps and a splitting headache every day if he could only see his friends again. His chest felt tight every time he thought of their names. How much fun he'd had on those precious few nights together, when the loneliness of being a subject of WICKED had receded, just for a while. Even the meetings with Teresa had stopped lately, really worrying him that the job inside the cavern was off also.

The days when they'd had basement get-togethers were long, long, long past. Surely some cosmic catastrophe had forever shifted the normal passing of time, stretching it out.

Thomas lay in his bed that night, his uneaten dinner sitting on the desk. He'd barely had a bite for hours, and his stomach had made sure to leave nothing inside. He was empty in every way.

He was also exhausted, yet unable to fall asleep. Instead, he closed his eyes, listened to himself breathe.

Something buzzed in his head.

He sat up, looking around the room. He'd heard . . . or more like . . . *felt* . . . a buzz somewhere deep in the pounding ache within his skull that had been plaguing him all day. He shook his head, pressed his fingers against his temples. He stood up to call Dr Paige, to ask for something to knock him out for the night, when the buzz came back, this time stronger.

He fell to the bed, rolled into a ball, and held his hands over both sides of his head. The buzz didn't hurt, really. It was just so strange, so foreign. What ridiculous test had WICKED come up with now?

Buzz. Buzz. Buzz.

Louder and stronger each time. It felt like an invasion of his body; it scared him, made him think of Cranks. Going crazy. Seeing and hearing things that weren't there.

Maybe they lied to us, he thought. *Maybe we're not immune.* They'd said Newt wasn't. Could it be possible—?

BUZZ.

He rolled onto his back and stared at the ceiling, his hands still glued to the sides of his head, as if that could do anything to help. Dr Paige. He had to call Dr Paige.

Thomas.

This time it was a voice. But at the same time, *not* a voice. A vibration, a rattling of his mind, a disturbance that felt like the buzzing had formed into a solid word. He slowly stood up, hands out for balance.

Thomas, this is Teresa.

He was going crazy. He was actually going crazy. It was the oldest and most common symptom – hearing voices in your head.

'Uh . . .' he said aloud.

Is this working? Is this working?

The last word landed between his eyes like a thunderbolt. The pain knocked his legs out from under him and he collapsed onto the floor. Never had the world felt so fluid beneath him, as if nothing solid existed, no form, no substance.

'Teresa?' he asked aloud, disorientated. 'Teresa?'

No answer. Of course there was no answer. He'd gone crazy. He had the Flare; he'd be a Crank soon. His life was over.

Listen to me, the voice came again, the series of words like a horse galloping in his mind. *If you can hear me, pound on your door. I'll be able to hear it.*

Thomas pulled himself to his knees. He supposed he had nothing left to lose, so, the world swimming around him, he crawled across his room towards the door. As strange as it sounded, the odd voice in his head was more like a presence, and he didn't know how to explain it, but it *felt* like Teresa.

He made it to the door, tall as a mountain as he knelt before it.

Thomas? came the voice. *Thomas, please. Please tell me this works. It's taken me months to figure it out. If you can hear me,* pound on your door!

She shouted the last part, another series of thunks in his

skull that hurt like an ice pick.

He steadied himself, raised his hands to rest on the door's surface, then squeezed his fingers into fists. *What you're about to do,* he told himself, *just might be the last nail in your Flare coffin. If you're wrong, you'll know you're truly crazy.*

The voice again. Teresa.

Thomas? Thomas? Make the sound.

He did it. He reared back with both fists, then banged them against the door, beat it like it might be the last barrier to his freedom. *In for a penny, in for a pound.* He'd read that in one of those classics they'd given him. For a solid ten seconds, he threw his fists forwards onto the hard surface until his knuckles ached and the pain shimmied up both arms

Then he collapsed to the floor again, struggling to catch his breath. He heard shouts down the hall, footsteps, someone coming to check on him. But before anyone arrived, one last sentence surfaced in his mind.

Good, got it, Teresa said, a sense of excitement somehow attached to her voice. *I'll teach you how to do this later.*

And then she was gone. Not just her voice, but her presence as well. Gone. Like an extinguished light.

The door swung open and Dr Paige stood there.

'What in the world's come over you?' she asked.

21

The next day passed in agony for Thomas. He could barely wait to see Teresa in the flesh – for just ten minutes. *Five* minutes. All he needed was enough time to look her in the eyes and ask her. *Was it you?* He'd know in an instant, and he needed the confirmation desperately. As he ate breakfast, had a check-up, went from class to class, the same question ran through his mind.

Am I crazy?

He'd even tried to ask Dr Paige about his fears when she'd first retrieved him that morning.

'So how do you *know* I'm immune?' he'd asked her, watching her expression carefully as she answered.

'It's fairly straightforward,' she replied easily, walking next to him down the hallway. 'There are very specific markers in your blood make-up, DNA and cerebrospinal fluid that are consistent among all those who are immune. The markers are missing in those who are *not* immune. It took a lot of study to get to that point, but it's solid now.'

He considered that. It certainly sounded like she was telling the truth.

'Also,' she added, 'it's doubly confirmed in someone like you and the other immune subjects we've gathered.'

'What do you mean?'

'Well, we can verify with brain scans that the virus itself has taken hold inside you, that it's made a home for itself. And yet it has no effect whatsoever on your physical matter, your mental capacity, your bodily functions. And you've had the virus for years, with no change. Unless it's some sort of massive mutation of the virus – which our studies have shown no evidence of – then we can say with almost certain scientific and medical accuracy that you're immune.'

He nodded, fairly confident she was being honest with him. 'So if I started showing symptoms of the Flare, say, tomorrow, how shocked would you be? On a scale of one to ten?'

She looked over at him. 'Ten, Thomas. I'd be beyond shocked. As shocked as if you sprouted a third ear. What's all this about?'

He stopped in the hallway and faced her. 'Dr Paige. Do you swear, swear on your own life, that I'm immune? That this isn't some kind of . . . I don't know, some kind of test? I know you guys are really fond of tests. How do I know I'm not like Newt? *Not* immune?'

Dr Paige gave him that smile – that smile that always made him feel a little better. 'I swear to you, Thomas. I swear on the graves of the countless loved ones who have died . . . I swear that I've never lied to you. You're as immune as science and medicine can possibly conclude. And if there was any chance of anything endangering your life, I wouldn't allow it.'

He stared into her eyes. He found that he truly believed her, and that made him feel warm inside – as if a little piece of the wall he'd built up to protect himself had crumbled away.

'Why are you asking me these things?' she asked. 'What's wrong?'

He almost told her the truth. That he'd heard a voice inside his head. He almost told her.

'Dreams,' he answered. 'I keep having these dreams that I go crazy. And the worst part is that I'm not even aware it's happened. Do any of the Cranks actually know that they've lost their minds? How do we know *we're* not Cranks?'

She nodded, as if that was a completely valid question. 'That sounds like something for your philosophy class. Next month, I believe.'

She'd started walking again, and the conversation was over.

Thomas sat in his room thinking over the morning's conversation with Dr Paige once more. Ever since the wake-up, he'd hoped that Teresa would talk to him again, while at the same time hoping she didn't. Maybe that in itself was another sign he'd lost his mind to infection.

But the more he thought about it, the more he believed Dr Paige. She was either sincere or the best actress the world had ever known. Finally Thomas was too tired to worry any more, and he turned off his lights and hoped sleep would beat the odds and take him away.

It was only an hour or so later, just when he'd begun dozing off, that Teresa spoke to him again.

Thomas, are you there?

It didn't shock him like it had the first time. This time there was no buzzing, and on some level he'd been expecting it, so it wasn't as disorientating. Even so, any trace of sleep vanished at her words and he sat up, got out of bed, went over to sit at his desk.

'I'm here,' he said aloud, once again feeling like an idiot for doing so. He had absolutely no idea how to respond to her with his mind.

I can feel you trying to answer, she said. *The implants they put in our heads – I've been trying to figure out what's felt different since they did it, and as soon as I pressed through to make contact to you, it all clicked.*

Thomas sat there, nodding to himself like a dummy. It didn't escape him how strange it was that it already felt somewhat normal to have a girl speaking to him telepathically.

You have to focus, Teresa continued. *Probe your mind to find the foreign object, then focus on it. Press through it. You won't know what I'm talking about until you try.*

Her words came in a rush now, no longer painful but still disorientating.

'Okay,' he said, knowing she couldn't hear him.

Try it as you go to sleep tonight, she said. *I'll contact you every night until I hear back. Don't give up!*

He could sense the weight she put on the last three words. The importance of what she was telling him.

'Okay,' he said again. Then, confident he'd heard the last from her, he lay back down in bed and started tinkering with his own mind.

For several days and nights he worked at it, and it was the most frustrating thing he'd ever done. All he had at his disposal were mental tools, nothing physical. Maybe if he could take a scalpel and open his own head up, it would've been easier to pick and probe until he found something like a huge old-school light switch that needed flipping. But no, he had to close his eyes and search with fingers that only existed in his own imagination.

Once he let go of thinking about things in such a black-and-white manner, he was able to start seeing his own thoughts and conscience as things he *could* mentally manipulate. That was when he started making progress. He let his thoughts disappear and focused on nothing, until suddenly it was clear – there was an area that didn't seem to belong. And then he pressed on, working against it and thinking the one word he wanted to send: *Teresa.*

Then finally one night he felt more than heard Teresa

receive his message. It was as if he'd poked her with a cattle prod.

He whooped, lying in bed, knowing he was close. Hoping he hadn't hurt her too much.

Keep going, she'd said in his mind. *You're almost there. And next time, try not to electrocute my eyeballs.*

He had no idea what that meant, but he smiled all the same.

And kept trying.

22

I can't fall asleep, Thomas said to Teresa. Almost a year had passed since he'd finally mastered the implanted telepathy.

Maybe that's because it's barely past eight o'clock, she responded. *And last time I checked you're not a seventy-year-old man.*

Hey, I like my beauty sleep. How do you think I maintain this fine specimen of a face?

She snorted. It felt similar to those buzzes she'd communicated when she'd first spoken to him this way. *Yeah, I swoon every time I see you.*

Which is never.

Exactly.

There was a long pause, but the great thing about their trick was that even when neither one of them spoke, whatever connection they had in their minds made them feel the other's presence. After months and months of practice, he could almost believe that she was in the room with him. He craved it every night, and missed it whenever he was idle during the day.

Whenever he happened to have a spare minute.

How's the plan coming along? he finally asked, even though he knew it would annoy her. He almost enjoyed asking her the same thing every night for weeks just *because* it annoyed her. But this time he didn't get the usual irritated response.

I think I figured it out, she said.

Thomas sat up. *Really?*

No, not really. Go get your beauty sleep.

Thomas just rolled his eyes. He could sense that Teresa got his response.

Even though Thomas's and Teresa's doors had remained unlocked, Thomas knew they were being observed, and that they were still feeling the aftermath of their trip outside. They'd tried to sneak out to meet their friends a few times since that night, but the moment they left their rooms a guard would appear and kindly but firmly tell them to 'Please go back. It's for your own good.' Always, everything was *for their own good.*

And even though they didn't have the best gourmet chef in the world, food was one of the few things Thomas looked forward to in life. At the very least, WICKED considered quantity more important than quality, and that was just fine with Thomas. Growing like crazy, he was always hungry.

But maybe he'd have more than food to get excited about very soon.

Teresa, learning more and more about computers and information systems – their studies track had been diverging lately, becoming more specialized – had been told that the physical construction of the mazes was almost complete and WICKED would soon be ready for their help with things like programming the false sky and testing the optical-illusion systems. Aris and Rachel, two people they still hadn't met, were also on the work schedule.

Teresa had a knack for the computer systems side of things,

so that was where most of her training took place. And she was much, much better at it than they knew.

Much better.

We can do it, she said one morning, waking him up from a dead sleep.

Thomas rubbed his eyes groggily, not bothering to ask her what she meant. She'd tell him soon enough. She always did.

I know the security camera system like the back of my hand now. I've cued up all the recordings we need to loop for the night, then backtracked and erased my movements. It's all set up.

Thomas was totally awake in an instant. His excitement made him almost laugh with happiness, but he was also scared to death. Their punishment the last time they were caught out of their rooms – the Crank pits – still haunted him, but after so long without his friends, he was desperate to try anything.

Are you sure we won't get caught? he asked.

Very sure. I know where the guards are stationed. Everyone else will be asleep. And the lighting at night is so low that it will be really hard for someone to notice the loops. We'll be okay.

One hundred percent okay?

Ninety-nine.

Good enough for me.

Then we go exploring tonight.

Open your door in twenty seconds, she told him just after midnight. *I want to be in your room as fast as possible.*

Thomas did exactly as she instructed, and less than half a minute later she joined him inside his quarters. It was the first time someone other than a WICKED employee had gone past his door. He surprised her – and himself – by pulling her into a fierce hug, squeezing her like she'd disappear if he let go. Thankfully, she returned the effort just as strongly.

Man, it's good to see you, he said, still speaking with his mind, he'd grown so used to it.

She responded by hugging him even tighter.

Eventually, sadly, they let go. He sat on the bed and she sat at his desk.

'Let's give it a few minutes, make sure the first loop is working,' Teresa said to him, smiling with anticipation. He'd never seen her so full of energy and excitement.

'What will we do if they catch us?' Thomas asked, relieved to use his real voice with her again. 'This might set us back. I mean, we'll be working more on the mazes and stuff. Are we *sure* we want to risk it? What if they take it away?'

He didn't know why he bothered. Teresa answered only by rolling her eyes. They were going to explore and that was that.

After a few minutes of silence, Teresa spoke into his mind.

Let's go, she said. *And let's stick to the telepathy just in case. The video will work great, but who knows who might hear us if we're talking out loud. We can only speak if we run into our friends, and then only whisper. Sound good?*

Sounds like a plan, he replied.

They opened the door to his room, looked both ways, then went for it.

I've got it all timed, Teresa said. *When I say we have to leave for the next area, no arguing. Or else someone is going to catch us when the loops run out.*

Thomas merely nodded, and then they were running, his chest on fire.

A few turns, a trip through the lift, a few more turns, always pausing to peek around corners, make sure no one was wandering the halls.

Their first stop was the sector of Group B. The goal was to meet Aris and Rachel – they had placards on their doors just like Thomas's and Teresa's. But when Teresa knocked on Aris's door, there was no answer. They tried Rachel's. Again, no response.

Teresa spoke with their special ability. *These guys are either heavy sleepers, extremely obedient, or they're out breaking the rules just like us.*

Thomas nodded. *Oh well. Should we go say hi to Newt and the others now?*

Teresa nodded and he took the lead, winding through the halls and stairways, glad for the dimmed lighting. Teresa communicated the pattern she'd set up with the camera loops to figure out the best route, and where to stop and wait. Finally they turned the last corner before the Group A sector and stopped dead. Thomas sucked in a breath. There was a young boy in the hall; he had to be only seven or eight years old, and was a little on the pudgy side. He sat with his back against the wall, arms wrapped around his knees. Tears covered his face. When he saw Thomas and Teresa, he went as pale as the moon and jumped to his feet.

'I'm s-s-sorry,' he stuttered. 'P-p-please don't tell on me.'

Thomas slowly crossed the distance between them and put a hand on the boy's shoulder, trying to reassure him. 'It's okay, man, we're just like you. Nothing to worry about.'

'What's your name?' Teresa asked. Their whole plan was now in jeopardy, but the kid seemed so young, so innocent, so scared.

The boy burst into another round of tears, then answered through one of his sobs.

'They're making me call myself Charles.'

Thomas shook his head. 'Well, that's lame. We're going to call you Chuck.'

23

'Are you staying in the barracks?' Thomas asked the boy.

'Barracks? No. I've got my own room. At least for now.'

Teresa looked at Thomas, and he knew what she was thinking even without the telepathy. Why did this kid have his own room? 'Is it close?' Teresa asked the boy. 'Maybe we can go in there to talk.' She glanced at Thomas again. 'We have other friends we could get. Would that help you feel a little better?'

Chuck nodded, relief filling his eyes. He probably thought he'd never have friends again. He turned around and led them to his room, and Thomas got comfortable in the chair by the desk while Teresa went to get Newt, Alby and Minho. According to her set-up of camera loops, they had a few hours before they needed to be back in their own rooms.

Chuck lay on his bed, and Thomas pulled the desk chair to within a couple of feet.

'How long since they brought you in here?' Thomas asked.

'A couple of weeks. I don't know if my parents knew about

it. I don't even know if they had the Flare!' He started sobbing again, and Thomas didn't know what to do.

'It's okay,' he said, a pitiful attempt to make the kid feel better. 'Teresa and I have been here for years. You get kind of used to it. I know they can be jerks when it comes to renaming you, but after that it gets a lot better. As long as you basically do what they tell you to do.'

Chuck didn't seem too appeased. A few more tears trickled down his face.

'What're they gonna do to me?' the boy asked, sniffing back more tears. 'So far they've pricked me with needles about a million times.'

'Well, yeah. They'll be doing that to you for years. You get used to it.' *Just be glad you don't know about the implants yet*, he refrained from saying. 'But most of what happens is like school. You'll go to classes, learn lots of stuff. It's fun, actually. Plus, you'll make new friends.' He wondered again why Chuck was in a single room, not in the barracks with the other boys in Group A.

Chuck sat up on the edge of his bed, curious about what Thomas could tell him, and started unloading questions.

'Why do you think we're immune? Did your parents get the Flare? Did you see them go crazy? Did you have any brothers or sisters?' A few other inquiries flew out, Chuck not allowing Thomas a single second to attempt an answer to any of them. Luckily, Thomas was saved when the door opened. In marched Alby, then Minho, then Newt, then Teresa.

'What's up, Tommy?' Newt exclaimed, his face filled with genuine happiness at the pleasant surprise that'd been sprung on him. Thomas couldn't remember exactly how long it'd been since the last time he'd seen Newt. 'You look bloody fantastic for three in the morning.'

'Who's the new kid?' Minho asked.

Alby, a bit more thoughtful, went up to Chuck and shook his hand. 'What's your name? Mine's Alby.'

'I'm Chuck. I just got here.'

Alby nodded. 'Cool, man. They'll probably move you into the barracks with us soon. It'll be fun, don't worry. This place is all fun and games.'

Thomas had never heard such kind lies.

The next couple of hours passed with light conversation, lots of laughs, and dreams of the future that no one actually expected to happen. But for a little while, anyway, it was nice to pretend, to relax, to let themselves think they *had* a future and could do whatever they wished with it.

It was the best night Thomas could remember having since he'd first met his friends. He laughed even more than he remembered laughing that first night. He also felt at peace as they talked, often over each other, many times needing to repeat what they'd said because of being drowned out. Chuck's demeanour had gone from blurry eyes and a tear-streaked face to the joy and wonder of a kid at a birthday party. And that made Thomas feel good.

This place, he thought. WICKED. There were a million ways it could be worse. He'd been spared having to watch his mom succumb to the Flare, been spared from the harsh realities of the outside world. Spared a terrifying death at the hands of a Crank. Spared a lot of sorrow and horror in his life.

And what was the price? Boredom? A few tests? Dealing with a bunch of strange grown-ups who didn't always know how to handle children? And here Thomas was, sitting with a group of friends, joking, laughing, feeling good. And hey, a cure. Why not?

'Tommy?' It was Newt, breaking him out of his thoughts. 'I can see your wheels spinnin' up there.' He tapped the side of his head. 'Care to share?'

Thomas shrugged. 'I don't know. We keep . . . well, *I* keep thinking that WICKED did something terrible by stealing us from our families.'

'Yeah,' Alby said, though the half-grin on his face showed

that he'd probably considered what Thomas was about to say next.

'But I'm not so sure that's true.'

'So WICKED isn't bad?' Chuck asked, perking up. There was so much hope in the boy's voice that it hurt Thomas a little.

Thomas looked up at his group of friends, then looked at Chuck. 'A man once gave us a message that we'll never forget,' he said. '"WICKED is good." I think our lives might have a lot more purpose than we could ever know. I think we need to remember to look at the big picture.'

That's some deep thinking, Teresa said telepathically. *Makes you look cute.*

Don't, not in front of the others! He did his best to shout it at her, and he felt a prick of pride when he saw her flinch a little.

'Thomas, dude,' Alby said, 'there you go again, drifting off. Staring into space like an idiot.'

He had too much on his mind to try to put it all into words. 'I just think we need to keep things in perspective. We're safe, we're warm, we're fed. We're protected from the weather and the Cranks.'

'You make it sound like a bloody holiday,' Newt murmured.

'It could be a lot worse,' Thomas countered. 'Not to mention the small fact that we're trying to help save the entire human race.'

'And that means you, Newt,' Alby added. 'I don't wanna watch you go all Crank on me someday.'

That sobered Newt right up. Even Teresa looked sad. Thomas had ruined it for everybody, even though he'd *tried* to be positive about their ordeal.

Thomas glanced over at Minho, who'd been quiet for a while. He sat in the corner, his back against the wall, staring at the floor. He caught Thomas's eye and stood up.

'Make up all the fantasies about WICKED you want,' he said. 'Tell yourselves this is all a good cause, that they treat us well. I'm not buying it, though. It looks like I'm the only one still working on . . .' Minho stopped midsentence and shook his head. 'I'm heading back to my room now. Later.'

Minho was at the door and had it opened before anyone had time to recover.

Alby found his voice before Minho disappeared.

'What are you talking about?' Alby asked.

Minho had his back to them, but he didn't even turn his head to answer.

'We used to talk about escaping before Thomas and Teresa came around,' he said. 'Well, I never stopped thinking about it. Or planning for it. We should be here by our own choice, not by theirs. Not treated like prisoners. I hope you guys'll come with me. When I'm ready.'

Then he left, shutting the door behind him.

24

That was the last Thomas heard of Minho's great escape plan for six months. During that time, life was fascinating and fun. About once a week, Teresa worked her magic on the security camera loops and they had a get-together in one of their rooms or, more frequently, in the old maintenance room, deep below everything else.

And it was always the same group: Alby, Minho, Newt, Thomas, Teresa. And sometimes little Chuck. He'd become their favourite. He was goofy, innocent and gullible, and he took all their jokes in his stride. He'd become like the little brother they'd lost or, in Thomas's case, never had in the first place.

Sometimes they smuggled in food and ate as they talked and laughed. After a few months of these nights, they'd mostly forgotten that fear they'd all had. The fear of Randall or Ramirez walking in at any moment. Of being sent back to the Crank pits. Maybe this time there would be no fences to protect them.

They forgot to be scared, and they felt safe. It was the best time of their lives.

Okay, Teresa said in Thomas's mind. *Let me know when you see a red dot flash in the exact centre of the ceiling.*

Roger that, he replied.

Would you please *stop saying that?*

Thomas held back a laugh. He stood surrounded by mountainous walls of stone that the heavy construction crews had built around skeletons of steel and fiberglass. At least half of the Maze was complete, and it was starting to look spectacular. As he waited for Teresa's signal, he tried to imagine what the place would be like when it was finished, especially with the optical-illusion technology in place. The technology would work alongside certain . . . powerful suggestions provided by the subjects' brain implants to make everything *seem* three times as tall, as wide, as long. And it was *big* already.

Even though he and Teresa were helping with the creation of it all, their WICKED overseers didn't share a lot of information about how exactly things would work once they opened the Maze for business. He'd heard the word *Variables* thrown around a lot, and he knew that the Psychs had spent years planning for these killzone experiments.

He also knew there'd be some harshness. Thomas and Teresa were far from stupid, and they took every opportunity to find out more about the project they were working on. Once, they'd come across a page listing preliminary Variables, and a couple of things really stood out. Words like *forced pain* and *attack* and *elimination of comforts*. Those were mixed in with a bunch of scientific writing that didn't always make sense.

But things were moving forward, if a little behind schedule. One day, maybe with just a few years of intense research and testing, WICKED would have its cure. And Thomas could always say he'd been a big part of it. He'd started telling himself this a lot. It was easy, and it made him feel better.

Have you seriously not seen it yet? Teresa asked, sending a jolt of annoyance along with her words.

Oh! Sorry. He was constantly losing himself in his thoughts lately. *Yeah, yeah, there's a bright red dot, practically right above me.*

Practically? Or is it exactly in the right spot?

Um, well. It might be about ten feet off, actually. And, um, maybe a dozen or so more are blurry and scattered. Sorry.

It had to be one. Just one red dot, centred.

Tom, we have to get this right before we can move on to another project. And I'm sick of this one.

Tell me about it. My neck is killing me from looking up at all these mistakes.

She ignored him, having learned that that was the best way to get back at him for lame sarcastic comments.

Let me try again, she said.

They'd been at this for at least two weeks, trying and failing, trying and failing. Ms McVoy had assigned them to the Sky Project, and their job was to programme and fine-tune the systems to look like a normal sky to those below. Blue sky, night sky, the stars, the passing of the sun, everything. Thomas couldn't wait to see the result in all its glory.

But first he and Teresa had to get the balance right. Thomas suspected that WICKED knew they'd been communicating telepathically before they were 'officially' told about it and 'taught' how to use it, but no one said anything. He supposed WICKED could only benefit from their having mastered the technique, as the instant communication made them ideal for these types of projects, which appeared to be plentiful.

Teresa was projecting a red dot from a thousand different sources around the vast interior surface of the Maze cavern, and until Thomas saw it as a single dot, in a specific location, the technicians couldn't move forward with the projecting software.

Half an hour later, Teresa tried it again. This time, there were only six red dots, and the largest one was only four or five feet from centre. They were very close.

Let's wrap this up tomorrow, Thomas said after the test. *I*

gotta get a nap in before our rendezvous tonight with the fellas.
Deal.

Only one word, not spoken aloud, but she sounded exhausted all the same.

They gathered in the maintenance room around one o'clock in the morning. Thomas had taken a good three- or four-hour nap but still felt groggy when Minho passed around some awful liquid concoction that made Thomas's throat burn. Alby had a giant bag of potato chips, stolen from where, no one had any idea – and no one bothered to ask. The salty, crunchy goodness of every bite was especially powerful at such a late hour. Chuck had way more than his fair share.

'I've got a new guy coming tonight,' Minho said, not ten minutes after they'd settled in to eat their junk food.

Thomas's hand froze halfway to his mouth, holding a tantalizing chip waiting to be chomped. Teresa leaned forwards. Newt raised his eyebrows. Alby simply said, 'Come again?' Chuck didn't pause for a second. He continued to eat as if a cure for the Flare might depend on it.

Minho, seeing how unexpected his pronouncement had been, stood up and waved an arm to say it was no big deal. 'Nothing to worry about, folks. He's a good enough guy.' He stopped talking, though his eyes showed he had a lot more to say.

'"Good enough"?' Teresa repeated. 'That's the criteria now for trusting our secret to someone new?'

The confidence and swagger that had defined Minho just twenty seconds earlier suddenly vanished. 'His name is Gally. And, he's, uh . . . You remember that plan I told you about? To escape?'

Thomas felt his heart sink a little at that. He'd assumed – *hoped* – that Minho's notion had died a quick and lasting death. 'Yeah, we remember,' Alby said. 'We also remember the Crank pits, and the beds we have, and the food we get, and the walls that protect us from the insane asylum they call the world. Your point?'

'Gally's going to help me,' Minho replied, looking sheepishly around the room. 'He should be here any second.'

With seemingly perfect timing, someone knocked on the door as soon as he'd finished his sentence.

25

Thomas felt sorry for Gally the second he walked into the room. Nothing really stood out about the kid – black hair, tall and skinny, pale skin. He had some ugly teeth, but that wasn't so unusual. Thomas couldn't remember ever going to a dentist himself.

Still, Gally seemed . . . pathetic somehow. His eyes, maybe. If you looked into his eyes, you could tell that something had broken inside him a long time ago.

'Everyone, meet Gally,' Minho said. 'Gally, meet everyone. Some of you know him, or at least have seen him around. I'm sure we'll all get along peachy.'

'Good that,' Newt said.

Gally gave everyone a nice-enough nod, a sincere attempt at a smile. Thomas and the others did their best to return it.

After a long, awkward silence, Alby asked exactly what Thomas was wondering.

'So how's Gally supposed to help with this idiotic plan to escape?'

'I'll let him tell you,' Minho replied, thumping the new boy on the back.

Gally cleared his throat. 'I work out on the grounds with a couple others. Mostly landscaping stuff – cutting down weeds, shovelling snow when the odd storm hits, trying to get bushes and flowers to grow. But I also do electrical work, maintenance, whatever. The three of us work under a guy named Chase.'

'And this will help you how?' Alby pressed, making it clear how he felt about an escape plan. 'You going to push Minho to the woods in a wheelbarrow?'

Newt sniggered, then caught himself. 'Sorry,' he mumbled.

Gally, instead of getting offended, smiled right along. 'If anyone gets to be pushed around in a wheelbarrow, it's gonna be me. Minho owes me.'

'Why?' Teresa asked.

Minho answered. 'Because he's the only way this thing works.'

Everyone looked to Gally for an explanation. Everyone except Chuck, who'd fallen asleep on the floor, a dirty mop as his pillow.

'Chase isn't the smartest dude at WICKED, let's just say that.' Gally stared at the floor as he spoke – Thomas didn't know how to interpret that. 'I've been setting up little things for weeks now, things that'll help someone get past the WICKED security measures. Truth is, WICKED relies on the threat of Cranks and the state of the world to prevent us from trying anything. It's a lot harder to get *into* WICKED than to get out.'

'And what in the world do you plan to do once you're out in the great Alaskan wilderness?' Teresa asked. 'Rent a car, go find a nice apartment in Juneau?'

'Man, you guys really like your sarcasm,' Gally said. 'I mean, do you think I'm stupid? Just because I don't sneak out and have little parties with the cleaning supplies?'

'Gally, chill,' Minho warned.

Gally threw his arms up. 'They're the ones who need to grow up!'

'Hey!' Alby shouted. 'Don't come in here all high and mighty. We didn't invite you.'

'That's it, I'm out,' Gally said as he walked towards the exit. Minho jumped in front of him, put a hand on his chest. Gally stopped.

Minho looked around. 'Come on, guys. Can you give me the benefit of the doubt, here? Why do you think I've waited months to pull the trigger? Because I'm patient and *not* stupid. Gally's figured out a way to communicate with a cousin in Canada – he's close to the border. Gally used Chase's transponder codes. We'll have people waiting for us a few miles into the woods – they're already on standby.'

Thomas couldn't believe what he was hearing. Minho really meant it. Despite all the things they had better off than the rest of the world, he wanted out.

'Why?' Thomas asked. That one word got everyone's attention. 'Just tell us *why*, Minho. We know you're not stupid, and I'm sure Gally isn't, either. But why would you guys want to leave?'

'Because we're prisoners,' Minho answered. 'Because we're held here against our will. That's all the reason I need.'

'But you'll never have it half as good as we do here!' Teresa almost shouted. 'And how can you just turn your back on helping the world?'

For the first time since they'd met, Minho looked like maybe he didn't like them so much.

'I guess we have different philosophies,' he said. 'If you don't get it, you don't get it. You don't take away my freedom without asking first.'

'Sorry we got off to a rough start,' Gally interjected. 'I guess I'm just nervous being down here. But I promise you guys this can work.' He looked around at the group then and added, 'Anyone coming with us?'

His words were met with graveyard silence.

'When?' Newt asked, breaking the quiet.

Minho and Gally answered at the same time.

'Tomorrow night.'

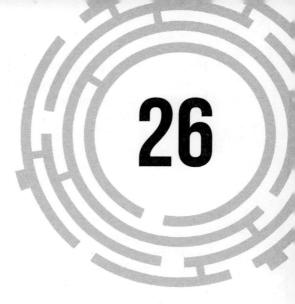

26

226.11.14 | 3:17 A.M.

They came for Thomas hours before dawn.

Randall, Dr Leavitt, and Ramirez. The three musketeers. Thomas knew, despite his grogginess, that the three of them coming together meant that something really bad had happened. Or was about to happen. He was on his feet seconds after they shook him awake.

'What's going on?' he asked.

'I have an inkling you know very well what's going on,' Randall replied, sharp and loud in the quiet of the night. 'And that's why you're coming with us, right now. We need your help.'

Thomas started to ask another question, but Dr Leavitt cut him off immediately.

'Come on, Thomas. Everything will be okay. Just do as you're told.'

'Quickly, now,' Ramirez added, the first time Thomas had ever heard the chief of security speak.

The three men escorted Thomas through the building, often

grabbing his arm at a turn in the hallway or getting off the lift, even though he didn't need it. They weren't rough with him, but they were clearly in a hurry.

They stopped when they reached a heavily fortified door. Ramirez pressed his fingerprint to a glass panel and said his name. The door opened. Randall gave Thomas a little nudge to go through.

Thomas wanted answers, but he decided to suck it up and remain quiet. Randall was being nicer than he had the night of the Crank pits, and Thomas didn't want to push him past some boundary he wasn't yet willing to cross.

Thomas looked around the room he'd stepped into. It was new to him – what looked to be a control centre for security. There was a large wall full of monitors showing everything from the medical rooms to dorms to progress on the Maze construction. Oddly, the video feeds for the Maze moved around skittishly, as if their cameras had been strapped to the backs of very angry cats. Nestled in the middle of the room, and facing the monitors, was a deck of equipment fitted out with more display screens and several chairs perched behind it. Two guards sat there now, their gazes fixed on a monitor to the right side of the wall.

Thomas looked closer and felt his heart drop. It showed Minho in a small room, strapped to a chair – the ropes digging into his skin – his face bloodied and bruised. He stared straight at the camera, unwavering, and his look of resolve made Thomas feel a little proud. And a little ashamed. He hadn't wanted Minho to run and doubted he'd actually try.

'Hurts to say this,' Randall said, 'but it looks like your friend didn't learn from his last attempt to go outside. I guess we were too easy on him, on everyone. Now we have no choice but to step things up. Don't you agree?'

Thomas stared at Minho. Minho stared back. Could it be possible there was a two-way camera? Thomas suddenly felt self-conscious.

'Silence is probably not your best option right now,' Dr Leavitt said. 'Sit down and we'll talk. People like Minho and Gally – people who think they're above the effort to help us here – have to be dealt with. Hopefully you can learn something by watching.'

Ramirez put a hand on Thomas's shoulder and gently helped him find a seat between the two guards.

'You're excused now,' Randall said.

For one split second Thomas thought Randall meant him, which would have been awfully strange since they'd just had him sit down. But it quickly became clear he was wrong when the guards got up and left.

Ramirez took the chair to Thomas's left, Dr Leavitt the one to his right. Randall stepped into the space between the controls and the monitors, then clasped his hands behind his back as if he were about to give a lecture.

'Thomas,' he began, 'let's be honest here. You know we've been watching you and your friends gather at night, correct? You might be young, but you're way too smart to think you were getting around us somehow.'

Thomas opened his mouth, then closed it. He'd at least *hoped* they were outsmarting them. He didn't know why they'd let them continue to gather, but as he thought about it, he realized it had been wishful thinking. He nodded.

Randall placed his hands on the outer edge of the control deck and leaned forwards, closer to Thomas. 'Listen,' the man said. 'We're not here to beat you up over Minho's mistake. If anything, we were able to see that most of you tried to talk him out of it. But there are some valuable lessons to be learned from all this, and we're going to take advantage of the situation.'

Thomas wished desperately that the guy would make his point already.

'You are going to sit with us and watch how we're going to teach Minho his lesson. We need witnesses, to be frank. We need the word to get around. We can't let something like this ever happen again. Our subjects need to know that actions have consequences.'

'What're you going to do to him?' Thomas shouted, really scared for his friend.

Randall flinched at the sudden loud noise, then continued as if he hadn't heard the question. 'After this is done, we'll bring in Teresa and show her. Same for Aris and Rachel over in the control room for Group B. But we wanted you all to be alone on this, all reactions your own and not influenced by friends.'

'It's also a big step in another way,' Dr Leavitt added. 'The Maze Trials will be only a year or two from now, based on our current pace, and this?' He gestured around the room. 'This is something you're going to see a lot of once we put the first batch of subjects into the mazes. So look at this little exercise as practice. Sound good?'

Thomas stayed quiet. Sometimes they could be so condescending.

'Thomas? Sound good?' Leavitt repeated.

Thomas felt a rage so strong he could barely contain it, like a fire starving for oxygen. He didn't understand how, but somehow he kept it all in.

'Sounds good,' he muttered.

Randall pointed to a different screen from the one showing Minho. In the new one Thomas could see an oval container of some sort. It had a seam along one side and hinges on the other. It looked like the coffin for a fat, very wealthy alien.

'What's that?' Thomas asked, falling right into their trap. Curiosity often won when it came to him.

'Those are pods,' Randall replied. 'Pods for a biomechanical creature that the military was able to help us design. At the moment we're calling them Grievers. They're still in the early stages of development, but huge progress was made with this last round. I think we're just two or more modifications away from having our perfect Maze monster.'

Thomas was so taken aback by the seemingly simple

statement that he could imagine the ridiculous look that must be on his face. He closed his mouth and forced himself to blink a few times.

'Not what you were expecting?' Randall asked.

'I . . . I don't . . . Expecting?' He was at a loss for words. 'What're you even talking about? Biomechanical creatures? Monsters in the Maze? What'd you call them? Grievers?'

Ramirez spoke up. 'You'll learn all the details soon enough. Honestly, we had no intention of sharing this with you for a while yet, but this opportunity arose and, well . . . I will say, as one who's been on the committee leading the development of these living weapons, that they're an achievement by any standard.'

'In short,' Randall added, 'if we're going to understand how the Munies' brains function despite being afflicted with the Flare, we have to be able to stimulate in them every kind of feeling and brain activity known to humans. Once we start the Maze Trials these creatures will help with that in a big way. You should see the Psych reports. Very interesting.'

Thomas felt like a dark shadow had passed over him. Something that sucked the life out of the air, and the air from his lungs. Everything these men were telling him – it was all feeling worse by the moment.

'Let's get on with it,' Randall said. He reached over and pressed something. 'Go ahead, Alice. Open the pod.'

Thomas watched as the seam alongside the oval pod split open. Jets of steam hissed from the opening, obscuring any clear view of the pod itself. Swirling, eddying mists filled the room on the screen. Thomas glanced over at the screen showing Minho really fast, and the true horror of what was about to happen became evident. Minho had finally broken his gaze and was looking anxiously to his right. Tendrils of fog slid along the floor from that side of the screen.

Thomas stood up, his skin now cold.

Minho was in the same room as that opening pod.

27

226.11.14 | 5:52 A.M.

'Stop!' Thomas yelled. 'Stop that . . . thing!' His imagination had run wild, trying to picture what terrible thing was about to reveal itself. 'I get the point, okay?'

'Sit down!' Ramirez yelled from behind Thomas, and the man grabbed both Thomas's shoulders and slammed him back down into his seat. Thomas had no idea when the man had moved from his chair.

Randall turned away from the mist-filled screen.

'If we don't act on our threats,' he said, 'then how will we ever have control in this experiment? If we let people escape – or try to – with no consequences, what does that tell the other subjects? Minho made his choice. Now things have to play out the way they're supposed to.'

'Please,' Thomas whispered, feeling the fight drain out of him. Minho – tough, reckless, always-joking Minho – had a look of such terror on his face that Thomas couldn't bear to watch any more. He turned his attention to the pod.

The mist had dissipated enough to reveal the container, its

two halves resting on the floor. Thomas stared mutely as something began to climb out.

Whatever he had expected, he never could have dreamed up what he saw next. It was impossible to tell its shape; the creature was wet and glistening, with patches of hair covering parts of its surface. But there was metal too – flashes of steel appendages, and sharp discs protruding from the quivering mass. Thomas watched the hideous creature push itself over the lip of the container and crash down to the floor, revealing a slug-like body about the size of a small cow.

He shuddered, watching the . . . abomination manoeuvre. He looked back at Minho, saw the boy thrashing against his restraints, screaming with no sound. The fog had washed over him. It was lingering in the background, melting towards the ceiling.

Thomas lost every bit of his restraint.

'Stop that thing!' he yelled, standing up. Ramirez was there instantly, pushing him down again. 'You can't do this!'

Randall glanced over his shoulder – he'd been watching Minho intently – and gave Thomas a tired expression.

'We have no choice,' the man said simply.

Teresa! he screamed in his mind. *You have to do something. They've got Minho tied up in a chair and . . . this . . .* thing, *this* monster, *is about to attack him!*

The words inside his mind felt strange this time, hollow. It felt like some invisible barrier was up and everything he said was bouncing back at him.

Of course, he thought. *Of course WICKED can turn it off. They can do whatever the hell they want.*

Minho continued to struggle and scream. He managed to move his chair, sliding it back until he hit the wall farthest from the Griever. On the left side of the screen, something flashed into view, a blob with spikes dragging it along the ground. Right before it ran into Minho, it stopped. The metal spikes receded into its skin and the creature flattened out.

Thomas was desperate now, seeing one of his few friends on the verge of serious damage – possibly even death.

'Randall!' he begged. 'Listen to me! Please, just . . . stop that thing. Just stop it! Just . . . hear me out! Let me talk, and then if you don't change your mind you can start it again. *Please.*'

Part of the creature's body was rising now, and several lengths of metal extended where the spikes had been. They were solid, covered in deadly objects – blades and saws and claws that snapped open and closed. Thomas watched, nearly in tears, as very slowly, the weapons extended towards Minho's body.

Thomas tried to take a calmer approach. He sucked in a breath. 'Randall, please. Minho is too valuable for this. If you don't stop that thing, I'm not helping you any more. With anything. I don't care what you guys do to me.'

The creature had risen on its hindquarters, and it now stood several feet higher than Minho's head. The metal arms that had extended from its skin wrapped around Minho, encircling him, trapping him against the wall he'd backed into.

'Randall,' Thomas said, fighting to keep calm. 'Go get Dr Paige. The Psychs. Go get the chancellor. Go get all of them! They need me, and they need Minho. He has too much potential to help your trial to waste him here.'

The creature lifted its saw appendage and the blade spun to life, the arm inching closer to Minho's forehead. He'd already pressed his head back against the wall. Thomas watched as his friend's face now contorted in pure fear.

'Last chance!' Thomas yelled. 'If he dies, I might as well—'

He cut off abruptly when Randall pressed the call button again.

'Pause,' he commanded, a little urgently, as if he'd let it go too far, too late to stop it.

The creature froze. And Thomas let out a huge, shuddering breath. He slumped back down into his seat and dropped his head into his hands. It took everything he had not to burst into tears.

'Look at him, please,' Randall said quietly. 'Look at the screen.'

Thomas raised his head and focused on Minho's display.

'You see that?' Randall asked. He was also watching Minho. The creature was draped over the boy, almost like a blanket. 'Did I not tell you that we're almost there, we've almost perfected the greatest soldier?'

Thomas didn't see anything besides his friend, literally inches from death, and a man who seemed to have lost his grip on reality – if he'd ever had it in the first place.

'I think this goes without saying,' Randall continued, his voice still imbued with a sense of awe. 'I need you to never forget what you've seen here today. I need you to understand the power and the danger of these creatures. The pattern of your empathy could end up being one of the biggest pieces of our puzzle.'

Thomas found it hard to focus on the man's words. All he could do was stare at Minho and his sweat-streaked face. The blade, even though it had stopped inching forwards, still spun as fast as ever. Thomas found it hard to breathe, knowing it would only take one word from Randall to end Minho's life.

The man pressed his magic button again and said, 'Okay, go ahead and call it back.'

Seconds later, the metal arms of the Griever withdrew, folding away from Minho and retracting into the moist, fatty body. The Griever seemed to melt into a flat slab of flesh on the floor, then wrapped itself into a rounded ball, traction spikes extending; finally it pulled itself end over end until it had rolled out of sight on the screen. Thomas turned his attention to the other screen and the creature appeared, spinning until it reached the pod, retracted its spikes, and oozed its way back inside. The pod hatch was closing even before the creature had disappeared into its home. A few seconds and a hiss of steam later, the pod closed and all went still.

Thomas looked back at Minho, hoping to see that some piece of his friend's rebellious nature had returned to him.

But not this time.

Minho's head hung low, and his body shook with sobs. Thomas just dropped his own head sadly. He was at a complete loss trying to understand what he'd just watched.

'Let's get you back to your room,' Randall said. 'We still have three more subjects to witness what you just saw. If I were you, I'd write down anything of importance you learned today.'

Thomas had missed something. 'Wait . . . what?'

Randall ignored him. 'You do realize that we never would have let the Griever hurt Minho, much less kill him. You're smart enough to know that, right? We only want everyone to learn a valuable lesson: the rules must be followed. Going outside, much less leaving the WICKED compound . . . Now you know the consequences.'

'But . . .' Thomas was so shaken, he couldn't put together the question he wanted to ask.

Dr Leavitt spoke up. 'Don't worry about your reaction today, Thomas. It was pretty close to what we expected, and it's not lost on us the passion you threw into trying to save your friend. I tell you what, the Psychs are going to have a field day with this one. Lots of data to analyze.'

Thomas finally realized what the man was saying. 'What do you mean you have three others to show . . . this?' He pointed to all the screens in front of him, the control deck, the ceiling above. 'You *do* mean a recording of it, right?' The next half second seemed to stretch out forever. *Please, please, please,* he thought. *Tell me that yes, you recorded it.*

'I'm sorry to say the answer is no,' Randall replied. 'It's more effective if Minho goes through it again.' He sighed. 'On so many levels, Thomas.'

28

228.04.03 | 7:00 A.M.

Thomas reached over, hit snooze on his alarm clock, and dropped his arm over the side of his bed. He hated the wake-up on days after a maintenance-room rendezvous, possibly hated that alarm more than a houseful of Cranks. *Hungry* Cranks.

But he did relish those ten minutes that followed hitting snooze, before the alarm blared again. It was like a little bonus to himself every morning.

He curled back into a ball, content, if just for a moment.

He hadn't seen Minho for over a year, even though he'd survived the punishment with the Griever. Well, at least physically. Alby said that mentally, emotionally . . . Minho was different. He wasn't as talkative, or reckless, and he certainly never mentioned the word *escape* again. The passing of time can certainly heal a lot of wounds, but the way Alby described their mutual friend, Minho would need about twenty more years.

The other members of their 'maintenance-room clan' met once a week. Everyone but Minho. He hadn't shown up once since the fateful day, and Newt said their friend wouldn't even consider it. He was a shell of the person they'd all got to know. It made Thomas incredibly sad. He'd really liked Minho, and everything about their situation seemed so unfair. Who could blame him for reacting this way after the horror show WICKED called his *punishment*?

Thomas believed in the cure – at least, he told himself he did. But WICKED treating them like lab rats – sometimes that turned his sadness into anger. Often he'd have to kneel by his bed and pound on the mattress with both fists until he collapsed from exhaustion. He wanted it all to be over, a cure in hand, and he did his best to stay positive in that regard. Dr Paige always said the data was plentiful and rolling in.

Maybe, just maybe, the end was in sight, no matter how distant the horizon.

He and Teresa were almost done with the Maze, just slightly behind the pace of Group B, from what they'd been told. But that was just it. Thomas had a harder and harder time *believing* them. WICKED continued to isolate him and Teresa, so he relied on the latest gossip from Alby, Newt, and his most plentiful source, Chuck. That kid had a brain like a sponge, soaking in every little comment he ever heard or overheard. They might tease him without mercy, but when Chuck spoke, people listened.

Thomas's daily ten minutes of morning bliss ended in a cacophony of klaxon sounds when his alarm went off again. He hated it more than solar flares.

Dr Paige showed up with breakfast, right on time. How long had he known this woman? Longer than his own mom, for sure. By years. And today he could read something different in her manner, a difference in her smile. A pain behind the bright intelligence her eyes always showed.

He wanted to ask her what was wrong, but their relationship had never quite recovered after what WICKED had done

- 144 -

to Minho. Still, of all the people who worked there, in whatever capacity, Dr Paige was the one he liked most, and he had to fight to keep any kind of wall between them. Though it was a very thin wall, and the mortar holding it together had begun to crumble.

'How are we today?' she asked him once she'd set the breakfast on his desk. 'Work day today, right?'

Thomas nodded, then sat down to eat. Normally they talked a little, about how tests were going, his classes, progress on the mazes, etc. But before Thomas could take one bite of his eggs, Dr Paige was headed for the door. She'd just opened it and was about to step into the hallway when Thomas stopped her.

'Hey,' he said. 'Can you come back in for a second?'

She paused, let out a heavy sigh. But then she closed the door and came back to the desk, took the other chair. She looked at him with sad eyes.

Thomas couldn't help himself – curiosity always won.

'I wasn't going to ask,' he said, 'but . . . is there something wrong?' For a long moment he was scared. What if one of his friends had died? Not Teresa, though. He would definitely have felt her absence, or her last moments. He would have had some clue.

'Thomas . . .' Dr Paige began. She looked around the room as if she might literally find words posted on the walls. 'We're getting very close to sending subjects into the mazes.' She let out a little laugh and met his eyes again. 'Well, you would know that better than anyone. How is your work going in there?'

She meant his and Teresa's efforts in the Maze cavern.

'It's going fine. Pretty fun. I don't know.'

'You sound less than enthused.'

'It's just been hard for me to get over some things. There are secrets – things you've been keeping from us. Some of it just doesn't seem right. And people could be nicer. Like Randall. Like Ramirez. Dr Leavitt.' It felt good to get some of this off his chest.

She crossed her legs and gave him a look of sincere concern.

'I don't know if you'll believe this, Thomas, but I've struggled with these very things myself. I could offer you excuses – but I'm guessing that's not what you want to hear.'

Thomas shook his head. 'Even the fact that you call us subjects. I mean, we're human, not a bunch of mice.' His voice had got a little firmer, but Dr Paige kept her cool, nodding as if she understood completely.

'I think it boils down to two things,' she said. 'First, even though everything we're doing at the moment is leading to the Maze Trials, that doesn't mean that the Psychs haven't been looking for every opportunity to seek out killzone patterns. Every second of every day matters, as I'm sure you understand. Just in the time we've spoken this morning, how many hundreds or thousands of people have caught the Flare out there in the world? How many have died?'

'So your solution is . . . take it out on kids?' Thomas asked, even though he knew it was a stupid thing to say. These people had saved them from almost certain death.

Anger flashed across Dr Paige's face. 'This is a harsh, brutal virus that needs to be dealt with by . . . *using* harsh and brutal will, Thomas. If you would just . . . stop thinking about how hard things are for you. You have no idea . . .' She faltered and a look of regret shadowed her face. 'I'm sorry. I'm . . . sorry. The truth is just too damn hard to talk about.'

She stood up, her eyes moist with tears. She appeared to be on the verge of saying something else, but then she turned her back to him and left the room, closing the door gently behind her.

29

Thomas had struck a nerve. He'd had her talking more honestly than ever before, and he wasn't going to waste the opportunity, no matter how much her sudden display of emotion surprised him. He got up and went after her.

She was walking briskly down the hall, almost jogging, so he had to run to catch up. He grabbed her arm to stop her.

She wrenched away from him, took a step back until she met the wall. Breathing heavily, she looked at him with something like disgust. Her eyes flared with a moment of anger. But then everything melted away and she was back to the same old Dr Paige he'd always known. Caring, kind Dr Paige. Although the sadness painted over her features almost made Thomas apologize and go back to his room.

'What's going on?' he asked. 'What aren't you telling me?' When she just shook her head, he kept at it. 'Every day I go out there and make your gigantic maze a little closer to test-ready. I don't whine or complain – I just do it. I work my butt off, and so does Teresa. We both know what the stakes are.'

Dr Paige nodded. 'Yes. You're right. I'm sorry.'

'But that's exactly what I'm talking about,' he continued. '*Because* we've had to grow up fast, we deserve to be treated like adults. Not like babies, not like mice in a cage, not like idiots. We all want the same thing. Why can't we be treated like partners instead of . . . subjects? Minho, Alby, Newt – everyone I know in here would be a lot more cooperative if you'd just show a little respect.'

Dr Paige had recovered from whatever had caught her off guard. She now stood tall and serene as ever, arms folded, eyes sharp and focused on him. 'Listen to me. Back in your room I told you it boiled down to two issues. First, some of these episodes of what you call *harshness* have actually been planned out by the Psychs. They are ways to stimulate brain patterns before we get to the big tests inside the mazes. Okay?'

No, not okay. Thomas didn't like it, though at least it *was* an explanation. 'Fine. And the second thing?'

'These people are survivors, Thomas. I know you were young – terribly young – but surely you remember the awful state of the world after the virus spread and reached us out here. Things weren't supposed to . . .' She paused, and something in her eyes told Thomas that she'd said something she hadn't meant to. 'But my point . . . the world became a place of horror and death and madness. By nature . . . by definition . . . anyone who survived those first waves of sheer terror had to be a little hardened. Tougher than normal. It's what helped them survive. The weak – they either died or will soon.'

Thomas, a little stunned by her flurry of words, didn't know what to say.

'So yes,' she continued. 'Most of the people here aren't the nicest you'll ever meet. They don't have the time or the inclination to worry about feelings. Okay? They've seen the depths of hell out there in the world, and they're ready to do anything and everything possible to find a cure and stop those horrors.

And you're just going to have to accept that.'

'Okay,' Thomas said, overwhelmed by all he'd just heard. Her impassioned speech had drained him of any desire to pursue the argument.

'Now buck up and get to work,' Dr Paige said. The corner of her mouth twitched in a semi-smile, which he figured was the best he could ask for that morning.

'Will do,' he replied, the words as sullen as he could make them.

Thomas walked along the corridors of the Maze, proud of the progress they'd made over the last few months. He couldn't take much credit for the majestic walls themselves – the cracked grey stone, the ivy that crawled like veins across their surfaces, the sheer magnitude of it all. Especially the advanced level of engineering that went into the moving walls, the changing configurations of the Maze itself. It was cool to watch, but he had no idea how it worked – the engineers weren't the friendliest folk in the world, and were too busy to get much information out of.

But so many of the finer details around him – the little things that really made the place come alive and feel real – were due to his and Teresa's tireless efforts.

He was thinking about all they'd done as he turned a corner and headed down a long stretch of the labyrinth. Even the doctors, Psychs, and technicians of WICKED were surprised at how valuable the telepathy had ended up being. Not only could Thomas and Teresa instantly communicate, they'd become much better at sensing the other's feelings, anticipating their thoughts, understanding things that were impossible to articulate. No one really believed him when he tried to explain it, so he'd stopped trying a long time ago.

You there yet? Teresa asked him from the control centre.

Give me a second, he responded. *I'm just enjoying our handiwork.* He looked up at the bright blue sky, the sun just peeking over the tall stone wall to his left. The sky on its own had taken countless days of painstaking effort to perfect, but seeing the end result – seeing that beautiful sky that looked so real – made him forget just how hard it had been.

The sound of little clattering metal feet approached from behind, and he knew what it was. One of the beetle-blade cameras that were now spread all over the complex, ready to record every single thing that happened during the trials. He was going to ignore the thing, until it jumped onto the back of his leg and crawled up his body.

'Ahh!' he yelped, and leaped into the air, twisting, reaching for his back, trying to swat the creature off. He spun in a circle as the thing scuttled all over his clothes, pecking his skin with those sharp legs. It reached his neck and latched on, digging in until it hurt.

You were saying again? Teresa asked. He felt every morsel of her evil glee. *That's a really nice dance you put on down there. Don't worry, I have it recorded, ready to show Newt and everybody else next time we get together.*

'Not funny!' he yelled out loud. The beetle blade was knocking its head into his ear, right in a spot that hurt like crazy. Thomas finally got a grip on the metal body and flung the creature off. It landed on its feet and scampered away, disappearing into the ivy of the wall to his right.

You win, he said. *I'm coming.* He tried not to smile, but he couldn't help it.

Next time I'll send a Griever, she replied. *Or worse – Randall.*

He laughed and so did she, one of those things he knew and felt without understanding how.

Okay, I'm here, he said. He'd reached the end of the corridor, which had a drop-off of about twenty feet to a black-painted floor. This was one of those weird areas inside the Maze where the optical-illusion technology wasn't yet complete, making you think you'd lost your mind. When he looked up, he saw a perfect sky. When he looked down, over the edge of the cliff,

– 150 –

he saw a black floor that led to a black wall – the edge of the Maze cavern. But straight ahead, the sky and the wall didn't exactly meet – the boundary between the two bounced here and there, blended and unblended, mixed and swirled. It made him dizzy and nauseous.

Can you see the Griever hatch? Teresa asked.

He'd closed his eyes to keep his stomach from swimming, but opened them again. Somewhere in the middle of that crazy kaleidoscope of illusion and real world mixing together, he saw a shaft towering up from the floor below, with an open circle at its top. This was the hole from which the Grievers would enter and exit the Maze.

I can see it, he replied to Teresa, *but it keeps swimming in and out of the illusion. It's gonna make me throw up.*

She didn't return a hint of sympathy. *Let me know when it disappears completely.*

He watched, squinting, hoping that would help his stomach. The image in front of him shimmered, went out of focus, bounced, then shimmered again. But soon the shaft of the Griever entrance vanished from his sight, and as long as he didn't look down, the illusion of endless blue sky opened up before him. Now, instead of dizziness, he felt an overwhelming sense of vertigo, almost like falling. He took a step backwards.

It worked! he yelled. *It looks perfect!*

She let out a big whoop, something he felt all the way to his bones. They'd been working on this section for a month, and now they were so close.

Good job, he said. *Seriously. What would these people do without us?*

They'd need another few years at least.

Thomas stared at the vista before him, in disbelief at how realistic it appeared. As if the corridor of the Maze ended in a cliff at the end of the world, at the end of existence.

I wonder who'll be the first one to see a Griever, he said. *And will they crap their pants? Should we bet on it?*

He was surprised by the sombre tone that rebounded back to him. And even more so by her words.

And who'll be the first to die?

They won't let it go that far, Thomas replied. *There's no way.*

Teresa cut off their connection without an answer.

30

229.06.12 | 10:03 A.M.

Thomas couldn't believe the people who sat around the table. Every important person he knew or had heard about, and then some. Psychs, doctors, technicians. Randall and Ramirez and Leavitt. Dr Paige sat next to Thomas and Teresa. Chancellor Kevin Anderson at the head of the table, Katie McVoy by his side. There were only two other teenagers in the room – Aris and Rachel. Even though they'd never met, Thomas knew exactly who they were.

Are they ever going to let us hang out with them? Teresa asked in his mind.

Thomas sent an image of himself shrugging. *I was just thinking that maybe it's a contest or something. Maybe they're hoping the two groups will do better if they're trying to . . . do it first. What if there's a prize!*

A lifetime supply of WICKED T-shirts!

Thomas sniggered under his breath.

Chancellor Anderson cleared his throat to get the meeting started.

'I'd like to welcome our lead candidates to their very first meeting of the Chancellor's Committee, an important step in their continued progress. Thomas, Teresa, Aris, Rachel . . . we're really proud of you. The work you've done during the Maze projects has been phenomenal. Just phenomenal. We pegged the four of you early on in this process as standouts, and we weren't wrong. Congratulations.' He beamed a smile that seemed about three orders too strong to be genuine, but Thomas imagined the man was under a lot of stress.

Thomas looked at Aris – olive skin, brown hair, eyes sharp with awareness – then Rachel – dark skin, tightly curled hair, smiling. Nothing stood out about them, but they were instantly likable. Their faces were kind, and they had none of the arrogance or haughtiness that Thomas would have expected.

'Now,' Chancellor Anderson continued, 'it's been ten years since the first inkling of WICKED was conceived by John Michael, and we've come a long way in our research since we began gathering those who are immune to the Flare. The progress in those first years was slow, of course. Trying to understand the disease itself, testing our subjects to ensure that they were actually immune, learning about the virus and how it interacts with your bodies and your brains. Slow but steady. Not a year has passed when we didn't have some kind of significant achievement, and I'd say that's better than anyone could have hoped for.'

Ten years, Thomas thought. That seemed like such a long, long time to him. And they obviously weren't close to a solution, or they wouldn't be bothering with this whole Maze thing.

'Thomas?' the chancellor said. 'You have the biggest look of doubt on your face I think I've ever seen.' He offered another one of those goofy smiles.

'Oh . . . um . . .' Thomas shifted in his chair. 'No, I just . . . it seems like such a long time you guys have been working on this. I don't know. I guess it just hit me that it's not going so well.'

Anderson nodded, lips pinched as if it were a reasonable observation. 'Dr Leavitt, you want to address that?'

The bald man seemed eager to do so. 'Read your history, son. I challenge you to find any kind of virus throughout the last few hundred years that was cured within *several* decades, much less one. Anything from the common cold to Ebola to HIV to the early stages of certain types of cancer. It's a long, long, *long* process. And those people didn't have a half-destroyed world with mind-sick Cranks running around. The fact that we've had the patience and endurance to work at this with a long-term strategy is pretty much a miracle. But even if there's only ten percent of the population left by the time we *do* find a cure, at least we'll have saved the human race from extinction.'

'What about Munies?' Aris asked. 'Could the human race continue if only they survive?'

Dr Leavitt scoffed, then seemed embarrassed that he'd done so. 'How many of those are going to survive a world full of Cranks?'

I really don't like him, Teresa spoke to Thomas.

Yeah, me neither.

'Dr Leavitt's points are well made,' Anderson said. 'We've done our best to gather the smartest people, the most advanced resources, and the best subjects, then ensured our protection from the outside world. We've planned for a long haul since we first began, and we don't plan to stop until an answer to this sickness is in our hands and ready to present to the world. And it should be no surprise to the candidates who are here today that we've been testing and running trials as often as possible since day one. Am I right?'

Thomas nodded, even though he thought it was an odd question to ask the very people they were testing. In fact, the whole thing – having them there in the first place – just seemed weird. Who knew, maybe that in itself was some kind of test. One of the Variables they always talked about.

'The Maze Trials are very close to beginning,' Anderson continued. 'And we've been prepping that for some time. But the progress we've made in the last few years towards our ultimate blueprint of the killzone . . .' He struggled to find the right words. 'I think we've laid a solid foundation through the smaller tests and trials we've accomplished with our subjects so far. The chances are slim, but maybe we'll have a blueprint after the Maze Trials. Who knows? Maybe we can avoid a Phase Two or Three. I'm feeling optimistic today.'

He paused, his gaze unfocused, as if his mind were several years in the future, imagining the perfect ending to what he'd devoted his entire life to. Next to Thomas, Dr Paige started clapping. Slowly at first, until others joined in. Soon the entire room was clapping, the sound of it even getting Thomas a little pumped up. He felt ridiculous.

Chancellor Anderson held up his hands and the clapping slowed to a stop. 'All right, all right. That applause, of course, is for all of us. And for all those subjects in Groups A and B. I really do feel like we're on the right path. I really do.' He smiled, seemed to gather himself, then let out a big breath. 'Okay, it's time to get to work. We're a month or two – four at most – from sending our first people into the mazes.'

Another one of his dramatic pauses – Thomas figured the man deserved a little moment in the spotlight after ten years of work – then he *really* began the meeting.

'The trials are upon us, folks. Let's dig in.'

31

229.06.12 | 6:10 P.M.

That night was the biggest change so far in Thomas's life. From that point on, Thomas and Teresa would be fully integrated with the other subjects of Group A, including meals, classes, and recreation time. It looked like slinking around would no longer be necessary.

Of course, that wasn't the greatest gift in the world, because most of Thomas's friends were slated to enter the Maze with the very first group, sometime within the next few months.

Ramirez, of all people, escorted Thomas and Teresa to their first dinner in the cafeteria, where all the other kids had been eating for years. When they entered the wide room – all stainless-steel serving locations and long plastic tables and cookie-cutter chairs – the place went silent, every eye trained on the newcomers.

'Listen up,' Ramirez barked, his voice echoing in the quiet. 'Many of you have heard of Thomas and Teresa – they've been considered elite candidates for years.'

He's giving us a death sentence! Teresa yelled in Thomas's mind, the anger coming through like an electric shock. *What the hell?*

'– be nice to them, they've worked really hard,' Ramirez was saying. 'The Maze Trials are starting soon, as you're all well aware, and there's a lot to be done. These two will be considered official liaisons between you subjects and the WICKED personnel overseeing the trial preparation. We'll be assigning the entrance schedule to the mazes very soon. In the meantime, take the time to get to know Thomas and Teresa, prepare yourselves mentally and physically, and let yourselves get excited for the fun changes ahead. Now, back to your meals.'

He nodded stiffly, then turned and walked out of the cafeteria, not saying a word to Thomas or Teresa.

That guy's just a boatload of charm, Teresa said.

Before Thomas could respond, he saw Newt and Alby coming towards them, faces alight with big grins.

'Well, look who the bloody copper dragged in,' Newt said, pulling Thomas into a big hug. He pounded his back a few times before letting go. 'It's a bit strange seein' you without sneakin' about and all. Welcome to society.'

Alby had already hugged Teresa, and then they traded, Alby squeezing the breath out of Thomas.

'Good to see you, man,' the older boy said. 'Your head big enough with all that crap they're sayin' about you? What're you, the chancellor now? No one here's going to like you much.'

Thomas opened his mouth to respond, but someone half tackled him from the left, almost taking him down. It was Chuck.

'What's up, you little runt?' Thomas asked, mussing the kid's hair in the oldest grandpa move in the books.

'Pretty much running this place, is all,' Chuck said, puffing his chest out. 'When I'm not sneaking over to Group B to get me some lovin' from the ladies, that is.'

This made them all bust up, and Thomas couldn't stop until he saw Minho sitting nearby, looking unsure of whether he should get up. Thomas walked over to him.

'Hey, man,' he said. 'Made anyone mad lately?'

Minho smiled, though he still seemed a little defeated behind his eyes. He was better, though, since the Griever incident. Thomas could tell.

'I'm a perfect angel,' he answered. 'Sometimes I make up words around Randall. You should see him – he always acts like he knows it's something bad, and he kinda half laughs at it. Such an idiot.'

Yeah, Minho was definitely getting better.

Tom, Teresa said, *look over there, to your right. Gally.*

Thomas glanced in that direction, searching until he found the black-haired boy who'd unwittingly caused all the trouble with Minho in the first place. Something was different about him, and it took a few seconds before Thomas figured it out. The guy's nose was about twice as big as it used to be, and totally deformed. Like some kind of squashed vegetable that had been glued there. Or worse, stapled – it *looked* painful.

Gally's eyes met Thomas's, and surprisingly, the boy offered what appeared to be an apologetic nod that seemed sincere. But he quickly returned his attention to the friends sitting with him at his table.

'What happened to *him*?' Thomas asked Minho.

His friend held up a fist. '*That's* what happened. His loose tongue gave us up, I'm pretty sure. Probably bragging in the showers or something. Even if it wasn't his fault, it sure made me feel better.'

Thomas expected him to laugh, or at least smile, but a darkness passed over his friend's face. Thomas just raised his eyebrows and shook his head. Alby, Teresa, Chuck and Newt had joined them.

'Let's get you some food,' Alby said. 'It ain't the worst thing you'll ever put in your mouth. Then we got some catchin' up to do, people to ridicule, plans to make.'

And for a little while, things like sun flares and Cranks were all but forgotten.

Weeks passed, and the official start of the trials grew closer and closer. Thomas found himself in the Maze as often as possible, seeing it as a sanctuary of sorts. He especially loved the central living area, with its wide-open spaces, its little forest; it was meant to become a place of rest and safety for those sent there. WICKED wanted most of it to be built by the subjects themselves – the farm, the gardens, the living space – probably a good opportunity to analyze their killzone patterns during such a productive time.

Thomas felt a significant sense of pride when it came to the Maze, and he wondered if he would ever be sent inside. He was madly curious about what it would be like, and every day he grew a little more eager for the actual trials to begin. Their lives needed a shot of change.

But as the day of insertion grew closer, he remembered he had a promise to keep. And one night he told himself tonight was the night. Although he had more clearance than before, he still felt a little mischievous as he made his way through the halls to the Group A barracks. He hadn't told anyone what he was about to do, figuring it would be better to seek forgiveness for something so harmless than to ask for permission in the first place. Most people were so busy, even during the evenings, that he doubted they'd be noticed anyway.

Newt was waiting for him by the door.

'You actually came, Tommy!' Newt exclaimed, probably only half kidding. Thomas always worried people were suspicious of him and Teresa because of their 'elite' status.

'Yep,' he replied. 'I'm a man of my word.'

They shook hands, and then the two of them set off, deep into the bowels of the WICKED complex.

32

229.10.28 | 11:04 P.M.

'**Y**ou probably know this place better than I even do,' Thomas said as they made their way around a corner and quietly set off down another long hallway. 'With all the sneaking around you guys have done.'

'Yeah, probably,' Newt agreed.

'Well, I think I found a quicker way to get over to the Group B barracks. And less chance of being stopped by security.'

Everything still look good? Thomas asked Teresa in his mind. She was helping out by guiding them through the least likely places to get caught. She'd studied video feeds earlier, and had made it very clear that Thomas would owe her big-time.

Yeah, she replied. *Go through that R&D lab I told you about and you should be totally fine. There's an emergency escape tunnel at the far end that goes right by the barracks.*

Got it, he said.

After a few more turns they came to a secured door marked research and development, one of the many to which he'd never been granted access.

It should be open now, Teresa said to him. It was as if she were watching them in real time. *And you should be fine on your way back. I'm going to my room and to bed. If someone arrests you or shoots you, too bad.* She cut off the connection before he could respond, but not before sending one last little mental image of a kiss on the cheek that she knew would embarrass him.

'Tommy,' Newt whispered. He'd hunkered down next to the R&D door. 'Wipe that bloody look off your face and let's keep moving.'

Thomas ignored him and pushed open the door, then quickly stepped inside the room, motioning for Newt to follow. Once the door was closed, they started to make their way across the lab. It was a large space, full of countertops cluttered with equipment and desks set up with workstations and monitors. The room was filled with glass containers and unusual machinery covered in an assortment of tubing and wires. The walls were hung with tools that looked like they belonged in a torture chamber from the Middle Ages: gleaming silver metal, and lots of it was sharp. Thomas and Newt stayed low as they made their way down the aisle that cut through the middle of the huge room.

'What're they *doing* in here?' Newt asked, his whisper sounding like a small explosion in the eerie silence.

Thomas jumped at the sound, then stumbled. Newt tripped over him, and then they were both laughing, legs and arms tangled in a pile on the ground. They were either stressed or starting to crack up.

'Are you sure WICKED knows what they're doing with you?' Newt joked as they picked themselves up and brushed themselves off. 'You seem a little more clown than elite.'

Thomas was searching for something smart to say when his eyes caught an unusual sight. Hidden back in the darkness of the room was a glowing green mass. It was mesmerizing and strange, and he couldn't look away.

Newt's smile faltered, then disappeared. 'What is it?' he asked, looking in the same direction. There was a misty fog surrounding the lime-green light.

Thomas knew he should walk away, keep moving and find the hidden passage to Group B. But there was no chance of that.

'Let's check it out,' he whispered, as if he might wake up whatever monster swam in the glowing goo.

Together, he and Newt slowly walked past several desks and workstations, step by step, getting closer to the eerie light. As they approached it, Thomas saw that the glow came from a large green plate of glass, maybe ten feet by ten feet, covering a container that stood chest-high. Wisps of white mist spilled out the edges and curled into the darkness of the room.

Thomas leaned over the glass, its top beaded with drops of water, and looked over at Newt. His friend's face was illuminated by the green light, and for a moment he looked sick. Thomas shook the thought away.

'We probably shouldn't mess with this,' Newt said, looking up from the vat. 'Looks bloody radioactive to me. We could wake up with three extra fingers and one less eye in the morning.'

Thomas smiled, only half hearing him, looked back at the otherworldly container below, feeling almost hypnotized. Mist churned beneath the surface, swirling in little whirlpools. But there was something underneath that. He could just barely make out a dark outline. He almost felt that if he just kept staring at it, whatever it was would reveal itself.

'Tommy?' Newt said. 'Let's move on, yeah? This thing gives me the creeps.'

Thomas couldn't move on. He desperately wanted to know –

A lumpy object moved in the container, bumping against the glass with a heavy thump, and Thomas jumped back. The object squeaked along the container's side for several seconds before vanishing into the fog again. The thing had been tan-coloured, with lines like veins running through it. An arm. It had looked like an arm.

Thomas shivered, and the hairs on his neck and arms stood straight up. He looked over at Newt, who met his gaze with one of horror.

'Why are we still standing here?' Newt asked.

'Good question.'

Thomas moved to leave when another lump of flesh pressed up against the glass. It appeared to be the torso of whatever creature was being held in the tank. It too had veins, and some-thing like mucus covered its skin. Thomas had to fight his stomach not to send dinner up his throat.

'Look, Tommy,' Newt said, leaning closer to the glass, pointing. 'It has . . . things growing out of its skin.' He stepped back from the container, shaking his head as he glanced away.

Thomas couldn't look away until he saw what his friend was talking about. With a sudden surge of bravery, he leaned on the edge of the container and wiped off some condensation. The meaty mass pressed against the window had large, bulbous growths – several of them. They looked like tumours or gigan-tic blisters. And unless his eyes were tricking him, Thomas could swear the growths were where the glowing light was com-ing from.

Finally he stepped back and rubbed his eyes. He'd seen a lot of strange things in his life, but this took the cake.

'What . . .' he said, drawing out his words, 'in the world . . . is that?'

'No bloody idea,' Newt replied, refusing to look back. 'Have we had enough yet?' Tendrils of mist cascaded up his shirt and parted around his head.

'Plenty,' Thomas agreed. 'Let's go.'

He'd had yet another peek behind the mysterious curtain of WICKED, and he didn't like what he'd seen.

A sombre mood hung between them as they made their way across the rest of the R&D room, the security tunnel Teresa had told them about, and then finally to a false wall behind a closet that led to the barracks of Group B. Every time Thomas thought he'd kind of got used to things around WICKED, he came across something like a glass container in which a hideous monster with glowing tumours grew like a foetus in a womb.

They obviously weren't telling him everything. Of course they weren't – he wasn't a naive idiot. But sometimes it seemed like they told him nothing, like they were playing him like everyone else. Like he was just another subject. Who knew what kind of horrors were in store for those sent to the two mazes. The Grievers, this thing growing in the R&D vat . . .

He sighed as Newt pressed against the wall and popped out a large panel. It revealed a small closet, mostly dark, with a door just a few feet away that led into the large barracks room. The door of the closet was ajar, and through the opening, Thomas could see bunk beds lined up along the walls.

'What if they freak out?' Thomas whispered. 'I don't want forty girls attacking me at once.'

'I thought you went for that sort of thing,' Newt whispered back. Thomas could barely see him, but he knew his friend was smiling.

Thomas shook his head and nudged Newt towards the opening, then followed him through to the other side of the closet. They peered through the door to Group B. The soft sighs of sleep were broken here and there by a sharp snore or the creaks of springs as bodies repositioned.

Thomas waited for his eyes to adjust to the darkness. He was scanning the room of bunks when a figure suddenly appeared in front of him. He stifled a yelp and stumbled backwards. The girl followed him into the shadows of the closet.

'What do you want?' she whispered fiercely. 'Who are you?'

Thomas finally recovered. 'Sorry to sneak in like this – we're from Group A. We're here so Newt can say goodbye to his sister before the Maze Trials begin.' He couldn't see Newt's face because of the darkness, but he imagined the boy laughing at him for being so startled.

'You could've given us a warning,' the girl replied, 'before creeping in like kidnappers. What are your names? Well, *your* name, if he's Newt. We know all about Newt. Sonya is one of my best friends.'

'I'm Thomas.'

'Oh.' She sounded disappointed. Or annoyed. Her group had probably heard just as much about him and Teresa as his friends had about Aris and Rachel. WICKED seemed to have spread the word. 'My name's Miyoko. Let me get Sonya.'

She slipped off into the barracks room, a shadow among shadows.

'I hope they're on our side,' Newt said. 'That girl'd take down half of us, yeah?'

Thomas didn't answer; the darkness of the closet suddenly felt menacing. He knew that WICKED had the subjects separated into groups of girls and boys for various reasons. It had to do with how they were going to run out the Variables later in the trials. But he also knew there was more going on, and he didn't like it.

Miyoko reappeared, this time with another girl right next to her. She was a blur as she ran past Thomas, streaking through the door and straight at Newt. They embraced in an unstable hug, stumbling back in the dark little room.

'Here,' Miyoko said, gently pushing Thomas out of the way so she could swing the closet door closed. Then she turned on a light that seemed as bright as two suns. He squinted and held a hand up to his eyes, temporarily blinded.

Newt was crying, and Thomas didn't need vision to know it. The boy sobbed, the sounds muffled by his sister's neck or shoulder. As Thomas's sight returned, he saw that both of them had tears streaming down their faces, and they were hugging each other fiercely. He didn't know how long it had been since the last time they'd seen each other, or if they were able to communicate somehow. But his heart hurt watching them.

'Come on,' Miyoko said to Thomas, grabbing his arm. 'Let's give them some —'

'I hate them,' Newt said loudly through his sniffles. He pulled back from his sister and wiped his cheeks. 'I hate every one of them! How can they do this? How can they steal us from our homes and keep us separate like this? It's not right!' He yelled the last word, and Miyoko winced, eyeing the door.

'No, no, no,' Sonya said in a soothing tone. She put her hands on both sides of her brother's face, looking straight into his eyes. 'Don't say that. You're looking at it all wrong. We've got it better than ninety-nine percent of kids out there. They *saved* us, big brother. What are the odds we'd be alive if they'd left us out there?' She pulled Newt back into a hug.

'But why do they keep us separate?' he asked, and the sadness in his voice broke Thomas's heart. 'Why all the tests and the games and the cruelty? I hate them, I don't care what you say.'

'It'll all be over someday,' the younger girl whispered. 'Remember, you're not immune. One day we'll be able to make you safe and then we'll be back together. Come on. You're my big brother. You're supposed to be the one comforting me.'

'I love you, Lizzy,' he replied, squeezing her hard. 'I love you so much.' He leaned back and looked at her.

She smiled and Newt shook his head, pulling her back into a strong hug, and Thomas had a feeling that was about the best things would get for a while.

33

229.11.12 | 7:31 A.M.

They were days away from insertion. Days. Thomas could barely sleep. He and Teresa connected via telepathy at bed-time each night, but often they just lingered in silence, without much to say. The mere presence of the other person, somehow *there,* was always a comfort, though. Aside from his mother, whom he would always love, Teresa had become the closest thing to family – the closest thing to what Newt had with Lizzy – Thomas could ever imagine.

The last thing he remembered before the knock that woke him up that morning was Teresa humming to herself. She seemed to do it without thinking. The vibration and tone and feel of it travelled through their connection, and it had sent him off to a deep sleep like he hadn't enjoyed in quite some time.

He groggily got up from bed and opened the door. Dr Paige was there, and she looked worried.

'Sorry,' Thomas said, rubbing his eyes. 'I slept in. But trust me, I needed it.' They'd been working themselves to the bone to get ready for the Maze Trials.

'It's okay,' she replied. She seemed distracted. 'Chancellor Anderson wants to meet with you and Teresa really fast this morning. Aris and Rachel will be there, too. It's urgent. Hurry and get dressed. You can have breakfast after the meeting.'

Thomas realized then that she was a little dishevelled, her face pale, and paused before answering.

'I mean it, Thomas!' she snapped. 'Hurry.'

'Okay, okay. I'll be ready in five minutes.'

'Make it three.'

It was the same conference room in which he'd seen Aris and Rachel for the first time a few months ago. That last time the room was filled with people. This time around, only three people were in attendance besides Thomas and the three other 'elite' candidates: Chancellor Anderson, the security officer, Ramirez and Dr Paige. They sat on one side of the table, and Thomas, Teresa, Aris and Rachel sat across from them on the other. No one in the room looked very happy.

'Thanks for coming,' Anderson began. They always started these things with statements like that – as if Thomas or his friends had a choice in the matter. 'I'm afraid I have some sobering news. And I'm not going to beat around the bush – I'm going to just come out and say it.'

Instead, he did the opposite. He went silent, trading looks with Ramirez and Paige. Thomas watched this until it almost became comical. But the dread in Anderson's voice had been real, and heavy.

'Then just say it,' Aris said.

Anderson nodded stiffly. 'We think . . . we *believe* that we might have an outbreak on our hands.' He sat back in his chair and let out a weary breath. Looked again to Dr Paige.

'An outbreak,' Teresa repeated. 'Of the Flare?'

'Paige, say something,' Anderson grumbled.

Dr Paige folded her hands on the table and looked at the

teenagers. 'Yes, the Flare. As you can imagine, none of the adults here are immune, so we've taken extreme caution to ensure our safety from the virus. A few months ago, however, we began to worry that we'd had a breach, even though none of our staff exhibited symptoms or tested positive.'

'Then what made you worry about it?' Rachel asked. Not for the first time, Thomas wished that WICKED would let the four of them work together more.

'You're aware of the Crank pits?' Anderson said, more of a statement than a question. 'That's the riskiest part of our facilities, but a vital one. It's a trap and a holding facility for Cranks that wander onto our grounds, and it provides biological material for our study regarding the virus.'

'So what happened?' Thomas asked.

'We keep a strict inventory,' Ramirez answered. It was always a surprise when the gruff man spoke. 'It's almost like an old-fashioned bee trap down there – they wander in but can't get back out. The holding facility is constantly monitored – we have cameras everywhere.' He paused, and made an awful phlegmy sound somewhere deep in his throat. 'There's a strict no-contact rule without a containment suit – actually, a twenty-foot-distance rule – unless you're a Munie, of course. Like you folks.' He sniffed, as if offended by his own words.

'You still haven't told us what happened,' Teresa said, not bothering to hide her disgust for this man – Thomas knew full well that she, like he, associated the man with all things Randall.

'One of the Cranks went missing,' Ramirez said. 'Three times a day we take an inventory, accounting for newcomers from the outside forests, less those who are removed for lab needs. There has never been a discrepancy, not once in all my years. Until a few months ago. One up and vanished.'

Those words settled for a moment, no one speaking. Thomas felt a shivery fear despite being immune. He wasn't really afraid of the virus – it was the Cranks that terrified him.

And to think that one might be hiding somewhere inside the WICKED complex made his stomach feel watery.

'We don't want to alarm you or anyone else,' Chancellor Anderson said, 'but we've brought you in to let you know we've made some decisions. Some hard decisions. For starters, we've decided to shorten the Maze Trials from five years to two. For all we talk about this being a long, slow process, the possibility of a breakout has given us pause. We might have to be a little more . . . intense with the Variables.'

Thomas had never felt so uneasy. Anderson was dancing around something here, but he wasn't sure what. Teresa didn't say anything specific in his mind, but she opened up her emotions to him, showing that she shared his ominous feeling.

'We've been working on several possibilities for a Phase Two, even a Phase Three if it comes to that. Once we get past the initial maze insertions, we'll see how things go.'

Thomas immediately thought of what he and Newt had seen in the R&D laboratory: the glass-topped container, the veined skin, the bulbous tumours . . .

Anderson sighed, then put his head in his hands before looking up again. Thomas had never seen him so frustrated.

'I feel like there's too much to do sometimes,' the man continued. He slapped an open hand on the table. 'Look, things can be worked out over the next few months as we study and analyze the results within the mazes. Suffice it to say we have Flat Trans technology, we have the potential for more human resources, and we're even scouting locations for further trials. It can all happen, and it will happen, everything in its own time. Reducing the Maze Trials from five to two years is simply the right thing to do.' He smiled a weak smile. 'I think half of my frustration with this change is that it took so much effort to build the damn things that it's a shame to see them utilized for less than half the time that we intended.'

He's stalling, Teresa said in Thomas's mind. *There's something he has to say that he doesn't want to say.*

Thomas gave her a barely perceptible nod. She was exactly right.

'What are you not telling us?' Aris asked.

Anderson at first acted surprised at the question, but then gave a knowing smile. 'Sometimes I forget just how perceptive you kids are. Here's the thing. I'm just nervous, okay? I shouldn't show you that, much less admit it, but there's the truth.' His eyes flicked around the room, then came to rest on the table in front of him before he looked up at each of the kids and let out a breath. 'I guess what I'm trying to say is that this is going to be hard, but I know you're all up to it.'

More things were said, more information exchanged during the meeting. But Thomas didn't hear much of it, because it was all dressing. Something had changed. Or someone had chickened out. Somehow Thomas knew that for some reason, at the last second, Chancellor Anderson and his two partners had decided *not* to tell them everything.

What's he hiding? Thomas asked Teresa when they were finally getting up to leave. But then he looked at Dr Paige, and the odd expression on her face made him realize that he had asked about the wrong person.

34

229.11.22 | 8:47 A.M.

L ook at Minho, Teresa said to Thomas.

It was the morning before the big day – the first insertion into the Maze. Forty boys from Group A were lined
up along the walls of the hallway, ready for their final medical
examinations. Newt, Minho, Alby, Gally – all the boys Thomas
had got to know over the last few years of his life would be part
of the group. Orderlies walked up and down the hall, prepping
them to enter the medical rooms – taking temperatures, blood
pressures, checking eyes, tongues.

Yeah, I see him, Thomas replied. He and Teresa were there
at Chancellor Anderson's request – to observe and provide
moral support. But all he felt was a heavy, heavy sadness at saying goodbye, and he'd stayed silent since arriving.

Minho was about ten boys away from where he and Teresa
stood, and he'd been fidgeting all morning. But now it had
turned into something worse – his body reminded Thomas of
a cocked gun, his muscles coiled as if he were about to spring
into action.

Man, Thomas said. *There's no way he'd try something again. Right?*

Although there were plenty of things to upset their friend. Inside the medical rooms, clearly visible from their place in the hallway, menacing devices hung over each bed – they looked like robot masks, metallic and full of wires and tubes. Thomas assumed they were meant to capture every type of killzone measurement imaginable, a foundation from which they could study progress within the Maze Trials.

Follow my lead, Teresa said. She pushed away from the wall and walked towards Minho. Thomas followed right on her heels. She had an air of authority about her, so the medical attendants barely glanced her way. She stopped when she got to Minho, and put a hand on his shoulder. He flinched, and for an instant Thomas thought he might actually strike out, but then his eyes met hers and a wave of calm seemed to wash over him, relaxing his muscles as it flowed through his body. To Thomas's surprise, tears formed in the boy's eyes.

'It's okay,' Teresa said to him. 'Don't make it worse by fighting them. Everything will be fine inside the Maze. You'll see.'

'Aren't you going in with us?' Minho asked.

The response took both Thomas and Teresa by surprise.

'Uh, w-well . . . ,'Teresa stammered.

'Not yet,' Thomas quickly interjected, leaving it at that. Hoping his friends wouldn't dig further.

A hint of anger flushed Minho's face again, but this time it set firmly. 'Seriously? So you're telling me not to fight *them*? Are you sure you don't mean *us*? What exactly are you doing here, Thomas? I don't see you being poked and prodded like cattle.'

Alby, just a few feet down the hall, turned to look at the three. 'Yeah,' he said. 'He's got a good point, if you ask me. You're just gonna throw us into a big experiment, then go back to your cush bed and relax? Were you ever going to tell us? Or just let us think you were going in, then, *surprise!*'

Thomas had no idea what to say. He'd been able to convince

himself that he was the same as his friends. That they didn't care that he'd been separated out, that he had different responsibilities than they did. How could he have ever thought it wouldn't matter? That it wouldn't blow up in his face?

'What? Forget the script you're supposed to follow?' Alby asked. 'Or are you just worried about upsetting your buddies?' He nodded towards the doctors and nurses, who all continued their work as if nothing was happening.

'Guys, come on,' Teresa said, finally finding her voice. 'We're no different from anyone else – we just do what they ask.'

'Say whatever makes you feel better,' Alby answered. He folded his arms and leaned against the wall, looked the other way. They were understandably on edge.

And then the truth was clear as day. Thomas's friends were being sent into the Maze and he wasn't. He didn't know if he'd ever be sent in. He was different from his friends, and no one could ignore it any more. They stood, backs against the wall, some glaring at him as if he'd known about this the whole time. As if he'd been lying to them. Even Newt, down at the end of the line, looked at Thomas, anger twisting his face.

Thomas was absolutely crushed.

Minho hadn't said anything, but the fierce, coiled-snake look had returned. Anger, fear, anxiety about what this new change meant – Thomas understood how they felt. And he was the perfect one to blame.

Minho flung Teresa's hand off his shoulder. 'Alby's right,' he said. 'I've tried and tried to give you guys the benefit of the doubt. Figured you were going to be able to help us. But now it's obvious what you were doing. You've been helping them the whole time. It's all been about getting ready to do *this* to *us*, hasn't it!' He pounded his chest twice as he emphasized the words.

'Minho, listen—' Teresa began.

'Get out of my face!' Minho yelled.

The world was falling apart, and Thomas could think of nothing to say. Alby, Minho, Newt. Until five minutes ago he'd considered them his best friends, and just assumed they understood his mind and heart. And now it had all collapsed and here he was, standing in front of them like a complete idiot. Anything he said sounded like a lie, even to himself.

Out of the corner of his eye, he noticed someone approaching down the hall. He looked and saw it was Gally. He'd left his place in line and his face was aflame with anger. Two nurses followed him, trying to catch up to him before he reached Thomas.

'Thomas!' the boy yelled, picking up his pace, only now that he was closer Thomas could see that his expression wasn't anger – it was fear. 'You have to help us! Can't you help us?' Two orderlies grabbed the boy before he could get closer, holding him back. 'We know you have some power with them. Help us!' He sounded desperate and struggled to keep his eyes on Thomas as orderlies roughly turned him around and dragged him into an exam room.

Thomas felt powerless. He looked down the line of boys who had been his friends, and his heart broke over and over. Minho, Alby, Newt – their eyes brimming with resentment. How had everything crashed so suddenly?

He had to say something, quickly. His chance would be over soon. He had to fix this! They had to know that they were all wrong, that he and Teresa weren't working with WICKED, really. They would help *them,* even go into the Maze themselves if they had to. He had to speak, now!

Thomas opened his mouth, ready to spill out his words, his pleas, his apologies.

But something happened. Something deep inside his brain clicked and it felt as if a hand reached within his actual body and began to manipulate him, play with his nerves, his thoughts, his everything. As if possessed by an evil spirit, he lost complete control – lost it to someone or some*thing* else. He spoke words against his will.

'I'm sorry,' he said, the tone and pitch of it sounding as foreign as if it came from another person altogether. 'There's nothing I can do.'

And then he watched, frozen, helpless, screaming on the inside, as they took his friends away.

35

The very next day, Dr Paige arrived right on schedule. Thomas had been awake all night thinking about what had happened, becoming angrier and angrier. By the time his alarm went off he was ready to unleash it all on her. But when he opened the door and saw the doctor's face, he wilted. What had happened to him made him feel half crazy, and he was scared to bring it up.

'Don't say a word, Thomas,' she said. 'There are reasons for things that you don't understand. Also know that I'm not the final say on any decision. But I did get you one victory today. How would you like the day off? You can spend it observing your friends in the Maze. I feel like you deserve that much.'

Thomas's spirit rose, then sank. 'The only reason you guys want me to do that is so *you* can observe *me* observing them.'

She sighed. 'Do you want to do it or not?'

He swallowed his pride. 'Yeah.'

Dr Paige led Thomas to the observation room in which he'd seen Minho tormented by a Griever once upon a time. This time the monitors showed various glimpses into the massive green space at the centre of the Maze – where most of his friends now resided. Dr Paige showed him to a chair at the control deck, and he sat down, already glued to the various scenes playing out across the many monitors. Without saying another word, she left him, softly closing the door.

Thomas leaned forwards.

He watched.

They'd had one night in their new home, though none of them had seen the actual Maze yet. WICKED had yet to open the doors that led to the Maze, saving that for the next day.

Thomas watched the boys wander about the large courtyard nestled within the giant walls of the Maze itself. Their faces said it all. Their *eyes* said it all, often visible when a beetle blade could get close enough. They had no idea where they were. They looked disorientated – and the more Thomas watched, the more something felt wrong. Everyone had peeled off, and really seemed to be on their own.

He zeroed in on two of the boys he didn't know very well, who were just crossing each other's paths.

'Hey,' one of them said in a shaky voice. 'Do you know where we are? How we got here?'

The other boy shook his head, looking on the verge of tears. 'I don't . . . I don't even know . . .' He didn't finish, but turned and walked briskly away.

Similar things were happening elsewhere. Most of the boys avoided each other, but when they did interact, it seemed as if they were acting like strangers. As if they didn't know who anyone else was. Or even who they were themselves. A few names were thrown about, but even those were said with uncertainty.

Those masks. *That* was what the masks had been for.

WICKED had done something terrible to their memories. Something to do with their implants, probably.

If that was the case, if this was something permanent, Thomas couldn't imagine anything more horrible. It was all they *had,* their memories. He thought back to when Randall had taken away his name – it had felt like losing part of his soul. And this was far, far worse. How deep did it go? Was it possibly temporary?

He found Minho walking briskly along the walls, studying every inch of the structure. He could have been doing it for hours, since before the false sun came up. He was scared – that much was obvious. Losing your memories, combined with being thrown into a stone prison – that had to fill you with a panic beyond what most could imagine. He walked and walked and walked, down one expansive wall to the next, then the next, then the next. It couldn't have been lost on him that he was going in circles.

On another feed, Alby sat near the copse of trees, his back against one of the skeletal pines. He was so still, he looked almost lifeless. He looked broken, and it killed Thomas. This young man, whom Thomas knew as fierce and determined, always ready to tackle what came at him. WICKED had been able to turn him into nothing more than a shell.

Newt was one of the wanderers. Aimlessly walking back and forth, from the barn to the fields to the small structure that was meant to be their home. It was nothing more than a shack, really. He had the same empty look in his eyes as Alby. Newt walked slowly to his old friend, as if he were approaching a complete stranger. Thomas pushed a button to get the audio feed from that monitor.

'Do you know where we are?' Newt asked.

Alby looked up sharply. 'No, I don't know where we are,' he snapped, as if Newt had asked him a hundred times and he was sick of hearing it.

'Well, bloody hell, neither do I.'

'Yeah, I think we all get that.'

They stared at each other for a long moment, neither dropping his gaze. Finally Newt said, 'At least I know my name – it's Newt. And you?'

'Alby.' He said it almost like a guess.

'Well, shouldn't we start trying to figure things out?'

'Yeah, we should.' Alby looked as mean as the night they'd been caught outside the WICKED complex.

'Well then?' Newt asked.

'Tomorrow, man. Tomorrow. Give us a day to mope, for God's sake.'

'Right.'

Newt walked away, kicking a loose stone to scatter across the dusty ground.

Late that afternoon, Minho tried to climb the wall.

The vines were tempting enough, beckoning those who dared to scale the leafy ivy. Minho did just that, gripping it with white-knuckled fists, finding perilous footholds as he inched his way up. Hand over hand, shifting his feet carefully, he climbed.

Ten feet.

Fifteen feet.

Twenty feet.

Twenty-five.

He stopped. He looked towards the sky, then craned his neck to look back down at the ground. A crowd had gathered, cheering him on. Another couple of boys had tackled the vines as well, trying to follow their fellow prisoner's lead.

Minho looked up again. Down. At the wall. At his hands. Up to the sky again. The ground. The sky. The wall. His hands. Then, without any explanation, despite the abundance of ivy above him, he started back to the ground. He jumped the last few feet, then brushed his hands on his pants.

'Can't be done here,' he said. 'Let's try another spot.'

Three hours and all four walls later, the sky almost dark, he gave up.

So did everyone else.

That evening, when Dr Paige came to get him, Thomas couldn't believe the day was over already.

'Time to go back to your room,' she said gently.

She'd had his meals brought to him throughout the day, so Thomas thought to take advantage of her accommodation by asking a favour. And he didn't want to risk upsetting her by asking about the apparent memory loss – he'd save that for another time.

'Can I come back here in the morning?' he asked. 'I feel like I need to see their reactions when the doors open for the first time. It's important.' He tried to insinuate that he meant its importance to the study.

'Okay, Thomas. That'll be fine. You can have breakfast in here.'

He stood up, his heart so heavy it felt as if it had stayed in the seat. After one last look at his friends – settling down for the evening, talking in small groups, eating some of the food they'd been provided – he turned away.

The next morning, he got into the observation room just in time.

The entire Maze shook and he flicked on the sound. The room he sat in was suddenly filled with the rumbling sound of thunder and the giant doors began to slide open, an impossible sight to anyone who had never witnessed it before. It was still an impressive sight to Thomas, who had helped *build* those doors.

Thomas's friends gathered, confused. Some crying in fear. Some of them with such bright expressions of hope on their faces that it just about broke his heart. It seemed pretty obvious that their memories were still lost to them.

He watched as they filed out into the corridors of the Maze proper and began to explore its vast array of halls, twisting and turning along their patterns. Thomas wondered what they would think the first time the walls out there moved, re-forming into a new pattern. He imagined the terrifying times that lay ahead for his friends, and then he remembered the gelatinous creature crouching over Minho, and what would happen the day WICKED decided to unleash that into the Maze for the first time.

'Thomas?'

He turned, startled out of his thoughts, to find Dr Paige behind him.

'There will be plenty of other opportunities to watch your friends,' she said. 'But your responsibilities here take priority, okay? You still have a full schedule. Let's go.'

He went, leaving his friends behind.

36

230.03.13 | 2:36 P.M.

Thomas sat in the chair, staring at the bank of monitors across from the control deck, feeling a little better than he had in months. Which wasn't saying much. At least he actually wanted to take his next breath instead of wishing that maybe it wouldn't happen, that some mysterious illness would strike him dead on the spot. It had been a long time since he'd felt . . . okay. And today he felt okay.

Dr Paige continued to let him observe his friends in the Maze as long as he kept up with his normal schedule of classes, tests, check-ups, and everything else. He no longer had workdays since the Maze had been completed, so he had extra free time and, even though he knew they were observing him as he sat and watched, this was the only place he wanted to be.

The techs had installed a new display system, and maybe that was part of the reason he'd finally been able to snap out of his doldrums, even if it was only for a fraction of each day. Now he could choose any of the beetle-blade feeds and throw it onto a much-improved centre screen, which was a full six feet across and had spectacular colour and detail and improved audio. He loved it, seeing and hearing his old friends in the Maze close up, almost as if he were there with them. The entire system was a hundred times better, and he knew that his whole life would now revolve around finding more and more excuses to be in this very room, watching. Observing. Digging for something to give him insight. Sadly, their memories had never returned, a thing that still galled Thomas to no end.

He chose beetle blade number thirty-seven and swiped it onto the main viewing screen. The display showed Alby and a kid named George standing at the east door of the Maze, talking and laughing, both of them eating peaches they'd just plucked out of the trackhoe's scoop. Thomas had never even spoken to George before, but these were the kinds of scenes he craved. Shots of the Gladers actually enjoying life. It always gave him hope, helped him forget for a while the terrible theft they'd experienced. And with nothing that interesting going on anywhere else, he sat back and watched, wishing he could be there. Just for a visit.

Someone knocked on the door.

'Come in!' Thomas called, not bothering to check who it was when the door opened, then closed. He knew by the sound of the person's steps. He definitely knew. 'Hi, Chuck,' he said without looking.

'Hey, Thomas!' the young boy said, his voice filled with the usual enthusiasm. He pulled a chair over and put it right next to Thomas, barely an inch away, and jumped up into the seat with a jovial grunt. 'Anything exciting happen yet?'

'You're looking at it,' Thomas replied. 'See that? Look really close. Look at what Alby and George are eating. You won't believe it.'

Chuck leaned forwards, his hair a wild eruption as usual, and squinted at the screen, searching with all the seriousness he could muster.

'Looks like peaches,' he finally said.

'Bingo,' Thomas replied, slapping Chuck on the back. 'You might be the best analyst in all of WICKED.'

'Hardy har har.' That was the kid's favourite response when Thomas teased him. 'You so funny.' That was his second favourite.

Thomas had begged Dr Paige to let Chuck serve as his assistant for an hour or two each day. It had become clear that WICKED appreciated the insights Thomas provided and he insisted that he needed someone to bounce ideas off during these work periods. Teresa was often too busy learning computer systems on top of her normal schedule to help him.

He claimed he was grooming Chuck to do great things, but the truth was that Thomas needed him. Being alone often brought his memories crashing in, and Chuck was a beacon that lit the darkness. Dr Paige seemed more than happy to acquiesce, considering the value of studying Chuck's reactions to the things he witnessed. It was pure selfishness on Thomas's part, but he couldn't let it go. He flat-out needed Chuck, like a kid with a security blanket.

Chuck was a constant bright spot in what had been a miserable couple of months since sending the first batch of subjects in, after stealing their memories. If it weren't for Chuck and Teresa, Thomas didn't know how he would have survived.

As if the thought had summoned her – which it very well might have – Teresa spoke in his mind.

Hey, what are you doing? she asked. *I just finished prepping the next kid to go in. It's Box time for him tomorrow morning. Poor guy.*

I'm in the observation room, he answered. *I'll give you three guesses who's sitting right next to me, and the first two don't count.*

Sweet little Chucky-Chuck? He could feel her beaming over the connection. They both had a soft spot for the kid. *Mind if*

I come join you guys?

Are you kidding? It's never the same without you.

She didn't respond right away, and he knew she was about to say something serious. He cringed, waiting.

I can tell you're feeling better, she finally said. *And that makes me very happy.*

He sighed with relief.

You and me both, he responded back. *Now get your butt over here.*

Teresa showed up at the observation room a few minutes later. She slipped inside without saying anything and pulled up a chair next to Thomas. The whole routine was as comfortable as a well-worn pair of shoes. Chuck looked over at her and winked – flirting with an older girl was his idea of hilarious – then gave a thumbs-up.

'How are you, Chuck?' she asked. 'Been sent to your room yet today?'

'No, ma'am,' he replied, batting his eyelashes. 'Perfect little angel, just like always.'

'I bet.' She reached over Thomas's lap and grabbed a piece of skin on Chuck's leg, then wrenched it hard.

Chuck screamed in agony and leaped from his chair, hopping up and down as he rubbed at the sore spot. 'Not cool!' he yelled. 'Not cool!'

'That's for stealing the devilled eggs from my lunch tray when I went back for a drink,' she said, one eyebrow raised accusingly. 'You know how much I love devilled eggs.'

'What?' he asked. 'How did you . . .' He looked at Thomas. 'She's some kind of mind reader.'

'Don't mess with Teresa,' Thomas said, slowly shaking his head back and forth as if in pure awe of her powers. 'If I teach you nothing else in life, my son, it's that. Don't mess with Teresa.'

'Come here, you little devilled egg,' Teresa said, now chasing

Chuck around the room, trying to smother him with hugs. For all his flirting jokes, the kid hated it when she did that.

Thomas leaned back in his chair, enjoying every second of it.

Yeah, he thought. *I feel good again.*

37

Another insertion day.

The boy's name was Zart, and it was his turn to enter the Box. It was Teresa's job to prep the new insertion this time. She'd prepped Zart the day before and he'd gone through the Swipe procedure early that morning. Thomas looked over at him, unconscious on the gurney. Whatever they gave the kids to knock them out seemed like it could fell a rhinoceros.

He looked up at Teresa and flashed her a smile. They were in the lift, along with Dr Paige, two nurses, and Chuck. Once again, Thomas had convinced Dr Paige to allow his sidekick along, which Chuck loved. He was always excited for a break from his normal schooling and testing. Thomas felt more strongly each day that the boy's future shouldn't be hidden from him, that it would be good to prepare his mind, even if much of it ended up being on a subconscious level.

The car hummed as they descended towards the basement of the facility. No one spoke the entire trip down, not even Chuck, which was a minor miracle. Thomas's mind wandered.

What's it like? he wondered, staring down at Zart's sleeping face. How weird it must be to wake up with your memories erased. Dr Paige had explained many times how it worked, but what did it *feel* like? That was what Thomas wanted to know. To have a completely intact picture of the world and how it was . . . but with everything that mattered scrubbed out. Friends, families, places. It was a fascinating and terrible thing.

The lift chimed and they were there. The basement. It pricked a little at Thomas's heart. It was where he and his friends had met one night a week for so long. Where he'd turned from a lonely, miserable kid to a relatively happy person with friends.

The doors opened and the nurses rolled the gurney out into the hallway. Thomas looked at Teresa and they followed Dr Paige out. Chuck tagged along, his eyes wide with anticipation. If what lay in his future bothered him, he never showed it.

The wheels of the gurney clacked against the tile floor as they made their way down the long hallway to where the Box waited.

'Why are you guys so quiet?' Chuck asked. Every few seconds he had to trot for a couple of steps to keep up with everyone else.

'Because it's the butt-crack of dawn,' Teresa replied. 'Before the usual wake-up, and we haven't had breakfast.'

'Or coffee,' Dr Paige added, showing a rare spark of personality. 'I'd kill a Griever with my bare hands for a cup of coffee.'

Thomas and Teresa exchanged looks of surprise, then amusement. The woman had just made a joke. Maybe the world *was* ending.

It scares me, Teresa said out of nowhere.

What scares you? he asked.

The idea of the Maze. Insertion. But it also kinda excites me, too. Sometimes I envy the boys in the Glade. Yeah, they rough it pretty hard, but they have fun.

– 190 –

Thomas shrugged, acting like he'd never given it any thought. The truth was, lately he'd been thinking about it a lot. *I don't know,* Thomas said. *You know the Psychs aren't going to let the fun and games last for very long in there.*

Teresa didn't respond at first. They walked on down the hall in silence.

The crap'll hit the fan soon enough, she finally agreed.

Finally they reached the wide double doors that led to the chamber holding the Box. For all the sophistication surrounding WICKED and their trials and experiments and technological wonders, there wasn't much fanfare to the Box itself. It sat in a wide, dusty room at the bottom of a shaft that led up to the Glade, connected to enormous gears on the surface by chains and pulleys. A magical lift to a brand-new world.

Thomas shuddered to think what it must be like to wake up in that dark box of metal, memories gone. It had to be terrifying.

'Here we are,' Dr Paige said as the nurses wheeled the gurney towards the looming wall of silvery steel. 'I know we've spent the last few weeks getting more subjects into the Maze as the Psychs make adjustments to the programme, but after Zart we're going to become a little more regimented. We'll be sending one boy a month into the Glade, same day, same time. Like clockwork. Unless something changes.'

They always keep their options open, don't they? Thomas said to Teresa.

They sure do. Somehow she projected the image of her sticking her tongue out and crossing her eyes. Made no sense, and yet seemed the perfect response.

The nurses stopped right next to the Box, which was about ten feet high. One of them went around the corner and came back dragging a large, sturdy stepladder on wheels.

'Where's the door to the thing?' Chuck asked, examining the seamless wall closest to them, then venturing around to the other sides. No one answered until he rounded the entire container and ended up back where he started.

'Just watch,' Teresa said, not hiding her disdain for the process.

'It's not what you'd call glamorous,' Thomas added.

'Can't wait!' Chuck said, a little too cheerfully. Sometimes Thomas thought the boy had a drier sense of humour than anyone knew.

'Okay,' Dr Paige said. 'Let's get him up the stairs. Everything should be set. They're all ready in the command room.'

The nurses grabbed Zart – one by his legs, the other lifting him by curling his arms underneath his chest – and lifted him off the gurney. Then they slowly and carefully walked up the rolling stepladder, which shifted under their weight precariously. They reached the top, and then it became an exercise in awkwardness as the nurse holding Zart around the chest hefted him to the top edge of the Box, struggling until he could flap the boy's arms over the lip of the metal to keep him in place. He waited, made sure the boy wouldn't fall, then leaned down to help the other nurse lift Zart by the legs.

So lame, Thomas said to Teresa. *They really couldn't come up with a better way to do this? They have implants in our brains, Flat Transes, little robot bugs with cameras on them. And this is how they—*

He cut off when the nurses accidentally released Zart's body too early and the boy toppled over and vanished from sight, crashing into the bottom of the Box with a rattling boom that echoed off the high ceiling. Chuck sniggered, then looked ashamed when Dr Paige gave him a nasty glare.

'Sorry,' he muttered.

'Is he okay?' Dr Paige asked, her voice filled with annoyance.

Both nurses were on their tiptoes, leaning over the edge as they examined Zart down below.

'Looks fine,' one of them said. 'He pulled himself up into a ball – he's sleeping like a baby.'

'Why not put a door in the side of the Box?' Chuck asked it in a voice so sweet that it was obviously meant to be the opposite. As in, *How could you guys be so stupid?*

'Everything we do is for a reason,' Paige answered, but she didn't try very hard to make it sound convincing. Had it maybe even been another joke? 'Come on, let's go watch his insertion.'

'What happens now?' Chuck asked as they walked back the way they came, down the impossibly long hallway. 'When will he wake up?'

Surprisingly, Dr Paige answered, for once humouring the boy's wild curiosity. 'In about an hour,' she said. 'As soon as he does we'll start the simulated ride up and begin our observations. We should see some new – and very interesting – patterns over the next day or two.'

Her mood had changed quickly, her tone and light step exuding excitement.

'Cool,' Chuck replied.

They kept walking.

Thomas watched, Teresa beside him. They'd made Chuck go back to his room, not wanting him to see the pure anguish the boys felt upon first waking up in the Box. No need to push it with preparing the boy for his future.

Together, Thomas and Teresa watched, and imagined what it must be like.

Zart awoke in darkness, the cameras in the Box barely able to catch his movements. He said nothing at first, stumbling around the metal compartment like a drunkard. But then he became aware of everything all at once. The loss of memory, the strange place, the movement, the sounds. He panicked, pounding on the walls, screaming, 'Help me! Help me!'

The hysteria went on; a cut on his fist burst open, slicking his hand with blood. Finally he collapsed to the floor, then crawled into a corner. There, he pulled his legs in close to his chest and wrapped his arms around them. At first, the tears were only a trickle, but soon the sobs came, his shoulders shaking as he cried.

The Box came to a stop and a bubble of silence filled the air, like something that might pop and explode at the slightest touch. Zart almost jumped out of his clothes when the ceiling suddenly popped and squealed, two doors grinding as they slid open. The light of ten burning suns blinded him from above. He pressed both hands against his eyes, rolling back and forth on the floor as he groaned.

He heard rustling, whispers, light laughter coming from the sky. Finally he peeked through his fingers, actually able to see. He saw a square of light, silhouettes of thirty boys wrapped around it, all of their heads bent, looking down at him. Some of them elbowed their neighbour, pointed, sniggered.

A rope dropped, the loop tied at its end landing right in front of him. He stood, put his foot in the loop, held on to the rope with both hands. They pulled him up, dragged him over the edge of the Box, lifted him to his feet. Three or four boys dusted him off, hitting him harder than they needed to, but their whoops and laughs made it all seem okay. Like old friends welcoming home a lost soul.

A tall kid with brown hair stepped up to him, held out a hand. Zart took it, shook.

'My name's George,' the greeter said. 'Welcome to the Glade.'

38

The day had gone much like the ones before it. Breakfast, a couple of classes, more time in the observation room. Lunch. Observation room. All the while, Teresa by his side. Chuck was allowed to join them once his afternoon classes were done.

Chuck on the left.

Teresa on the right.

Thomas didn't know exactly what his role with WICKED was developing into. They seemed to let him do whatever he wanted, go wherever he wanted. He usually ate his meals in the cafeteria with the subjects who hadn't yet been sent into the Maze. He didn't click with them like he had with Newt, Alby and Minho, but they were mostly cool. Two guys named Jeff and Leo were especially nice, although they were obviously pre-occupied with what lay in store for them – they'd heard rumours about what the Maze was like and what it might become. Mostly, though, they kept to themselves.

As Thomas watched the monitors, he decided he was okay.

Satisfied with the status quo until something better presented itself.

'What's going on over there?' Teresa asked, snapping Thomas out of his thoughts. She pointed at one of the monitors on the right. Thomas threw it onto the large central display to get a better look.

A group of boys, led by Alby and Newt, were standing suspiciously around a lean-to of lumber scraps against the stone wall near the northwest corner of the Glade. WICKED had started the boys off with a small, simple structure for them to take shelter, with hopes that the subjects would add to it as supplies were sent in, take some initiative and better their living conditions. They'd already started messing around with the idea the last couple of weeks, and they'd collected all the spare wood they had and leaned it against the wall. Some boys had even slept under there the last few nights.

But now the group standing at its opening nearest the corner of the walls looked . . . troubled. They stood oddly, for one thing, too close together, as if they didn't want the beetle blades to catch a view of what was inside the lean-to. Their heads twisted this way and that, scanning the area around them like criminals waiting for a getaway car. Alby and Newt whispered furiously to each other, either arguing or mutually worried about something.

'What're they up to?' Thomas said quietly, leaning forwards to see if he could make out anything in the shadows. Nothing from that angle.

Teresa beat him to the punch by pushing a communications button that linked them to the command room – where the *important* people worked.

'Any way we can get a beetle blade in there?' Teresa asked whoever was listening.

'Nope,' replied a man. One of the Psychs, probably. They didn't interact with the subjects much, if ever, even with Thomas and Teresa. 'We want to see this play out before we let them know we're watching closely.'

That made Thomas even more intrigued. 'Can't we at least zoom in from where it's at right now?'

'We'll do our best,' the man replied curtly. 'Command room out.' There was a loud click that he obviously made audible on purpose. In other words, *Leave us alone.* They got that way sometimes.

Movement on the display stole Thomas's attention. Alby had leaned into the triangular shelter and was struggling with something, his body tense with exertion. Newt joined the effort, and then they were dragging something out of the darkness and into the grey light – the false sun had already been eclipsed by the huge wall on the west side and thrown that area of the Glade into shadow.

'What . . .' Teresa said. 'What is that?'

'It's a person!' Chuck yelled, making Thomas jump a full inch above his seat.

But the kid was right. Alby and Newt both held on to one leg each, dragging a person to the junction of the north and west walls. When they got there, Alby knelt next to the boy and punched him in the face. Teresa yelped in shock and Thomas scooted a couple of feet backwards without thinking. Alby reared back and punched the boy again, then again. Newt grabbed him by the arm and pulled him away.

'Can you tell who it is?' Teresa asked.

Chuck had walked around the control deck so that his eyes were only a few inches from the screen. 'I know him,' he said. 'That's George.'

'The one who welcomed Zart into the Glade?' Thomas asked. 'That was barely over twenty-four hours ago. How could everything have gone wrong since then?'

'*What* went wrong?' Teresa added. 'I mean, what in the world's going on? Why is Alby trying to beat the hell out of George?'

Thomas noticed one of the camera views on the left side of

the main display blur into motion, the beetle blade scuttling as fast as it could through the growth of vines.

'Chuck, get back over here,' Thomas snapped. 'I can't see all the views.'

Chuck obeyed, the look on his face somewhere between fear and glee. Thomas quickly grabbed the screen he wanted and swiped it onto the main display in the centre. Just as it settled there, the camera angle popped out of the vines and showed a bird's-eye view of Alby, Newt and George. Despite the noise the beetle blade must've made in its hurry, none of the boys seemed to notice.

Now Thomas could see everything in perfect detail, and could hear their every breath and movement.

George was a mess. He squirmed on the ground, his muscles clenched as if they'd been permanently locked that way, cramped and tight. His eyes bulged; his lips pressed together into a pale line; the skin of his face looked as if it had been ripped off, boiled, then stapled back on. Thomas blinked, rubbed his eyes. George appeared almost animated, a product of studio special effects. As he writhed as if going through the worst pain imaginable, he let out sharp moans through his closed mouth that sounded rabid.

'What the bloody hell is wrong with him?' Newt shouted.

Another kid stood by him now, someone Thomas didn't know. That boy said, 'I told you guys. We were out exploring the Maze. He was always ahead of me. I heard all these mechanical sounds, and then Georgie screamed. I could barely get him back here.' He looked angry, seething as he spoke.

'Who's that?' Thomas asked. He almost felt like he was there in the Glade with his old friends.

'His name's Nick,' Chuck replied. 'Picks his nose.'

Thomas tore his eyes away from the display to look at the kid. 'Seriously? Now?'

'That's all I know about him!'

'I didn't want the others to see him,' Alby said, bringing

Thomas's attention back to the large screen. 'Get everybody spooked. Fat chance of avoiding that now.'

'Well, why were you just hitting him in the face?' the boy named Nick asked, still hopping mad. 'He's my friend, you know. He needs medical help, not some hothead beating on him.'

'He was trying to freaking bite me!'Alby yelled in Nick's face. 'Back off!'

'Boys, slim it,' Newt said, stepping in between them. 'Let's figure this out. What do we do?'

They stood over George, who'd got worse. His head actually looked like it might explode from the swelling. He was beetroot-red and puffy. Veins bulged along his forehead and temples. And his eyes . . . they were enormous. Thomas had never seen anything like it.

'Did you see what attacked him?'Alby asked Nick, seeming to have forgotten that a few seconds ago they were on the verge of a fight.

Nick shook his head. 'Saw nothing.'

'Did George say anything?' Newt asked.

Nick nodded. 'Well, yeah, I think so. Not sure, but . . . I think he kept whispering, "It stung me, it stung me, it stung me . . ."' It was weird, man. He sounded like he was possessed or something. What're we gonna do?'

Thomas slumped back in his chair. For some reason, those words really chilled him.

It stung me.

39

230.03.15 | 5:01 P.M.

'Come on,' Alby said, leaning down to grab George's legs. 'No use trying to hide this any more. Let's get him out to the middle of the Glade and gather everybody. See if anyone knows what to do.'

At that exact moment, Newt looked up, straight into the camera. Thomas leaned back, for a second thinking his friend had somehow spotted *him*.

Newt cupped his hands around his mouth and shouted. 'Hey! Whoever sent us here! Send us some medicine. How 'bout a bloody doctor? Better yet, why don't you take us out of this hellhole!'

Thomas went cold. It was crazy that Newt and the others really didn't know who'd sent them there. Or even that something called WICKED existed. All they knew was this strange life they now lived at the centre of a maze – and that there were cameras on the tips of robot insects running around the place. Only now, it looked like they were going to know all too well about the Grievers, too.

It stung me. No one had mentioned anything to Thomas about being stung. It had to have something to do with one of those metal appendages that extended from the creatures' bodies.

The boys had picked George up – it took four of them because he was thrashing so hard. And the sounds he was making. Moans so haunting Thomas wanted to cover his ears.

The group rounded the small structure they'd started calling the Homestead and headed for the centre area of the Glade near the opening to the Box. Other boys – some working in the gardens, some in the farm animal area, others just milling about – noticed the situation immediately, and soon the other Gladers were gathered around George, who was half placed, half dropped on the ground by his very frustrated bearers.

Because they'd been noticed anyway, WICKED had dropped any pretence of not observing and swarmed in with the beetle blades. Various angles of the scene flashed up on the monitors in the room, and Thomas chose the best one – wishing he still had an overhead view – and put the display front and centre.

'Listen up!' Nick yelled. Thomas was a little surprised that Alby hadn't taken charge. 'Georgie and I were out in the Maze, running the corridors, and he got up ahead of me. Something attacked him. He keeps saying he got *stung.* Anybody know anything about this?'

'Minho's seen some kind of creature out there,' Alby said. 'Where's Minho?'

'Still running,' someone answered. 'Probably taking a nap in one of the Deadends.'

'It was one of those creatures he talked about, though,' Alby said. 'Had to be.'

'It doesn't really matter what it was.' Nick pointed down at George, who was curled into a tight ball, rocking back and forth on his side. 'What are we going to do with him? All we have is a bunch of aspirin and bandages.'

'There was something weird in the cooking supplies they sent up last week.'

Thomas hadn't seen who'd spoken, but then a tall, dark-skinned boy stepped out of the crowd until he stood right next to Nick.

'What are you talking about, Siggy?' the leader asked him.

'His name's Frypan!' someone called out. 'You're the only one who doesn't call him that.'

A few sniggers broke out, which couldn't have been more incongruous to the situation, given the boy writhing in agony at their feet.

Nick ignored everyone, though Thomas noticed Alby throw around a few harsh looks.

'It was in the bottom of a cardboard box,' Siggy, Frypan, whatever-his-name-was, said. 'Some kind of syringe, had the word *serum* printed on it. I figured it was a mistake – somebody had accidentally dropped it in there, whatever. Threw it out with the sausage leftovers this morning.'

Alby stepped up to the boy and grabbed him by the shirt, pulled him close. 'You threw it out? Didn't bother telling anybody? No wonder you wanna cook – ain't got brains for noth-in' else.'

Siggy smiled. 'If that makes you feel smarter. Anyway, I'm telling you now, aren't I? Slim it.'

'Where'd you throw it away?' Nick asked. 'Maybe it's not broken. Let's at least take a look at it.'

'Be right back.' Siggy jogged off towards the Homestead.

It only took three or four minutes, but by the time the tall boy returned with a slender metallic cylinder gripped in his hand, George had plummeted from bad to worse. More like from worse to worst.

He'd gone still except for his chest, which moved rapidly as he gasped for air. His jaw had gone slack, his limbs loose, his muscles relaxed from their clenched-state form earlier. The boy wasn't long for this world.

'WICKED won't let him die, right?' Chuck asked. 'This is just some kind of test. They want to see how everyone reacts.'

Teresa reached around Thomas and patted Chuck on the back. 'That's what the syringe is for. I'm sure of it. They just better hurry.'

She looked at Thomas, spoke to his mind. *This is not going to end well.*

He gave a slight shake of the head, then returned his attention to the screen. Siggy had given the syringe to Nick, who now knelt by George's side. The sick boy – the *stung* boy – hardly moved at all now, barely breathing. His eyes looked empty of life.

'Anyone know how to do this?' Nick called out. 'Where to stick it?'

'Anywhere!' Alby yelled. 'Just hurry and do it! Look at him!'

No one else even bothered replying, so Nick took the syringe, braced his thumb against it, then stabbed it into George's arm. The boy didn't even flinch. Nick pressed the plunger down until all the fluid was gone; then he dropped it on the ground, stood up, and took a couple of steps back. Everyone gave George some space but stayed close to watch what might happen, cutting off Thomas's view of the body.

'Come on, Georgie,' Nick said, barely loud enough to hear. That and the rustling of a soft breeze were the only sounds in the Glade.

A long moment passed. Teresa squeezed Thomas's knee, her hand warm through his jeans. She was as nervous as he was.

Then the boys parted, scrambling backwards, and an inhuman roar filled the air. George was on his feet, his mouth open, his face stretched in a painful grimace. He shouted in a strained voice, 'Griever! It was a damn Griever! They'll kill us all!' The words came out of him like the percussion of distant explosions.

He suddenly ran at the boy closest to him, jumped on the

kid, started pounding on him. Thomas watched in total shock, barely able to believe what he was seeing. Alby and Nick tried to pull George off the boy, but he swatted them away, lunging at Nick with his teeth bared.

'What the . . .' Teresa whispered.

George clawed at the boy, drawing blood on his cheeks, on his mouth. Now he went for the eyes, screaming the whole while. The kid under him fought back, screaming as he tried to twist his body out from under his attacker. But George seemed to have the strength of ten men. He pressed his victim down with one hand and punched him in the face. Then he went for the boy's eyes again, howling like an animal.

It was insanity. As if George had gone from the flu to a fully-fledged Crank in a matter of minutes. Other kids stepped in, tried to pull him off, but no one could get hold of any part of his wildly thrashing body. Thomas saw movement come in from the right, saw that it was Alby, running at full speed. At some point he'd left the scene, and now he returned at a charge.

In his hands, held up next to his shoulders, as if he were a seasoned warrior of ancient days, he held a long, thin shaft of wood. It appeared to be a broken broom or shovel handle, its end a splintery, sharp point.

'Get out of the way!' Alby yelled, his feet thundering across the dusty ground.

Thomas looked back at George, saw that his hands were digging into his victim's eye sockets, the kid screaming in pain.

Alby reached him and thrust the makeshift spear into the back of George's neck with enough force that it burst through to the other side. George's cries turned into choking gargles as his body fell to the side. The kid scrambled out from under him, his hands covering his injured face.

George twitched, moaned, then went still.

Blood darkened the dirt and stone below him.

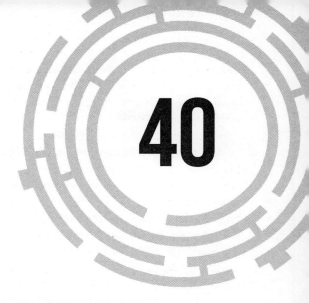

40

'Holy crap,' Thomas breathed, as stunned as he'd ever been. Teresa let go of Thomas's leg and slumped back into her chair with a loud release of breath. 'Holy crap is right. What's going on?'

Thomas looked over at Chuck and felt his heart break a little. The boy had curled his legs up into his seat and wrapped his arms around them, his face pale, two clear lines of tears glistening down his cheeks. He was trembling. An unbearable guilt swarmed around Thomas's heart – he'd never expected his friend to see something so awful. He'd never expected to see something so awful *himself.*

'Hey, hey,' Thomas said, turning to face Chuck. He gripped the boy's shoulders. 'Hey, look at me. Look at me.'

Chuck finally did, eyes filled with sadness.

'We'll figure this out, okay?' Thomas said. 'I'm sure that . . . I don't know. Something went wrong. Someone screwed up. It wasn't meant to happen. This *isn't* how the Maze will be, okay?'

Chuck spoke through a lurch of a sob. 'I was just having

fun. I didn't . . .' His voice cracked and he kept crying, quietly.

'I know, man, I know. That was tough to watch.' He pulled Chuck into his arms. Teresa was already there, embracing him from the other side. Their little group hug went on for a minute or so; then Thomas looked over his shoulder to see how the Gladers were reacting to the violent death.

Some of the boys had dispersed, most of them wandering off alone. Alby was on his knees, leaning against the wooden spear he'd used to kill George, staring at the ground, completely still. Newt was near him, sitting cross-legged in the dirt, head in his hands, eyes closed, as miserable as a person could look.

A beetle blade had skittered closer to George's body, and Thomas put that view in the centre display. Of all the kids present, Nick seemed to have held it together better than anyone, even though George had obviously been a close friend. He'd called him Georgie, after all. Nick knelt next to his dead companion – rummaging through his clothes, looking into his eyes, studying his limbs. He suddenly froze, his eyes focused on a spot in the middle of George's back.

After a second or two, he reached out and grabbed the dead boy's shirt, fingered it until he found a small rip. Then, with several quick jerks of his arm, he tore a larger hole and leaned in to stare at something. Thomas leaned in, too, in the observation room, focusing on the big screen in front of him.

The beetle blade moved in closer until it was right next to the body, its view pointing at the very spot that had interested Nick. The skin there was red and swollen, and several thick black veins sprouted out of a wound, an almost perfect circle of darkness cut into George's flesh. It looked like the body of a spider with broken legs coming from its body. The vicious wound was hard to look at for too long.

'*Stung*,' Teresa said. 'That looks like one hell of a sting to me.'

Thomas stood up. 'That's it,' he said. 'Come on.' He turned away from the hideous display projected onto the wall and headed for the door.

'Where are we going?' Teresa asked, right by his side.

Thomas turned to Chuck, who was close behind them. 'Actually, you need to stay here. I mean, I *need* you to stay here.'

'What? Why?' He was either offended or terrified to be left alone, Thomas couldn't tell.

'Someone needs to keep an eye on those monitors for me. If anything happens – if a Griever comes out or if someone gets stung or the whole place explodes, anything – you come find me. Okay?'

Thomas knew that Chuck was too smart to buy his explanation for leaving him behind, but he accepted it without putting up a fight. 'Fine. But where are you going? How will I find you?'

Thomas opened the door and waved Teresa through.

'I'm going to get some answers.'

Thomas banged on the door. 'Let us in!' he yelled.

The main command room was off limits to anyone younger than twenty-one. He'd heard someone say that once, but it sounded like a formality invented to keep them out. He, Teresa, Aris and Rachel were part of the 'team' when it was convenient. He knew they were all being analyzed just as much as anyone in the Glade.

And after what he'd just seen, Thomas was beginning to feel very uncomfortable about things.

He was about to pound on the door again when there was a click, followed by a hiss; then the big metal slab swung open. A man he'd never seen before stood there, short and stocky with dark hair. And he looked none too pleased.

'What's the problem, Thomas?' the man asked in a surprisingly calm voice. 'Things are a little crazy in here right now.'

'You keep saying we're important, that we're a part of all this,' Thomas said. He pointed at Teresa, then himself. 'We helped programme your maze. And helped send all our friends there. And now we just watched one of them die and you did nothing to stop it. Why? Why didn't you guys go in and help? Someone needs to explain what happened, and someone's going to do it right now.'

Thomas was shaking, trying to hold himself together. He sucked in a quaking breath, waiting for the man to answer.

Several emotions passed across the man's face. The last was anger.

'Hold on,' he said, then closed the door without waiting for a response.

Thomas reached out to bang on the door again, but Teresa grabbed him, shook her head.

They'll talk to us, she said in his head. *Just show a little patience. We have to act as calm as they do in these situations if we're ever going to get anywhere.*

Chagrined, annoyed that she was right, feeling stupid over his ridiculous act of bravado, he let out another breath and nodded, then waited.

The door opened less than a minute later. Dr Leavitt stood there, as bald and unhappy as always, but before he could say anything, Dr Paige appeared at his side. She practically pushed the man out of the way.

'Thomas,' she said kindly. 'Teresa. I'm sure you must be as concerned as we are.'

He hadn't expected those to be her first words to them, although he couldn't say why they struck him as strange.

'Well, yeah, we are,' Teresa replied. 'You guys are okay with killing kids now?'

Thomas didn't know if he would have been brave enough to say it so bluntly, but he agreed. However it had happened, WICKED had just murdered George. A kid who wasn't even eighteen.

Dr Paige stepped to the side, opening the door wider. 'Come in. We'll explain to you what happened. What went wrong. You deserve to know.'

'Yeah, I think we do,' Thomas heard himself say, though he was a little lost at the moment. He'd been struck by a realization that had never felt truer: it didn't matter what they did or what they said. Anything and everything could be a test set up by WICKED.

It was too much.

He followed Teresa into the command room, suddenly wary of his surroundings.

'Follow me,' Dr Paige said, letting the door swing shut.

Leavitt still stood to the side, eyeing both Thomas and Teresa when they moved past him as if they were enemy invaders.

After walking down a short, narrow hallway, they entered a vast room that opened to both sides. To Thomas's right was an array of monitors, workstations, control desks and chairs. It looked like their own observation room on steroids, at least ten times bigger. Twenty people or so went about various duties in the huge space. To Thomas's left were several desks, a glass-enclosed meeting room and a few closed doors, hiding who knew what mysteries. It made Thomas remember that he really only saw a tiny piece of WICKED's vast operation.

'I don't want anyone else talking to you about this right now,' Dr Paige said over her shoulder as she walked through the middle of all the activity. 'Let's find a quiet spot and I'll explain to you what's happened. I wish you trusted us – trusted me – a little more than you've shown just now. Maybe gave us the benefit of the doubt.'

'Benefit of the doubt?' Thomas repeated, surprised by her reaction. Could she really expect that of them? After what they'd just seen?

The doctor came to a small glassed-in room with a table and four chairs at its centre. She opened the door and ushered them in, gesturing for them to sit. Thomas didn't like how this was going – he'd wanted to stomp in there demanding answers, and now somehow they were on WICKED's terms again.

'We didn't come for a nice sit-down,' he said. 'We don't want lies. We want actual *answers*. Please.'

'You killed someone,' Teresa added, in a much calmer voice. 'We didn't sign up for this. We didn't sign up for you killing our friends. Are we next?'

Dr Paige didn't look angry, or guilty, or even embarrassed. Instead, she seemed . . . sad. Distressed.

'Are you finished?' she asked, her voice tired. 'Can I please talk now? You're sick of lies and half-truths? So am I. But you came here for answers, and all you're doing is making accusations. That has to stop if you want me to talk.'

Thomas sighed. It seemed they always ended up treating him like a child and there was nothing he could do about it. Most annoying, he *was* still a child in their eyes, though he sure didn't feel like one.

'Fine,' Teresa said while he stewed. 'Then talk.'

Dr Paige gave a slow nod of acknowledgment. 'Thank you. Now, here's the truth. We mutated a version of the Flare virus that can take hold in the immune in . . . interesting ways. Ways that will help us understand the main virus better. That altered version is what the Griever injected George with, and it's also what the serum is for, to stop its effects. Sadly, the serum hasn't been perfected yet, and you saw the . . . unfortunate result.'

She paused a moment, eyeing Thomas for a reaction. Thomas was too shocked by her candidness to gather his thoughts. Teresa stayed silent as well.

Dr Paige folded her arms. 'We'll keep working on it. We didn't mean for George to die – that's the honest truth. We'll correct the serum.' She paused to take a breath before continuing. 'But I can tell you this: we measured some very significant results in the hours after he was stung – results that we need and will continue to need. Not just from George, but from everyone who saw what happened and reacted to it.' She stood up, then put her hands on the table and leaned towards them. 'And that's what matters.'

She walked towards the door and opened it, then looked back at them. 'I've grown to love the both of you. Like my own children. I swear to you that nothing on this earth could be more true.' She paused, on the verge of choking up. 'And I'll do anything – *anything* – to make sure that you have a world to return to someday.'

She looked down, a shimmering tear perilously close to dripping from her eye, then stepped out and closed the door.

41

230.04.8 | 7:15 P.M.

Thomas ate dinner quickly. He had the observation room scheduled for the entire evening, and he didn't want to waste a single minute of his available time. It was the closest he could get to actually being with all those friends he missed so much. He wolfed down his last few bites of food, then ran until he got there.

He sat down, made sure all the monitors were up and running. Did a quick scan of the controls and the different perspectives up on the screens.

Then Thomas leaned forwards.

And he watched.

Minho and Newt had been partners today, Runners out in the Maze. He watched them come in through the east door, headed for the hulking turtle of a building they'd transformed into a map room of sorts. They'd requested old-school paper and pencils by leaving a message in the Box after it delivered its weekly supplies, and their request had been granted.

They didn't stop jogging until they'd reached the menacing door of the concrete-block building. It had always had a locking wheel-handle, like something you'd see on a submarine – which was why they'd chosen it to store the maps they drew. Minho inserted a key, then spun the wheel until something clicked and the door popped open. The two of them went inside, the first Runners to arrive back home. A beetle blade followed them in and Thomas switched that view and audio to the main display.

As Minho grabbed pieces of paper for them, both boys were chanting words under their breath. It sounded like they were saying, 'Left, left, right, left, right, right, right' and 'two-fisted rock, then three rights' and 'rainbow crack, left, bald ivy spot, left, right, right.' They wrote furiously on their respective papers, recording their words before they forgot.

'Phew!' Minho said, dropping his pencil; he stretched his arms up over his head and yawned. 'Sweet run today.'

'Not too shabby,' Newt muttered, grinning to himself.

Then they grabbed new pieces of paper and started turning their words into a visual map.

Alby sat on the bench by a flagpole, alone. Night had fallen, and the doors had long since closed. An empty plate sat next to him; crumbs dotted his shirt. His eyes were closed; his body was perfectly still.

'Alby?' someone said, walking up to him.

'Shh!' Alby hissed. 'Leave me alone. I want to listen.'

'Fine.' But the kid stayed close, closing his eyes like Alby.

Outside the huge enclosure of their home, the walls of the Maze began their process of changing positions. The ground trembled, and the distant roar of stone against stone filled the air. Alby had something close to a smile on his face.

'Thunder,' he whispered.

'What?' his visitor asked.

'Thunder. I remember thunder.'

A tear trickled its way down his cheek. He didn't wipe it away.

Thomas sat in his chair, silent and sullen as Dr Paige worked on measuring his vitals. He had a full load of classes today, and he dreaded it with a heaviness that made him want to cry.

'You're quiet this morning,' the doctor said.

'I need to be,' he replied. 'Please. Today, I need to be quiet.'

She whispered her response. 'Okay.'

Thomas pictured his friends going about their various activities in the Glade. Tried to imagine what they were doing that very second. And he thought about something he'd been thinking for a while: someday he should probably join them there. It would be the right thing to do.

Dr Paige stuck a needle in him, and this time he felt it.

Thomas went along in his weird, boring, sometimes heartbreaking, sometimes uplifting life. Watching his friends tough it out inside the Glade and the Maze. But also watching them prosper, work hard to make it a better place. Rules were established, jobs assigned, routines worked out. The Homestead was three times bigger than when they'd started, and Minho had been named Keeper of the Runners.

All these things and much more happened as the days turned into weeks turned into months. Teresa and Chuck were his constant companions, and he loved having them around. They made his life bearable, even fun at times. But it was hard to get too flippant when the place where you lived constantly reminded you of two things: your friends were in an experiment, and that experiment existed because an awful, hideous disease rampaged in the outside world.

And so he lived. Day in, day out. Getting his body monitored, attending classes, doing as he was asked. Like helping Teresa prep the new boy each month for insertion. The basement, where he'd made so many fond memories, was now a place he visited only once a month. It seemed darker and danker than it ever had before. He did whatever he could to find time for the observation room, taking his own notes on what he saw, sharing those with Dr Paige. The better the analysis, the more sessions he got.

Mostly, it was a life of boredom, interrupted by sweet times with Teresa and Chuck. Made tolerable by the ever-increasing kindness of Dr Paige, who seemed to be the only member of WICKED with a heart, the only one who remembered what it was like to be a kid. She didn't shy away from repeating what she'd said that day, about loving them like her own children. But it was always laced with a sense of danger, as if she knew on some level that letting herself feel that way might be the biggest risk she'd ever take.

It was a strange world. But Thomas was alive, and he lived.

42

His crazy day started with a knock on his door during a morning break.

When he opened it, a boy he'd never seen before stood there, with Randall, of all people, right next to him. The man had been scarce lately – in fact, Thomas was pretty sure he hadn't seen him since the day George had died. And he didn't look so good. He was thinner than before, and his complexion looked grey. As for the new boy, he was a touch taller than Thomas, with blond hair, and his eyes were as wide and curious as a baby's.

'This is Ben,' Randall said. 'He's one of the new subjects we picked up the last few days, and he's the perfect age for insertion. Dr Paige wants you to prep him before you run through your daily check-ups and tests.'

Randall turned away without waiting for a response, walking quickly down the hallway, as if late for an appointment. Poor Ben stood there, blinking nervously.

'Don't worry about that guy,' Thomas said, opening his

door wider. 'He's always been a weirdo. Come on in. Believe it or not, I can remember what it feels like to be brand-new here.'

'Thanks.' Ben entered the room timidly and sat down at the desk when Thomas motioned to the chair. 'They found me in Denver.'

And then the kid transformed in an instant, bursting into tears. He put his hands over his face, and his shoulders lurched with each sob.

Denver? Thomas had studied plenty about the city – how it was a safe zone, a gathering place for those who didn't have the Flare. They evidently had put extreme precautions in place to make sure no infected ever entered, and it was surrounded by heavily fortified walls. The fact that Ben came from there struck Thomas as . . . odd. Didn't this mean that his parents had been healthy? And yet WICKED had taken him away?

Thomas realized the boy was still crying. 'What happened?' he asked, not sure how to act. 'I mean, take your time, but I'm here to listen.' He almost rolled his eyes at the lame choice of words.

'We'd finally found a place to live,' Ben said through his tears. 'Somewhere nice. And neither one of my parents had the Flare – I know it! They wouldn't have let us in if they did.' It was all coming out in a flood now, his tears evaporating into anger. 'They asked if I would join their study and my dad said no and they grabbed me and took me anyway. They pushed my mom down and threatened to shoot my dad. Who are these people? Why am I here?'

Thomas sat on his bed, frozen. He had absolutely no idea what to say. He'd always wondered about everyone's parents, and it seemed like his suspicions had been true. WICKED said they all came from families with two sick parents and no other care available. Was this some anomaly or one of many lies?

Ben started crying again, burying his head in his arms on the desk.

'I'm sorry, man,' Thomas said, feeling the boy's sadness deep within himself. 'They're trying to find a cure for the Flare, and they're desperate.' That was all he had. He didn't have the heart or words to try anything else. 'But hey, things aren't so bad, I promise.'

Ben picked up his head, wiped his tears, then nodded.

'Come on, let me show you around.' Thomas stood up and walked to the door, opened it, and escorted Ben into the hallway. Calling himself a big fat liar the whole time.

After giving Ben a tour of the complex, Thomas sat with the new kid in the observation room, introducing him to the Maze. He didn't have the heart to come right out and say that he'd be sent in shortly, not after the tearful display earlier. But he was sure the kid wasn't stupid.

He tried to keep it positive.

'Most of the guys love it. Sleeping in the outdoors with their friends.' It wasn't lost on Thomas that here he was, telling lies as easily as WICKED seemed to. It bothered him, but he didn't know what else to do. He wanted the boy to feel better.

His thoughts fizzled away as something developed on the right side of the main display. On one of the screens, a beetle blade was following Gally, who kept looking over his shoulder as if he were up to no good.

'Uh-oh,' he whispered, placing the view of Gally on the huge screen in the middle.

'What's wrong?' Ben asked.

For a few seconds, Thomas had completely forgotten that Ben existed, much less that he was sitting right next to him.

'Um, nothing,' Thomas answered absently. 'Just, uh, I want to see where my friend is going.' Worried something bad might happen to traumatize Ben on one of his first days, he quickly escorted him into the hallway. He made him stand several feet from the door. 'Listen, wait here, okay? I'm going to call a friend over to finish up your tour. It was great to meet you.'

'Okay,' the boy said, obviously feeling stupid.

Thomas felt bad but rushed back into the room, leaving the door open a crack so he'd hear when Teresa arrived. He found his seat again.

Gally had made it all the way to the south door and was just now turning back towards the Glade, searching the area, obviously wondering if anyone was watching him. Evidently he didn't care about the beetle blades, just the other boys. Looking confident that he hadn't been noticed, he focused his attention on the left side of the enormous door itself, the row of protruding spikes towering above him.

'What are you up to?' Thomas whispered. 'Come on, you stupid beetle blade, get me a better angle.'

As if the little mechanical creature had heard him, it scurried faster, crawling next to Gally along the wall. Then it turned around and scuttled backwards so that any observers could clearly see the boy's face.

He was crying, his cheeks so wet it'd obviously been going on for a while. Thomas didn't understand that at all. What was he doing sneaking around forbidden territory? Not being a Runner, he wasn't allowed in the Maze itself, and he looked intent on entering it.

Thomas suddenly remembered Ben, waiting out in the hallway.

Hey, you there? Thomas immediately called out to Teresa. Then he turned down the volume so Ben couldn't hear what was going on. *Come get this new kid out of my hair. His name's Ben, and he's just outside the observation room. Gally is up to something weird.*

Okay, was her simple response.

Gally had just broken the rules and stepped around the edge of the door. He was now officially outside the Glade. He closed his eyes, started taking deep breaths. A strange smile spread across his face. His arms came up from his body, sticking out at his sides, as if he were imagining that he could fly. And suddenly Thomas understood. Gally had stepped outside the

Glade just for the rush of it.

Then the display screen erupted in a blur of movement. Thomas sucked in a breath of air when a Griever appeared out of nowhere, its grisly wet skin suddenly filling the screen, Gally covered by its body. There was an inhuman moan and a surge of machinery. The beetle blade bolted; its camera now showed nothing but vines and stone, all of it shaky. But Thomas heard Gally scream. And it wasn't a scream of fear, it was a scream of pain.

The camera view tilted back into place, and the Griever had disappeared. Gally clutched at his side with one hand, pulled himself along the ground with the other. It took a few agonizing seconds, but he finally got himself back into the Glade proper. Boys were running towards him. One named Clint was at the front of the pack, hauling a first-aid kit. WICKED had finally figured out the proper dosage for the serum, and Clint held a syringe in his free hand as he ran.

Gally's screams were something Thomas thought he'd never be able to forget.

He heard a gasp behind him and spun around to see Ben peeking through the narrow gap of the open door. The boy's eyes had widened in horror.

'What just happened?' he asked in a timid voice.

Thomas fumbled for words. 'Oh, that? They, uh, sometimes they do these drills, test their response times. Nothing to worry about.'

He didn't fail to realize he'd just used one of Dr Leavitt's favourite phrases.

Teresa arrived just then to whisk Ben away.

Poor kid, Thomas thought.

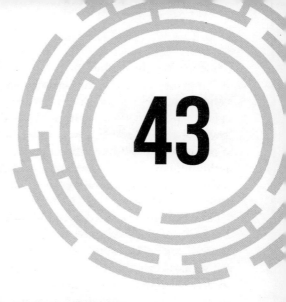

43

230.12.17 | 9:06 P.M.

Thomas waited patiently for Dr Paige to come back after taking his latest blood sample to the lab. In a rare occurrence, there was no one else in the room with him, not even an assistant. After a couple of silent minutes, he got curious.

He got up from his chair and went over to the counter. He opened a few doors, pulled out a few drawers. Nothing looked too out of the ordinary. Vials, syringes, paper-wrapped products. But then, in the last drawer to the right, he found an absolute gold mine.

A research tablet.

The thin foot-long rectangular device had a shiny grey screen, ready to reveal a world of information. He knew he'd probably need passwords, but this was an opportunity that might never present itself again. Refusing to consider the consequences, he tucked the device into the back waist of his pants, flopping his shirt over the remaining portion to hide it.

He was in his seat well before Dr Paige returned.

That evening, he told an orderly he was feeling a little under the weather and wanted to bypass his usual session in the observation room. No one made too much of a fuss about it.

He wanted to dive into his pilfered research tablet. He'd also grabbed a few snacks in the cafeteria to make it a full night of entertainment. Sitting at his desk, no one around to bother him, munching on potato chips, he powered up the tablet and got to work. He hadn't told Teresa about it yet. He wasn't going to take the slightest chance of someone taking his treasure away from him before he at least had one shot at it.

To his great disappointment, and just as he'd suspected, most of the information portals on the device required passwords. And he could forget about remotely accessing the main WICKED systems. But there were enough things in plain sight to keep his attention, all filed in an open-access tab labelled *History.*

He dug through the documents, memorizing as much as he could. He learned the original names of his friends, laughing at some of them. Siggy, aka Frypan, had been named Toby by his parents. Toby. Thomas didn't know why that struck him as so funny.

There was other interesting information. Schematics on the WICKED complex and its various buildings. An early military report on what would become the Grievers. Climate data going back to the year of the sun flares, as well as comparative charts to the averages before that time. Tons of information on the Flare, its symptoms, stages, prior attempts at treatment.

One seemingly random remark in a memo caught his attention – two staff members reminiscing about the time they had to 'tinker with poor A2's memories because his first meeting with Teresa had been such a disaster.' This made Thomas stop reading. He stared down at the tablet, thinking back.

He remembered the day he'd first officially met Teresa. How

he'd been dizzy with déjà vu. Had WICKED been experimenting with their implants and memories that long ago? It made sense, in light of what they did to his friends when they sent them into the Maze, something they'd have to be well prepared for. But Thomas felt dizzy considering the possibility – to think that there could be an entire meeting with Teresa that had been erased from his mind. What else might they have taken from him?

The more he thought about it, the more upsetting it was, which wasn't helping anything, he told himself. So he returned to perusing the tablet for information.

After a few dead ends, he saw a file labelled *Deleted Com*.

He opened it.

It was a series of memos and correspondence that he had to think had been left out of the secure area by mistake. Communication between higher-ups at WICKED and several other entities that he could only guess were predecessors of the organization. There were a lot of acronyms, some of which he recognized from his various history classes. FIRE (Flares Information Recovery Endeavour), PFC (Post-Flares Coalition), AMRIID (Army Medical Research Institute for Infectious Diseases), and more he didn't recognize. He scanned them, fascinated at what it must have been like living through that time period.

He stayed at it for hours, his eyes stinging from reading for so long. At a certain point, he started skimming, reading too fast to catch much of what the documents actually said.

Then he stopped on something interesting. A couple of acronyms he'd never seen before, along with the words *TOP SECRET* in red letters. This just might be something. He scanned a memo or two, his heart rate picking up with each word he read. Things he couldn't believe. About a virus. About it being man-made. About it being released on purpose. About a population that had got too big to feed.

'Oh, man,' he whispered, reading through the last one again. He could barely believe what it said.

Post-Flares Coalition Memorandum
Date 219.2.12, Time 19:32
TO: All board members
FROM: Chancellor John Michael
RE: EO Draft

Please give me your thoughts on the
following draft. It goes out tomorrow.

Executive Order #13 of the Post-Flares
Coalition, by recommendation of the
Population Control Committee, to be
considered TOP SECRET, of the highest
priority, on penalty of capital punishment.

We the Coalition hereby grant the PCC
express permission to fully implement their
PC Initiative #1 as presented in full and
attached below. We the Coalition take full
responsibility for this action and will
monitor developments and offer assistance
to the fullest extent of our resources. The
virus will be released in the locations
recommended by the PCC and agreed upon
by the Coalition. Armed forces will be
stationed to ensure that the process ensues
in as orderly a manner as possible.

EO #13, PCI #1, is hereby ratified. Begin
immediately.

Wow.
That was all he got from Teresa after spilling everything to
her.
Yeah, he replied. Wow *is right. They thought the virus would*

only kill a certain percentage of the population – make it more manageable. They had no idea it would mutate and become this monstrous thing that's basically wiped us out. I just can't believe all this. Can't believe it.

Teresa was quiet. She didn't even broadcast how these revelations made her feel.

The worst part, he continued, *is that there are several direct links to WICKED. Like, remember John Michael? That guy we saw at the Crank pits? He was the one who ordered the virus released!*

The past is the past, Tom.

Her words stopped him cold.

At least they're trying to fix what they screwed up, she continued. *I mean, there's nothing we can do about that now.*

Teresa . . . he started to say, but then stumbled over a void. He had no idea how to respond. *Did you . . . did you already know this stuff?*

I'd heard rumours.

And you never told me? He was stunned. How could she have known this and never said anything? She was his best friend. The first person he went to with everything.

I just don't see the point. Yes, we have reason to hate these people. But how is dwelling on the past going to help anybody? The solution is what matters.

Thomas had never been so blindsided in his life. *Didn't you learn anything from our puzzle lessons with Ms Denton? To know a solution, you have to know the problem through and through. This is a problem.*

The response he got from Teresa was emotionless.

Yeah, I guess you're right, she answered. *I'm really tired, Tom. Can we talk about it tomorrow?*

She was gone from his mind before he could respond.

The next day, Teresa refused to talk about it, emphasizing that she'd rather focus on the future than the past. Dr Paige also blew it off, saying that those decisions had been made well before her time. It was almost like they were both determined to forget.

Thomas wouldn't forget.

He swore to himself that he'd always remember this.

That he'd always remember that WICKED was trying to fix a problem their predecessors had created in the first place.

44

231.05.04 | 10:14 P.M.

Winter came in spurts that year, like old engines being restarted after years of sitting in the maintenance heap. But it finally settled in, lasting long past what should have been the onset of spring.

Thomas didn't venture outside very often – and then only by special permission and with at least two armed guards by his side – but he saw enough to know that ice, cold and snow had returned to the world with a vengeance. The resident WICKED climatologist said that weather patterns were slowly resuming their cycles on Earth – winter, spring, summer and autumn – but that in places farthest north and south of the equator the seasons were far more unpredictable and extreme than they'd been before the sun flares. He described the world's climate as a pendulum that now swung faster and farther in both directions.

Thomas enjoyed it when he could, enjoyed the feel of snow on his face, the tingle of icy cold on his nose and fingertips. It felt like a way of spitting in the sun flares' face. *See? I'm cold.*

Now go suck it.

In early May – winter still refusing to loosen its grip – Thomas took a walk outside with Chuck and Teresa, two of the guards right behind them, weapons out. Thomas was in a sour mood.

Everything about WICKED had worn him to the bone, hardened his heart. The Psychs, the Variables, the killzone, the patterns. Everything. He'd felt that way ever since the night he'd discovered the truth about their predecessors – that they'd unleashed the very virus to which they wanted to find a cure. Going outside for a while was a tiny escape.

Teresa shivered and rubbed her arms through her coat. 'Are we sure this is planet Earth? WICKED didn't throw us through a Flat Trans, put us on an ice planet?'

'That'd be cool,' Chuck replied. 'Ice aliens. I wonder if your tongue sticks to their skin when you lick them. Ya know, like a flagpole.'

Thomas tousled his friend's curly hair, trying to put his bad feelings aside. 'Yeah, we know, Chuck. You don't always have to explain your jokes to us. Sometimes they're actually funny. Like that one. It was funny. I'm laughing so hard it hurts on the inside.'

'Me too,' Teresa added. 'I'm snorting, I'm giggling so hard. On the inside.'

Chuck oinked like a pig and giggled. He often reacted to things like that. It only made him more likable.

'Might want to bring it down a notch,' Teresa said. 'We don't want to wake the Cranks down in the pits now do we?'

'I never got to see them,' Chuck replied, faking sadness. At least, Thomas *hoped* he was faking.

They rounded a corner of the complex and stopped, a spectacular view having opened up in front of them. The lights on the outside of the WICKED building were bright enough to illuminate the surrounding forest, the pine trees dusted with snow glowing in the reflection. Specks of snowflakes lit up the sky, the crashing of waves below the cliffs more distant than ever. Thomas felt like they were standing inside some sort of man-made set, the chill breeze coming from giant fans.

A fake world like the Maze.

'Man, it's so pretty,' Teresa whispered.

Thomas expected a joke to pop out of Chuck, but he was just as caught up in the wonder of their surroundings. 'Our world isn't so bad,' he said. 'Once WICKED figures out how to make everyone well again, life'll be pretty good, don't you think?'

Thomas just nodded, a hand on Chuck's shoulder. Using his stolen tablet, Thomas had done his own research about the Scorch, a place where WICKED had set up some kind of secret operation. If Chuck could see the pictures of that desolate hell-hole, he might change his tune a little. But the kid was right. The world had a lot of places like this forest on a cliff, the majestic ocean crashing against it. Places where humanity could settle in and rebuild.

'Tom, over there,' Teresa said, her tone urgent. He followed her sightline to a group of trees about a hundred feet away.

A figure had stumbled out of the woods and fallen. Whoever it was got back up, brushed off the snow, then started walking straight towards Thomas's group. The guards quickly put themselves in front of the kids, raising their weapons.

'We better get back,' one of them said.

'It's a Crank, isn't it?' Chuck asked. He said it calmly, bravely, and Thomas burst with pride, so much so that it almost hurt.

'Bingo, little man,' the other guard replied. 'Don't worry, you're safe. Let's get inside.'

'Wait a sec,' Teresa said. 'That's not a . . . I mean . . . that's *Randall*.'

Thomas squinted against WICKED's bright lights. And she was right. It was him. Randall. Lurching through the snow as if he'd lost something there and hoped to kick it into the air.

The first guard lowered her gun. 'I'll be damned. It *is* him.'

'What's he doing out here?' Thomas whispered.

'What should we do?' Chuck asked, way too loudly. Thomas tried to shush him, but it was too late. Randall had stopped, his head snapping up. He saw them, and for a long moment no one moved.

Then Randall broke into action, struggling to get through the snow to them.

'Sorry,' Chuck muttered.

'Let's get back,' the guard said more urgently. 'We need to tell Ramirez.'

They turned their backs on Randall and jogged briskly towards the closest entrance to the looming complex. They were right in front of it when Randall shouted at them from behind.

'Stop! Marion! Moureu! I just need to say something!' At hearing their names, the guards turned around, once again placing themselves in front of the kids and raising their weapons.

Randall stepped out of the snowy grounds and stumbled onto the pavement, about twenty feet away from them. He looked awful. Eyes bloodshot. Nose bleeding. His cheeks hollow and gaunt. The skin at the right edge of his brow had split open, a streak of red painting the side of his face. Thomas stared at the poor man. What could he possibly be doing out here?

'Speak fast, then, Randall,' the woman said. 'You don't look well. We need to get you some help.'

'Can't hide it any more, can I?' Randall said, now bent over, leaning on his knees. 'It's the darndest thing!' He lurched upright, swaying left, then right, before getting his balance. 'The darndest thing, trying to hide the Flare from your bosses.'

Thomas grabbed Chuck by the hand. The snow seemed to freeze in midair, no longer swirling, no longer dancing, no longer falling.

'All right, we're done here,' the female guard said. 'Open the door, Moureu. Get them inside and find a doctor. Quick.'

'You think you're special?' Randall yelled. 'You really think they're not gonna do the same thing to you they're gonna do to them all?'

Moureu punched in the security code. There was a loud beep. The colour on the display changed from red to green; then a click rang through the air. The door popped open. The guard pulled it wide and stepped back.

Thomas practically shoved Chuck through the entrance, then grabbed Teresa's arm and pulled her with him, running through. He didn't want to spend one more second out there with Randall, whom he could still hear yelling.

'You hear what I said?' the sick man shouted. 'You're runnin' from the wrong guy. I'm not the one you should be scared about. You hear me?'

The guard pulled the door closed on Randall's ramblings. Thomas peered through the small safety window and watched the man turn around and stumble back towards the forest.

'You can sleep on my floor tonight,' Thomas said to Chuck. They stood in the hall outside his door. 'I don't care if we get in trouble.'

Teresa had gone into her room to use the bathroom but had just come back out to join them. She had a troubled look on her face.

Thomas looked at her, concerned. 'You wanna sleep in here, too? I'm a little freaked out myself.'

'Actually . . .'

'What's wrong?' Thomas asked.

She flicked her eyes at Chuck, who was lost in his thoughts. She spoke in Thomas's mind. *Let's get him to sleep in your room. Then we need to go. Now.*

Wait, what? Thomas said back. *Go where?*

Things are worse than you think, she said. *Look . . . just get him to sleep, tell him bedtime stories for all I care. Whatever it takes. Tap on my door when you're sure he's out.*

What's wrong? he asked again.

'You know what?' she said aloud, ignoring his question. She gently brushed a strand of Chuck's hair out of his face and he looked up at her, his eyes filled with the weight of all he'd just seen. 'I'm tired. Why don't you two go have your sleepover and I'll see you in the morning. And don't worry.' She leaned over a little to be able to look him in the eyes. 'Seriously. Randall is sick and they'll take care of him. We're immune, remember? There's nothing to worry about.' She smiled a big warm smile at the boy. She was so reassuring, Thomas almost believed her himself.

'Good night,' Thomas said to her. 'Come on, Chuck.'

'Good night,' she said back, then slipped into her room.

Thomas closed the door behind him and threw a couple of blankets on the floor for Chuck. As he was settling into his makeshift bed, the boy once again reminded Thomas that he was far smarter than they often gave him credit for.

'Yeah, she's right – *we're* immune,' he said in the darkness. 'But what about all those people who work for WICKED?'

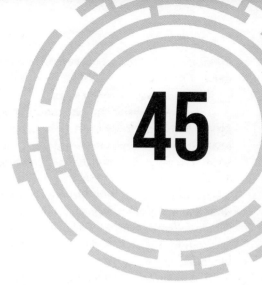

45

231.05.04 | 11:41 P.M.

Teresa opened the door before he even tapped twice.

'Come in,' she whispered urgently, though her calm focus scared him.

He stepped inside and she closed the door. 'What's up?'

She held up a piece of paper. Thomas took it. A few words were scribbled on it in pencil:

Come see me. ASAP.
Dr Paige

Thomas looked up at Teresa. 'Okay, now, really – what's going on?'

'That note was slipped under my door while we were outside.' She paused, breathed. 'I'm pretty sure Dr Paige knows what happened out there tonight. It has to be related to Randall somehow.'

Thomas leaned back against the wall. Something was terribly wrong, he just knew it. A horrible fear was clawing its way up his chest. He felt an overwhelming uncertainty, a shifting of the world.

'What do we do?' he asked.

Teresa put a hand on Thomas's shoulder. 'Let's just go find Dr Paige. She's the smartest person I've ever met. If she wants to talk to us, then we need to go.'

'Okay,' Thomas said dully. 'If there's anyone we can trust, it's her.'

Teresa gave him a nod of encouragement, then opened the door and left the room.

He followed her.

He knocked softly on Dr Paige's door. The last thing they wanted to do was wake up any of the other doctors or Psychs along the same hall. When she didn't answer, he knocked a little harder. Finally he heard a soft voice from the other side.

'Who is it?'

'Thomas,' he said, a thought suddenly striking him. What if the note hadn't actually been from her? 'And Teresa. We got your message?'

The door opened a crack. He'd never seen Dr Paige so . . . dishevelled. Her hair was down and tangled from sleep and her face was clean of make-up. She opened the door wider and nodded for them to enter.

'I'm glad you came.'

Dr Paige sat at her desk, Thomas and Teresa both on the bed, side by side, waiting for her to speak. He found himself thinking of Newt, maybe the one he liked most of all of them, not immune. There were only two futures for Newt: they found a way to treat this sickness, or one day he went insane, ending up like Randall.

Dr Paige finally spoke. And while she seemed as calm and contained as ever, her eyes said something different. Thomas saw fear in them.

'I've been dreading this day for months, wishing we could last just a little while longer,' she said.

She stood up, stood quietly for a moment, thinking, then turned to look at them.

'There's a reason I've fought for you and sought your help so many times,' Dr Paige said. 'You are part of this organization. You've grown up here, as one of us, and I know we have the same goals. I know that I can trust you to do anything to help us achieve our mission. And now I need you to trust me. Can you do that?'

Thomas looked at Teresa and she looked back. He could feel what she was thinking.

They both nodded.

The doctor flashed them a warm smile. 'Yes, I thought so,' she said. 'Okay, well, we have no choice now. Once we start this, there's absolutely no going back.' She took a second to look each of them in the eye. 'So, I need to ask you both: are you ready?'

Thomas stood. Teresa stood. They both nodded again.

'Okay, then,' Dr Paige said. 'I've been suspicious for a while now that certain WICKED officers have been hiding information from us that can potentially undermine everything we're doing here. Some of our top people haven't even shown their faces in weeks. It's time to initiate the protocol.'

She paused before she spoke again. Took a breath. 'It's time for the Purge.'

46

231.05.05 | 12:33 A.M.

D r Paige marched down the hall, confident step after confident step, her whole demeanour different from anything Thomas had ever seen before. It was like she'd accepted some woolly mantle of responsibility and wore it high on her shoulders. He found himself believing she could save this situation.

'We have to get everything done in the next twenty-four hours,' she said quietly over her shoulder. 'I have plenty of help on my end, and Aris and Rachel will help you on yours.'

'Where are we going?' Teresa asked. 'What's the Purge?'

Dr Paige stopped at the lift, pressed the call button, and stepped in when the car arrived, speaking as the door closed. 'First things first. At the end of every day WICKED requires a mandatory blood test of its members. We've always understood the importance of monitoring for contamination.' She entered the floor number and the lift started moving. 'But over the last several months, I've noticed some strange activity – there's been an undercurrent of suspicion – and then I discovered some of our personal health data has been breached. Chancellor Anderson finally decided that all results would have to go through him before being disseminated to the medical staff. Well, I receive a general report every night, and not *one person* has tested positive. *But* . . . that's according to the reports I'm seeing through the chancellor.'

The lift came to a stop, the familiar chime dinged, and the doors opened. Thomas and Teresa followed Dr Paige out and down yet another hallway.

'But I started noticing symptoms recently,' she continued. 'Even the chancellor himself is showing signs of infection. I'm almost certain now that our beloved leader has been fudging the reports. I saw Randall on the security feeds tonight. And if Randall is sick . . . well, it's impossible he's the only one.'

Dr Paige stopped in front of a door that Thomas had only seen once before. The time he'd been invited there to meet the chancellor himself.

'But why haven't we noticed anything?' Teresa asked. 'I mean, besides Randall, we haven't seen any signs people are sick.'

Dr Paige nodded as if she'd anticipated the question. 'It may be early for some. Others further along may be in hiding somewhere. Makes me wonder if Randall got out from wherever that is. What happened tonight with him made me realize how serious our situation has got. If the results are being faked like I think, I need to initiate the safety protocol to ensure we remain healthy and we can continue our work. I have to take charge. Tonight.'

Thomas couldn't believe how quickly things were escalating.

The doctor had never looked so grave, so determined. 'First we have to get every last one of those results from the blood tests – from the *original* results, not the summary report. We'll find out who's sick and who isn't. And then we'll deal with things.'

Thomas was trying to sort through the whirlwind of information. 'How do we get into his office? Aren't the security feeds following us?'

She smiled, a brief break in the clouds. 'Which question should I answer first?'

'The second one,' Teresa said for him. 'Security.'

Paige nodded. 'Let's just say there are many people who owe me favours here. That and everyone is so scared about getting sick, they're depending on us to guarantee their health. Ramirez is terrified of succumbing to it, and he thinks I'm best suited to make sure the cure actually *happens*. The sad truth is that Chancellor Anderson's time leading WICKED has to come to an end.'

Thomas didn't know what to think of that. 'And . . . this office? How do we get in without Anderson knowing about it?'

At some point, Dr Paige's smile had completely vanished. 'Oh, he'll know about it. He's in there right now. Shall we go in?' She reached into a pocket and pulled out a surgical mask, slipped it onto her face. 'I guess you guys don't need one of these, eh?' Her eyes showed the smile had returned.

Dr Paige opened the unlocked door and stepped inside the office of the chancellor.

Another room was attached to the back of his office, a private space to relax or hold more intimate meetings. They found Anderson in there, asleep, half of his body draped on a couch, the other half hanging precariously towards the floor.

'How did you know?' Teresa whispered, so quietly that Thomas barely heard her.

The doctor motioned for them to go back into the main office, and then she gently closed the door to the private room where the chancellor slept.

'You can't imagine the precautions I've taken to avoid catching the Flare,' the woman said, her words muffled through her mask. 'Extreme. I wear this mask almost twenty-four-seven now, and always when I'm in a confined space like this with

– 238 –

others who are potentially infected. I wash my hands and face every half hour. I prepare my own food. . .' She looked down at her hands. 'I have to take *some* risks, of course. Every day. I could hardly call myself a doctor if I didn't.'

'But what about . . . this?' Teresa asked, pointing over her shoulder in the direction of Anderson's private room.

'He's one of the reasons I'm so cautious. I've come here to visit him once a week or so for months. We'd developed a . . . friendship . . . even before all this started. We've talked for hours upon hours. About our former lives, WICKED, the blueprint's progress. He stopped bothering to lock the door over a month ago. But my point is, over that time he's changed.'

'Who else do you think might have it?' Teresa asked.

'We're about to find out – if he hasn't destroyed the original test results.' She went to the chancellor's desk – scattered with the framed photos of his lost loved ones they'd seen on their previous visit – and opened up his display screen. 'For all his security fears, he hasn't been very original with passwords.' She smiled at that, then got to work, using the keyboard as well as the touch functions on the screen itself. A blue glow filled the room with a ghostly pall.

'Shouldn't take too long . . .' she said absently.

Thomas was struck with a sudden thought: what if he wasn't really immune like they'd always told him? He did worry about that every once in a while, but surely he would've got the disease by now. A memory of the horrible Crank pits flashed through his mind.

Dr Paige manoeuvred her way through several layers of security on the chancellor's computer until she finally got to a spreadsheet listing the full roster of WICKED employees in the complex, from cafeteria workers to doctors and Psychs to the test subjects themselves. She scrolled through a few records until she got to a tab for administration; she clicked on it and an image of Chancellor Anderson's face flashed onto the screen.

His beaming smile couldn't have been more incongruous with the situation at hand. Dr Paige dived deeper into the data and found the test results from the end of the day before. Although he'd basically already accepted what it would be, when Thomas saw the verification literally flashing right before his eyes – in red, no less – it sent a chill to every corner of his body.

Chancellor Kevin Anderson had the Flare.

And, as it turned out, so did a few others at WICKED.

47

231.05.05 | 3:42 A.M.

Nineteen of the one hundred and thirty-one doctors, Psychs, scientists, technicians, nurses, and other staff inside the WICKED complex turned out to be sick. All high-ranking officials, mostly in Anderson's circle. No wonder they'd conspired to keep it from everyone else.

Dr Paige had whisked Thomas and Teresa back to her room and locked them inside, explaining that she now had to fully initiate the Purge protocol and make sure everything was in motion. That she'd return soon. Two hours later she came back, and she had Aris and Rachel with her. As they came in from the hallway, Dr Paige dropped four loaded backpacks onto the floor.

'What are those for?' Teresa asked.

'I'll explain everything,' the doctor answered. 'I'm going to need the four of you desperately today.'

Thomas gave them a friendly nod, which was returned. Aris seemed to have grown older, lines crossing his face like little marks of worry. Rachel had cut her hair even shorter, and there was a sadness in her dark eyes. But she stood confidently, and something about these two encouraged Thomas.

Dr Paige showed no signs of wearing down. She'd taken charge with gusto.

'This is what my people have figured out,' she said. 'Anderson has all the infected hidden away in Sector D, and judging from their symptoms, a few of them appear to be pretty far along. It explains why we haven't seen their faces around lately. I've locked down that entire wing of the complex.

'I've checked and rechecked the original medical tests from yesterday. Other than Anderson, who's still in his office, and Randall, somewhere out in the forest, it seems that we have all the infected contained. Everyone outside of Sector D is clean.'

She paused for a couple of deep breaths. 'But we can't waste a single second. We need to clear those people out, and we need to do it fast. I have some brave guards who are willing to risk infection, but I just can't bring myself to lose another life to this disease. Which is where you come in.'

She stopped speaking, letting her words hang in the air, and the realization of what she was saying suddenly hit Thomas like a lightning bolt.

'You mean . . .'

She nodded, her expression showing how hard it was to say what came next. 'You're all immune, and you're the oldest and strongest of those not in the Maze. We're dealing with people who are very sick and weak – more important, though, is that most of them are asleep, which is why we have to act right now. These backpacks have syringes filled with a solution that's been prepared for this task – all it takes is a quick plunge into their necks and the job is done. You should be able to do it with no problems'

Thomas felt his knees go weak, and sat on the floor to hide it.

Aris finally said the words no one else could.

'So . . . we're just going to kill them all?'

'They'll die anyway,' Teresa said immediately, shocking Thomas out of his thoughts.

'Whoa, whoa, whoa,' he said, standing back up. He looked at his friend, wondering if this was some attempt to relieve herself of guilt or if she'd really grown such a hard shell around herself for protection. 'We have to think this through.'

'No, Tom,' Teresa snapped. 'It's *be tough now* or everyone dies later.'

Thomas slumped back to the floor, so dazed his vision had gone a little blurry. He had no response. She'd also cut off their mind connection. All he could do was look at her.

'I'm sorry,' she said, the fierceness melting away. 'I'm sorry, Tom. Really. I just . . . I know this whole thing is awful, but it'll be less awful if we just accept it and get it done.'

'She's right,' Dr Paige said. 'The four of you will be adults soon. You can handle this. We know exactly where the infected are – you just need to go from room to room and inject them.' She gestured towards the backpacks. 'We've packed guns, and we have Launchers for you as well. Just in case. I need to stress that. Just in case. I think you'll be able to do this to them as they sleep. And I'll have guards posted, despite the risk of infection, if things go south.'

The room went silent for a long time. Dr Paige was at least allowing them a moment to think through it.

'Count me in,' Teresa finally said.

'Me too,' Aris added.

'The ends justify the means,' Rachel said somewhat bitterly. 'It should be WICKED's official logo. They should have a giant banner draped across the front entrance. *The ends justify the means.* But I'm in.'

'Well, it's true, isn't it?' Aris asked. 'If you could save a billion people by killing a million people, shouldn't you do it? You know, hypothetically speaking? If you really had that choice and said no, then aren't you *actually* killing a billion people? I'd rather kill a million than a billion.'

Now it was Aris's turn to get a perplexed look from Thomas. It seemed like the world had started spinning in the opposite direction.

Dr Paige nodded at the three who'd accepted her challenge. 'Thomas?' she asked.

He didn't respond. He stared at the floor.

'Tom?' Teresa said. 'I need you with me on this. With *us*. Please.'

He didn't feel well. He didn't feel well at all. He stood up. His thoughts raced as he searched for the perfect words. He knew that they would do what Dr Paige needed them to do. They'd come too far to turn back now. He had friends out in the Maze, Chuck to think about, a world to think about.

He'd do it. The Purge. It had to be done. And now he needed to say something smart, something profound, something that would bind them together and start the terrible journey.

'This sucks.'

48

231.05.05 | 4:15 A.M.

After the four of them had agreed to the mission, Dr Paige went to get a few security guards to give them instruction on the syringes and weapons and to go over the best plan of attack to coordinate the entire effort. While they waited, Teresa reopened their connection.

You okay? she asked.

I just . . . I don't know how I feel about this.

She paused for what seemed like forever, and he could sense her mind racing. He waited, even though he wanted to say more.

Look, she finally replied. That word always meant she was about to reveal her soul to him. *Remember when I told you everything about where I came from? When my name was Deedee?*

A sharp pain came across with that name, so strong that Thomas had to shift in his seat. *Yeah. I remember.*

It was a horrible place, Tom, she continued. *I can't even . . . it was horrible. I saw countless people catch the Flare, remember running from Cranks, remember . . . The point is that I keep telling myself that so many parts of the world are like that right now. So many little girls, just like I used to be, are watching it happen. Dying in the middle of all those horrors. And WICKED wants to save the world from that. Save all those little girls and all those little boys.*

I know, Thomas said. *We all saw bad things.*

Not like I did. I was basically at ground zero. The infected were concentrated in one place and the virus hadn't been diluted yet. We're going back to that as it spreads. One day the whole world – every town and city – will be like it was in North Carolina. And then everyone will be dead.

Thomas stood up, wishing he could somehow escape this depressing talk. *I get it, Teresa. I get it. We need to find a cure. You really think I haven't heard this speech a thousand times?*

He could tell she was frustrated with him. *Tom, the speech isn't empty. We have to find a cure, and we can't look at things in the short term any more. We're talking about extinction. All that matters is the end result. How we get there . . . we just do it. Okay? Whatever it takes.*

So we kill them? Thomas asked. *That's what you're telling me? The four of us are going to walk around these buildings and just slaughter every last person who has the Flare?*

Yes. That's what we're going to do.

Thomas tried to offer another solution. *Can't we just move them to the Crank pits?*

Seriously? You think they want to be thrown into a cage with monsters? Tom, you're not even thinking straight. A wave of frustration crashed through their connection, powerful enough to make Thomas wince.

So we kill them. It felt like letting go of some vital part of being human.

We make sure Dr Paige can get these facilities under control, keep both mazes running. It's not about killing anyone. It's about saving.

Thomas sighed. *I'll do my best.* What else was he going to do?

She came over to him, leaned in to whisper in his ear. 'This is so important,' she said. 'The most important thing in the world.'

'Yeah,' he breathed. 'Because WICKED is good.'

A few minutes later, the door opened. Several uniformed guards came in, followed by Dr Paige.

'Let's get you prepped,' she said. 'Time is running out.'

49

231.05.05 | 5:44 A.M.

Thomas's backpack was heavy. He and his friends had full packs carrying everything they'd need. Two guns each, replacement cartridges for the Launchers they had strapped across their shoulders, and enough syringes to put down a zoo full of elephants. Better to have too much than not enough.

They ran through the hallways of the complex to their first target – Chancellor Anderson. A good man with whom Thomas had never had much of a problem. A good man who was now utterly insane. They had to take care of him first before heading down to Sector D.

They'd been running for a good five minutes when Aris halted and held a hand up. Teresa almost ran him over before she stopped.

'Did you hear that?' Aris whispered.

Thomas listened, trying to pick out something unusual over the hum of the ventilation system and the sound of their heavy breaths from running.

'Nope,' Thomas said, even as the others shook their heads.

'Just keep listening,' Aris responded, his gaze shifting to the ceiling, as if what he'd heard had come from above. 'There.'

A low wail, like a child crying. Now that he heard it, Thomas couldn't believe he hadn't noticed it before. High-pitched, sad, it echoed along the corridor, making it impossible to tell what direction it came from. Thomas imagined a child at the bottom of a well.

'Maybe it's coming through the vents from Sector D,' Rachel suggested.

The pitiful noise ceased.

'Or it could be one of the kids,' Thomas said. 'Dr Paige has them all hiding somewhere.'

Teresa spoke up. 'We need to get Anderson resolved before we can think about anything else. Let's go.'

Aris had no objection. The four of them set off running again.

The door to Anderson's office was closed, not locked. Teresa stepped forwards and opened it. Thomas held his breath, half expecting the man to jump out at them like a zombie.

Nothing but quiet and dark. And a smell. A horrible smell.

Teresa nudged the door wider and stepped inside, Launcher held out in front of her, ready to fire. Aris went next, then Rachel, Thomas last. The blue glow of the workstation still shone – nothing had changed since they'd last been there. Except for the putrid stink of body odour and urine, even faeces. The smell assaulted Thomas and he gagged, falling to one knee, as his throat closed. He tried to pull himself together.

You okay? Teresa asked in his mind.

Yeah. Is he in there? He nodded towards the back room.

Let's go see.

But Aris had already moved to that door and lightly kicked it open. Another wave of wretched stink came wafting out of the darkness. Thomas got back to his feet and stood behind

Aris and Teresa, staring inside, trying to make things out. Rachel was right next to him, holding her nose.

'Is he dead?' she asked.

'No,' came a rasp of a voice. Anderson. It barely sounded human. 'No. Not dead. Not your lucky day.' He let out a series of wet, wracking coughs.

'Oh, man,' Thomas said. His stomach was not handling all this very well. 'Get a light on in this place.'

'It might hurt his eyes.' This from Aris, who fingered the panel anyway. Lights blazed, as bright as noon.

Anderson screamed, clawing at his eyes. He writhed on the floor in front of the couch, which looked like he'd been lying on it for months. 'Turn it off! Turn it off!'

Aris dimmed the lights, which Thomas silently thanked him for. The sight before them was almost too much for Thomas to bear. He stared at the man who'd once been their leader. Blood covered his face and his clothes, and his hair was matted and greasy. He'd lost weight, his skin pale and sweaty. He lay on his side, his mouth set in a permanent grimace, baring teeth that were rimmed in red. And then Thomas saw why.

The man only had two fingers left.

Bloody nubs remained where the others had once been.

'Oh my . . .' Aris said when he noticed, covering his face with the crook of one arm. 'He didn't. He didn't.'

'He did,' replied Rachel, her voice cold.

Thomas couldn't look. He turned away from it all and went to the display screen on the former chancellor's desk. It showed the communications system, and there on the screen was a memo that Anderson had been writing. Luckily, it appeared to have never been sent. Because the memo itself was harrowing.

'Guys,' he said. 'Listen to what Anderson almost sent to everybody while we were gone.' And then Thomas read it to them.

WICKED Memorandum, Date 231.5.5
TO:
FROM:
RE:

I only have two fingers left.

I wrote the lies of my farewell with two fingers.

That is the truth.

We are evil.

They are kids.

We are evil.

We should stop, let the Munies have the world.

We are evil.

We can't play God.

We can't do this to kids.

You're evil, I'm evil.

My two fingers tell me so.

How can we lie to our replacements?

We give them hope when there is none.

Everyone will die.

No matter what.

Let nature win.

'He's so messed up,' Teresa said over Thomas's shoulder as he read Anderson's last words.

'I'd say it's beyond that,' Thomas replied.

'My fingers,' Anderson moaned from the other room. 'Why'd you eat my fingers?'

Thomas felt a crushing heartbreak as he followed Teresa to Anderson's side again. The man had curled himself up into a ball and was rocking back and forth.

'Only two left,' the man said, his words floating with delirium. 'I hope the other eight were tasty. I always thought it'd be me that ate them. But no. It had to be you, didn't it?'

Thomas shared a glance with each of his friends. After all they'd seen, was this the saddest? To see a man who'd led this giant operation with such vigour turn into a snivelling lunatic?

Anderson's body contorted, seemingly every muscle twisting in on itself. He twitched for a few seconds, then relaxed. His wild glare slowly left the floor and followed the line of Thomas's body from his feet to his thighs to his torso and finally met his gaze.

'They'll take your brain in the end,' Anderson said. 'They'll take it out, look at it for a few hours, then probably eat it. You should've run when you had the chance.'

Thomas couldn't move; the sudden clarity in the man's eyes scared him more than anything else that day.

'What do we do?' Aris asked. Their former chancellor kept talking, but he'd shrunk back into a foetal position and his words were lost in his moans of agony. He stared at the floor right in front of his face.

'We have to put him out of his misery,' Teresa answered. 'And then I think it'll be easier for us to . . . take care of everyone else. But we need to get moving.'

A month or two ago Thomas would have been shocked at her callousness. Even a few days ago. But not any more. They were now dealing with the cold, hard truth of their situation. Whoever these people had been – they were no more.

Thomas suddenly decided that he had to do it. He had to be the one, right here, right now. If someone else did the deed, he might never build up the nerve again.

'It has to be me,' he whispered, mostly to himself. He wasn't even sure they'd heard him. But they certainly noticed when he swung the backpack off his shoulders and set it beside him. He knelt down right next to Anderson, and blood from the man's injuries seeped into the knees of his pants.

The others made no move to stop him.

Thomas unzipped his pack, rummaged inside it, and pulled out one of the syringes filled with Dr Paige's concoction. He snapped off the protective tab of plastic on the end of the needle, then positioned it in his hand, his thumb lightly pressed against the button that controlled the electronic plunger.

'Are we sure about this?' Rachel asked. 'I mean . . . we're sure?'

'Yes,' Thomas replied, short and curt. Nothing else to say.

Anderson rolled over onto his back, trembling now. His eyes widened as he stared at the ceiling, murmuring unintelligibly. Thomas leaned in closer, syringe out over the man's head. There was no sign of awareness in Anderson's expression, no sign of humanity left.

Teresa touched Thomas on the shoulder, startling him. He looked back at her, and her eyes were brimming with tears.

Sorry, she said in his mind. *I'm with you on this. You can do it.*

He nodded, then turned to Anderson, still shaking ever so slightly on the ground, nothing more than simple shivering. Thomas brought the silver tip of the needle to the side of the former chancellor's neck. Hesitated.

Anderson's gaze shifted, his eyes falling on Thomas. He whispered something, a word. Repeated it, over and over. Saliva foaming at the corners of his mouth.

'Please, please, please, please, please, please . . .'

Thomas didn't know if he was encouraging him to do it or begging him to stop. But he slowly slid the needle into the soft flesh of the man's neck and pressed the button that controlled the plunger. A hiss sounded as the deadly fluid in the vial drained out of the syringe and into Anderson's body.

They all watched in silence as the former leader of WICKED grew still, let out one last, long breath, and closed his eyes.

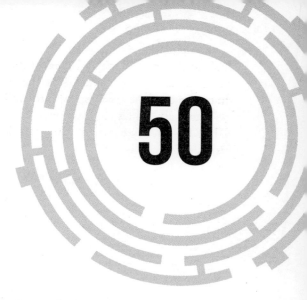

There were eighteen left.

Thomas and his friends stood in the security room once governed by Ramirez and Randall. Dr Paige and a few of her new staff analyzed the rooms and hallways of Sector D.

'Everyone is still in the same positions,' Dr Paige said, scanning the security feeds. 'Maybe we make a goal for you to reach five of them, then come back here and regroup, assess whether anything has changed.'

Thomas absently watched the camera feeds coming from the Maze while the others focused on Sector D. Near the Homestead, despite the late hour, Alby and Newt were locked in an argument with Nick, who'd long ago separated himself from the others as the clear leader. Without sound, the tussle didn't have any context. At least no punches had been thrown. Most of the other Gladers were asleep.

'They have no idea what's going on in here,' Thomas said, a little surprised that he'd spoken aloud. 'I guess that's a good thing.'

Teresa looked his way. She seemed ready to reproach him – they had slightly more pressing matters – but then softened. 'I know. For once, life is tougher out here than in there.'

'I guess the tables have turned,' Rachel said.

'Guys?' Dr Paige cut in. She gestured towards the cameras focused on the WICKED complex itself. 'The plan?'

'Sorry,' Rachel murmured.

Thomas focused his attention back on the relevant feeds.

A guard pointed at one in particular. 'Room D-17. A rec room. A few of them are sleeping on the floor in there. That should be your first stop after entering the Sector.'

'Maybe they're dead,' Teresa added.

Dr Paige leaned closer to the screens, her lips moving as she counted. 'And there's our five. It's a good plan. Go take care of them, then come back here and we'll show you where to go next.'

Take care of them, Thomas thought. What a nice way to put it.

They grabbed their backpacks full of death and headed out of the door towards Sector D.

After a guard let them through the locked-down entrance, Thomas and the others headed for the assigned room. They'd almost made it when movement in the hall ahead stopped them in their tracks. Aris had taken the lead and suddenly jumped back, pushing the others around the closest corner.

'There's a couple of people up there,' he whispered, his back to the wall, panting.

'I saw them, too,' Teresa said. 'Which means they probably saw us.'

With perfect timing, a shout rang through the hall.

'Hey, you kids!' A man, his voice on the edge of hysterics. 'Come here, my little subjects!'

This filled Thomas with a feeling of such horror that it made him shiver. Sweat broke out on his arms and forehead, a flush of heat making him unbearably hot.

'How many?' he asked.

Aris peeked around the corner, then jerked back to face the others. 'Two men. One's crawling on the ground, the other's walking, but he's using the wall to hold him up. They're getting really close. And, man, they look seriously messed up.'

Thomas appreciated the detailed report, but it only made him feel worse. 'Do we go back and regroup?'

'No, we rush them,' Teresa said. 'Why put it off? The four of us can take these two easily.'

Rachel was nodding as she spoke, and one look at Aris showed he agreed as well.

Thomas sighed in defeat. 'What do you mean by "messed up"?'

'The crawling dude is totally naked,' Aris answered, 'scratches all over his body. The one stumbling along the wall looks like he puked up about seven breakfasts all over his shirt. And his hair . . . I think he ripped some of it out. It's nasty.'

'You think they're all like this?' Thomas asked, overwhelmed by the task they had before them. 'I didn't know they were so near the Gone.'

A terrible wail of anguish sounded down the hall, a long, mewling sound that ended in something close to giggles. They were getting closer.

'You saw Anderson,' Teresa whispered. 'Those left have to be as bad as him or a couple of steps away from it.'

Thomas nodded, trying to encourage himself. 'Okay, okay. What do we do?'

Teresa swung her backpack off her shoulder just enough to unzip it and look inside. She pulled out a pistol, then two syringes. She handed the syringes to Thomas.

'I'll be the last resort,' she said, hefting the gun in her right hand, finger already on the trigger. 'Aris and Rachel, you hit them first with Launcher grenades. Once they're down, Thomas, you run up to them and inject the poison. I'll be right beside you. If they make a move, I'll take care of them.'

Thomas stared at her, half impressed and half terrified of his closest friend. But mostly he was thankful she'd taken charge.

'Okay,' he said, too smart to argue. Nothing about this was going to be pleasant, and the sooner they got to it, the sooner they'd be done.

'Sounds good,' Aris replied. 'You guys ready?'

Thomas, one death-tipped syringe gripped in each hand, nodded. Rachel held up her Launcher in answer. Teresa said, 'Go.'

Aris pushed off from the wall with a grunt and ran around the corner, yelling with adrenaline. Rachel went next, her weapon held ready, then Thomas, then Teresa, her gun the last line of defence. The sound of the Launcher charging filled the air, followed by the burst of power as a grenade catapulted towards the man moving along the wall. His hair had indeed been ripped out in spots, leaving red, bloody welts.

The grenade hit him square in his chest. He let out a howl as tiny tendrils of lightning danced across his body, and he fell to the floor. There he suffered spasm after spasm as the Launcher's power tried to fry him from the inside out.

'Your turn, Thomas!' Aris yelled as he stepped forwards, already aiming for the other man in case Rachel missed.

Thomas ran towards the first victim, then slid along the tile floor, coming to a stop just a foot or so from the man's head. He gripped the syringe, letting it hover just inches above the man's face, waiting for the streaks of white powder to fade. He heard a second Launcher shot, then a third, followed by rapid thumps of contact. A cry like that of some primal beast pierced the air.

Thomas saw his chance below him, the charges of electricity dwindling. He stabbed the needle of the syringe into the Crank's neck and released the poison. He scrambled away, kicking at the floor with his feet until his back met the opposite wall, where he stood up. The man's eyes rolled back in his head and he flopped over – the syringe bounced back and forth as if dancing on its needle, pivoting in the soft folds of the neck.

Seventeen, Thomas thought. There were seventeen Cranks left in the complex.

'Over here!' Rachel yelled. 'Hurry!' She stood above the second man, who was still convulsing from her Launcher shot. His battered, purpling body was like a dark storm cloud, sending little bolts of lightning down to die in the floor tiles.

Thomas ran to him. Static and sparks filled the air as he fell to his knees. He knelt forwards and plunged the second syringe into the man's neck, releasing the vial of liquid death.

Teresa was there, two hands tightly gripping her pistol, aiming down at the man's head just in case. Rachel and Aris stood right behind her, struggling to catch their breath.

'I think that does it,' Thomas said. 'We just killed two people without any of us getting a single scratch.'

'Cranks,' Teresa replied, finally letting herself relax as she dropped the gun to her side. 'Not people, Cranks.'

Thomas got to his feet. 'I didn't realize those were two different things.'

She gave him a hard look that scared him.

'Room D-17,' Aris said between breaths. 'Stick to the plan.'

Teresa turned away from Thomas to lead the way.

51

'**D** . . . seventeen . . .' Aris said, scanning the rooms as they jogged past. He pointed. 'Here it is!'

Thomas, who felt like everyone else had taken much more initiative so far that day, stepped up to the door and placed his ear against the flat surface. He pressed in, hoping to hear nothing. He wanted them asleep or dead.

'Anything?' Teresa asked.

Thomas shook his head. Then, 'No, wait.' He pressed his ear to the door again. A low moaning sound was clearer. 'Yeah – there's at least one awake.'

They prepared themselves much as they had for the encounter in the hallway. According to the cameras, five Cranks were on the other side of the door, immobile. Thomas squeezed three syringes in his right hand, two in his left, and Aris and Rachel both held their Launchers, fully charged and loaded behind him. That left Teresa with the gun again, and Thomas had a feeling that this time she'd be forced to use it.

When everyone was ready to go, Teresa used her free hand

to push open the door. It swung open into a dimly lit room, the scents of body odour and rotten breath wafting out like a diseased wind.

Thomas scrunched up his face at the foul smell, fighting his gag reflex as he slipped inside. Rachel, Aris and Teresa followed. Weapons ready. A quick sweep established the scene for Thomas, and his rapidly thumping heart slowed. The room was a gathering spot, filled with chairs and couches, entertainment screens, tables for pool and ping-pong. The five people they'd spied earlier were congregated in the corner to his left. A man lay on a couch, arm dangling off the side, another man on the floor at his feet. Two women were sprawled side by side, also on the floor, at the foot of two chairs, their arms draped across each other as if to comfort. The last person, a man, sat in a chair, his head lolling back in sleep, great, booming snores erupting from his wide-open mouth.

Aris and Rachel quietly stepped up to the group, aiming their weapons. A long moment of silence passed; then that familiar electronic whine filled the air, immediately followed by a series of cracks as the Launchers fired in quick succession. Five distinct thumps meant that they'd hit their marks. Blue lightning lit up the air as the Cranks' bodies convulsed with electricity.

'Now!' Aris yelled at Thomas. 'Here, I'll help you.' He came up to him, took syringes, passed one to Rachel. Teresa kept her gun trained on the five spasming figures as the three approached.

Thomas ran to the two men on the floor by the couch, their spasms lessening as the little tendrils of electricity faded to a few sparks here and there. Gripping a syringe in each hand – his thumb pressed against the dispenser button – he knelt down and stabbed the two needles into the Cranks' necks. Released the poison. He scooted away and got back to his feet, shocked at how smoothly things had gone down. Rachel had taken care of the man in the chair, and Aris was just finishing up with the women on the ground.

That meant there were only eleven left in the entire Sector. Aware of the horrors of it all on some level – the fact they were murdering actual human beings – Thomas pushed it away, focused on the necessity. He felt an elation that filled his chest. They just might succeed.

The door from the hallway banged open.

Four Cranks burst into the room, all of them looking healthy enough for a fight. They scattered in different directions.

One jumped on Aris before he could get off a shot from his Launcher – he sprawled onto his back as the female straddled him, reaching for the boy's throat. Rachel gave up trying to aim a shot without hitting her friend and ran in, using the Launcher as a battering ram, slamming its hard tip into the side of the woman's head. She shrieked and toppled off Aris; then Rachel shot a grenade into her chest.

Aris himself seemed traumatized by the attack, snapping from the strain. From somewhere within his pockets he pulled out a knife and, screaming with rage, swung off his back and rammed the blade's tip into the chest of the electrified Crank lying next to him. The electricity hadn't dissipated enough to do this – a jolt of energy made him cry out and fly backwards, knocking Rachel to the floor.

All this, happening so fast. Thomas could see only two of the remaining Cranks, running around the room with no logic to their movements. Thomas had nothing in his hands. Teresa randomly aimed her gun without taking a shot. Probably scared that she'd miss and hit Aris or Rachel.

Someone crashed into Thomas from behind.

Arms wrapped around him as he hit the floor face-first, his nose cracking in pain, the breath whooshing out of his chest, leaving him empty. He panicked, squirmed to get away from whoever had tackled him.

Teresa yelled his name. He saw her feet right next to him.

'Help,' Thomas tried to say, but it came out as nothing

more than a muffled grunt. The Crank behind him had released his grip and now put a hand on the back of Thomas's head, pressing his lips into the carpet to silence him. Thomas had no other thought now than taking his next breath – he couldn't get the slightest wisp of air into his lungs. Knees dug into his back, pressing his ribs so hard they'd surely break.

The boom of a gunshot rocked the room.

The pressure lessened on top of Thomas. And then it was gone completely. He lifted his head just in time to see the Crank topple off him and slump to the ground. A bloody hole marked the side of his temple, and signs of life had already fled his eyes. Thomas looked up at Teresa, who was trembling, still aiming the gun at the same place where she'd shot it.

'There's two more,' Thomas said, feeling the detachment in his voice.

Teresa recovered, took a deep breath, and positioned herself defensively, aiming her weapon at the other sections of the room. Thomas, hurting all over, forced himself to his feet, looking around to make sure he didn't suffer another surprise attack.

There were no signs of the remaining two Cranks – they must've hidden behind one of the many couches or chairs clustered around the rec room. Thomas pulled off his backpack to look for syringes while his friends carefully made their way from chair to chair, couch to couch, peeking behind them. So far nothing. Then Teresa screamed, and just as Thomas looked in her direction he saw her disappear behind a couch, dropping with a hard thump.

Thomas ran for her, his heart erupting into a rapid drumbeat. He'd left everything behind him – his pack, all the instruments of death it contained. It felt as if the air solidified, slowing his speed. No other sound had come from Teresa's direction, and Aris and Rachel were too far away to help.

He reached the wall, slammed his shoulder into it as he looked behind the sofa, saw Teresa on the ground, a man's arm wrapped around her throat. She fought him with both hands, to no avail. He squeezed and squeezed, making her eyes bulge and terrible sounds escape her open mouth. Choking, gurgled sounds.

'Let her go!' Thomas shouted. Words would mean nothing to this Crank – a bald man, sweaty, a huge gash across his forehead. Dr Leavitt.

It was Dr Leavitt.

Blood mixed with sweat, dripped down into his eyes, which were red-veined and fierce. Teresa, struggling, reached for something on the floor, just beyond her fingers.

The gun.

Thomas picked it up, felt the life of his best friend fleeing as if through the air, leaving her rapidly in the arms of death. He'd never actually fired a pistol before, worried about his ability to aim. Placing his finger lightly on the trigger, he returned his attention to Teresa and the Crank once known as Leavitt. The man hadn't relented, his arm a closing vice of flesh, and Teresa's skin had turned a frightening shade of purple.

Thomas threw aim to the wind and jumped on top of them, landing stomach to stomach on Teresa, her face mere inches from his. Their eyes met, sharing the pain and fear. Leavitt used his other arm to swat at Thomas, his meaty palm slapping him in the side of the head. Thomas pulled up his hand, sliding the tip of the gun along the floor beside Teresa's body. Up and up, past her ear, to the Crank's head, to the side of it, to the temple.

Leavitt's face suddenly transformed, losing all its malice and empty hate, turning into a pitiful, childlike plea. His arm's grip on Teresa loosened.

'Please,' the man whimpered, 'please don't hurt me.'

Thomas pulled the trigger and ended it. The shot was like a crack of thunder, the crack of the world splitting. His ears ringing, he grabbed Teresa and pulled her off her dead attacker. Thomas had never much liked him anyway.

She trembled in his arms, a rare show of weakness after such a terrifying ordeal. He wrapped himself around her and held her tight. Aris came up behind him, put a hand on his shoulder, but Thomas didn't turn to look.

'Where's the other one?' he asked, barely able to speak. 'There should be one more.'

'Rachel got him,' Aris replied. 'Don't worry. They're all dead.'

Thomas held on to Teresa as if he'd fall to the centre of the world otherwise. 'I can't take much more of this.'

Rachel responded from somewhere nearby.

'Six,' she said. 'There's only six left.'

By lunchtime they'd killed the remaining Cranks. Compared to the nightmare of what they'd had to do in the rec room, the rest were a piece of cake. All asleep, their lives ended with the stab of a needle and the flow of poison.

And that was it.

The Purge was over.

52

What a world Thomas lived in. Illness, death, betrayal. His friends subjected to cruel trials that might never mean a thing. A world baked, lying in ruin. A month ago, he'd helped murder more than a dozen human beings in a matter of hours. And every day since, he'd lived in a pit of self-loathing and guilt, avoiding his friends at all costs. Even living in a complex bursting to the seams with so-called Psychs, no amount of therapy had helped him cope with the horrors of the Purge. Nor would it ever.

He was changed. At least he understood that.

He'd even stayed away from the observation room lately, too depressed to watch the Maze. But today, he'd forced himself to come in and catch up. The first thing he noticed was a display that showed Alby and Newt walking beside one of the huge Glade walls, but something was off. Newt leaned into Alby, who had an arm draped across Newt's back, helping him stand. Newt could only put his full weight on one leg. He lurched with each step, his face grimacing in pain.

Thomas sat down at the controls, took a moment to settle his mind on how to go about what he wanted to do. Then he started the meticulous process of finding the correct camera angles he'd need to put together a story.

What in the world had happened to Newt?

Less than two hours later, Thomas had spliced together a series of camera clips from various beetle blades, the closest to a continuous feed that he could accomplish. It showed a tale that just about broke Thomas's heart. On the large display screen in the middle of the wall, he started it up again from the beginning.

Early in the morning of the previous day, Newt had been totally fine. He said goodbye to Minho and the other Runners – it was Newt's day off from running, apparently. After the different groups disappeared around their respective corners, Newt spent some time walking around the Glade, checking on the various sections as if everything in the world was normal with him – as normal as things get living inside a giant maze. He spoke to Winston over at the Blood House, then chatted with Zart by the small cornfield in the Gardens. Newt even laughed a little, once slapping Zart on the back as if he'd just told a great joke.

Newt wandered over to the Deadheads next, the grove in the southwest corner outlined by dying skeletons of trees which, to Thomas, always seemed like a premonition of bad things to come. There, Newt plopped down on a bench and sat for at least thirty minutes. Thomas forwarded the feed to the point when Newt finally stood up and walked into the tiny forest. The view switched to a beetle blade's low perspective as it crawled along just a few feet behind him. Newt headed straight to the cemetery, where wooden posts marked the places they'd buried those Gladers who'd met their demise since entering the Maze.

He knelt on the ground there, staring numbly ahead, eyes glazed over, his face sinking further and further into despair. He sat that way for a long time, and Thomas thought he could guess what was going on inside his friend's head. Debilitating guilt over all those who'd died. Thinking that maybe he could've saved them somehow. Sadness over the situation as a whole – the danger, the boredom, the frustration at not knowing why they were there. Frustration at the loss of memories. And, perhaps on some deep level, he was remembering the sister they'd wiped from his mind.

Newt stood up. He turned away from the graveyard and marched out of the Deadheads, walking so swiftly that the beetle blade providing the camera view bounced as it hurried to keep up. Newt left the woods without slowing down, heading straight towards the west door, the closest one. Several Gladers waved at him or called out a greeting, but he ignored them, staring straight ahead with grim determination. Thomas sat up straighter, already knowing the end result of this and maddeningly curious as to how it happened.

Newt left the Glade proper and entered the corridors of the Maze. His gait didn't slow, his pace hurried but steady. He turned left, then right, then left again. Several more turns. Finally he came to a long stretch where thick ivy covered the walls on both sides. He stopped next to the one to the left and faced it, leaning forwards onto his hands, which disappeared in the greenery. He paused for a moment with his head down, then looked up, craning his neck as if he wanted to see the very top of the wall.

Newt reached out and started climbing the ivy.

His muscled arms made it look easy. Gripping one vine, he'd pull himself up high enough to find purchase somewhere in the stone with his feet. Then he'd grab another vine, and another, using both hands, both feet, and all his strength. He scaled the stone and ivy, reaching the halfway point between the ground and the false sky in a matter of minutes. Thomas knew that this was where he would think he couldn't go much farther. A combination of built-in optical illusions and preprogrammed repressors within his implant would guarantee he'd never make it to the top. He did climb several more feet; then he stopped, looking towards the sky, beaten.

Thomas watched, and waited.

Newt clung to the ivy on the wall, his whole body almost disappearing behind the greenery. A beetle blade that had been scaling the wall at his side crawled up and stopped within just a few inches from the boy's face. Not for the first time, Thomas wondered about the software that ran these little mechanical creatures. How did it know what to do, when no one was around to feed them instructions?

Newt looked directly into the camera, and for the first time in this constructed feed, spoke so that Thomas could hear what he said.

'I don't know who you people are, but I hope you're happy. I hope you get a real buggin' kick out of watching us suffer. And then you can die and go to hell. This is on you.'

Newt let go of the vines and kicked away from the wall, plummeting out of the camera's view. The beetle blade hurried to reposition itself, and all Thomas heard was the rustling of its movement and then a distant hard thump. The view bounced its way down to the ground, then locked on Newt. He was lying on his side with a leg pulled up, arms wrapped around it. He rocked back and forth, groaning. Those groans turned into sobs. A deep, painful cry that made Thomas's chest hurt.

Newt suddenly let out an anguished howl, then screamed into the air. 'I hate you. I hate you!'

Thomas turned off the feed. He couldn't take it any more. He already knew that someone had saved him, pulled him out of the Maze back to the safety of the Glade. And he couldn't bear to watch one more second of it.

Newt, Newt, Newt, Thomas thought, feeling as if the very air around him were turning black. *You're not even immune, man. You're not even immune.*

53

231.09.22 | 11:17 A.M.

Thomas heard a gentle knock on his door and opened it to see Teresa. Things were almost back to normal at WICKED headquarters, as much as possible after something like the Purge had happened.

'Hey,' he said, groggy. 'You could've just buzzed my head. I was taking a nap.'

In answer, she held up a tablet. 'Did you see this?'

'Huh?' He had no idea what she was talking about.

She stepped into his room, brushing past him as he closed the door, and sat down at his desk. 'Come here and look at this. Did you send a mass memo out? Or did Dr Paige ask permission to use your name?'

'What? No.'

'Well.' She gestured to the glowing screen.

Thomas leaned in to take a look.

```
WICKED Memorandum, Date 231.5.22
TO: The replacements
```

```
FROM: Thomas [Subject A2]
RE: The Purge

I take total responsibility for what we've
had to do over the last few days.

What we have to keep in mind, though, is
that WICKED is alive and stronger than
ever. The Maze is up and running, and our
studies are in full swing. We're on the
path and we can't stray from it.

All I ask is that what we've done here
remain within the organization and never
be referred to again. What's done is done,
and it was a mercy. But now, every waking
thought has to be devoted to building the
blueprint.

Ava Paige is the new chancellor of WICKED,
effective immediately.
```

Before he had time to process it completely, Teresa took the tablet back from him.

'And look at this other one I found,' she said as she searched for something else. 'Supposedly sent by Chancellor Anderson the very *day* before he typed up that crazy one we saw on his workstation about his fingers. There's no way he wrote this. Check it out.'

She handed the tablet back to him.

```
WICKED Memorandum, Date 231.5.4
TO: Fellow Partners
FROM: Kevin Anderson, Chancellor
RE: My farewell to you all
```

I hope that each one of you will forgive me for doing this in such a cowardly manner, sending you a memo when it's something I should do in person. However, I have no choice. The effects of the Flare are rampant in my actions, embarrassing and disheartening. And our decision not to allow the narcotic Bliss within our compound means I can't fake it long enough to say goodbye properly.

Typing these words is difficult enough. But at least I have the ability and time to write and edit in the small windows of sanity left to me.

I don't know why the virus affected me so quickly and so viciously. I deteriorated far quicker than almost all of the original group. But no matter. I've been decommissioned, and my replacement, Ava Paige, is ready to take charge. The Elites are well into their training to serve as the link between us and those who will continue to run WICKED. Ava herself admits that her purpose is almost more like that of a figurehead, with our elite subjects the true rulers.

We are and will continue to be in good hands. The noble cause we began over a decade ago will see itself to fruition. Our efforts, and for almost all of us, our lives, will have been spent justly and for the greater good. The cure will be built.

Honestly, this is more of a personal note.
To thank you for your friendship, your
compassion, your empathy in the face of
implementing such difficult tasks.

One word of warning: it gets bad in
the end. Don't fight the time of your
decommission. I did, and now I regret it.
Just leave and end the suffering.

It's become too much.

Thank you.

And goodbye.

'What *is* this?' Thomas said, completely bewildered. 'That's
not how it happened at all. What's she trying to do, rewrite history so she looks more legit in the future?'

Teresa shrugged. 'I thought you'd want to see it.'

'Come on,' he said. 'We're going to talk to her.'

Thomas knocked on Dr Paige's door until she finally opened it.
He was so upset he could barely catch a decent breath.

The doctor looked surprised. 'Is there a problem?' she
asked.

'Why'd you do it?' Thomas asked, trying to stay calm. He
felt betrayed, confused, and above all, angry. 'Writing memos
from other people's accounts is your thing now?'

'It helps the others deal with our current situation,
Thomas,' Dr Paige said, her surprise transforming to a
bemused understanding. 'Gives them a better sense of order. It
also shows how involved you are in this organization and how
mature you've all become.' She smiled at Thomas. She looked
proud of him. 'And I think it's a simple but symbolic way to

create a bridge in everyone's mind. A link. Between the old and the new.'

Thomas didn't know how to respond, what to say. Why would she make him seem so important? And why would she send something from his messaging account without asking? Not to mention from Anderson's, their leader at the time?

'This does all that,' she continued, 'while having a focal point of one person. It's the best of both worlds.'

Still he didn't respond.

'You could've at least asked him first,' Teresa said.

Dr Paige gave them a genuine enough look of regret. 'You're right. I'm sorry. I got way ahead of myself.'

'It's not okay,' Thomas said. He turned and walked away, scared he'd say something he might regret. Dr Paige was full of lies. Just full of them.

Thomas went straight back to his room. He told Teresa that he wasn't feeling well and he returned to his bed. He closed his eyes and tried to calm his thoughts, rolled onto his side, wishing for sleep. Everything felt different. He couldn't tell Teresa what he was thinking, and almost everyone he knew or cared about was inside the Maze. And now these emails. It was just *weird* – if Dr Paige was devious about that, what else was she hiding from them? He wished he'd said more when he confronted her. But instead, he'd chickened out.

And here he was, staring at the wall of his room, thinking.

Thinking.

That was the worst part. If only he, Teresa and Chuck could run away and start a new life together. But then he thought of Newt. About his friend falling from the wall and how he wasn't immune. They needed a cure. And if they found one, everyone would be released – Alby, Minho, Newt, Chuck, Teresa, even Aris and Rachel. Maybe they could all live in the same neighbourhood, grow old together, sit around and stuff themselves with food and tell their kids stories about the time they'd saved the world. He pictured Minho in front of a big group of kids, acting out the life of a Runner, but for some reason he kept making giant ape movements, tickling his armpits, pounding his chest.

If only it were that easy. Imagine Minho acting goofy in front of future grandkids and all would be well. That thought came up again – what now, more than ever, felt like the right thing to do. He wanted to go into the Maze. Anything to be out of this place, back with his friends, and on to the next stage. Anything to get this cure done and done. Get to the happy future. He just wanted to lie to himself and do it.

The future, a Crank-free world, he and his friends living in paradise.

Talk about a load of crap.

He let out a deep breath, and then, despite its being the middle of the day, he fell asleep.

54

Thomas was back in his haven, the observation room.

Over the last few weeks, the guilt and anger had continued to build, slow trickles that joined to become a deluge,
and now he was drowning. There was only one way he could
ever bring the air back into his lungs. Being here, watching his
old friends in the Maze.

He and Teresa had grown distant lately – she seemed to have
coped with her own difficulties after the Purge by throwing
herself mind, body, and spirit into work, work and more work
– but Thomas didn't mind. They spoke often enough through
their telepathy to keep each other informed. Enough to know
that they both were doing what was best for them.

And for Thomas, that had been to stay out of sight as much
as possible. He had to stick to the normal regimen of tests,
check-ups and classes, but other than that he made himself
scarce. Unless Chuck or Teresa were available to hang out,
Thomas spent most of his free time in his room, reading or
sleeping, or observing his friends in the Maze, watching their

every move. Those moves had become pretty routine, the Gladers establishing themselves in a pretty impressive little community. Law, order, routine, safety. No one had died or been stung for a while now.

Thomas still loved eavesdropping whenever he could. Listening in when Alby, Minho and Newt would sit down for meals. It made Thomas feel like a part of them, almost like he was there.

And that was exactly what he'd been doing all afternoon, switching between views and microphones when one scene grew boring. At the moment, over by the east door, Newt was talking to Minho, who'd just returned from running the vast maze itself.

'Anything new out there?' Newt asked, the sarcasm obvious. 'Did a bloody Griever come out and ask for a snog?'

Minho leaned against the stone, still catching his breath. 'How'd you know? I told him maybe some other time – not really my type.'

These two had some variation of this conversation almost every day, mocking the monotony of what the Runners found in their daily excursions. They'd started walking towards the Map Room when Thomas heard a knock at the door behind him. Sadly, he pulled himself away from the world of the Maze and returned to WICKED.

'Who is it?' he asked.

The door opened, and Chuck's curly head poked through. 'Hey, Thomas. Dr Campbell said I could have two free hours to help you with your notes. So . . .'

'Come on in, you shank. You don't have to act like it's a big deal every time.'

He and Chuck had started using some of the slang words invented inside the Glade, just between the two of them. Chuck's favourite was *klunk* by a long shot. Dr Paige said the Psychs were really interested in how the memory loss affected the Gladers. Sometimes there were surprises, like the invention of totally new words. A few of them came from Minho, who'd had quite the mouth even before entering the Maze. The Swipe seemed to heighten the trait, which the Psychs also found interesting.

Of course, the Psychs found *everything* interesting.

Chuck came in and sat beside Thomas, plopping down in his seat with an exaggerated sigh of contentment. 'They sent Frank in today, which means I only have one month left.' The mix of excitement and fear in Chuck's eyes always broke Thomas's heart a little. He shared as much blame for the fear part as anyone – it'd been his own selfishness having Chuck in here so often, seeing some of the bad things that happened inside the Maze. But the kid was his brother in every way but blood – without him in his life, Thomas would've broken long ago.

'It'll be here before you know it,' he said.

'Which *means*,' Chuck said, 'that all of this'll be *over* before we know it, too.'

'Yep. You got it.'

'What'd you do today?' Chuck asked. 'Let me guess – medical check-up, classes, critical thinking, observe the Maze.'

'Yep. You got it,' Thomas said again, making the boy laugh. 'Pretty exciting life I lead, am I right?'

'Just wait until I get to the Maze,' Chuck replied. 'I'll liven that place right up.' He said it with an enthusiasm that Thomas could only guess was genuine – kids that young had a knack for remembering only the good parts.

'Yep. You got it.' The third time made even Thomas laugh. Then he stood up. 'Sorry, I have a meeting I'm supposed to go to.'

'Aw, come on, I just got here! I was hoping to watch the Gladers eat dinner. I think Gally and Alby are finally gonna beat the klunk out of each other tonight.'

'Sorry, bud,' Thomas said. 'And you know you can't be in here without me, so head to the barracks. Later we'll grab food, come back here, and do more Glade spying. Maybe the Psychs'll send a Griever in to dance for them.'

Chuck paled a little at that but did his best to cover it up. Sometimes, in his excitement to get to the Glade, he forgot about the monsters.

'Sorry,' Thomas said, wanting to kick himself. 'Terrible joke.'

The meeting was in a small conference room, and Thomas arrived knowing absolutely nothing of its purpose. Dr Paige sat at the head of the table, with two people to her left who were obviously Psychs. One was from the days before the Purge – a lady named Campbell. The other was a newbie, from Seattle or Anchorage or who knew where. Thomas purposely didn't bother learning details like that. He couldn't put his finger on why.

To Dr Paige's right, a middle-aged man with dark hair and brown skin sat with a girl who could have been his daughter age-wise, but not genetically, by the looks of it. She had fair skin and dirty-blonde hair, and the man leaned towards her as if he knew her well, as if they'd just been whispering.

Thomas stood there for a long moment, everyone in the room assessing everyone else.

Dr Paige stood up. 'Thanks for coming, Thomas. You've made yourself scarce lately. Helping Chuck prep for his big trip to the Maze next month?' She smiled innocently, as if she didn't know every single move he made, every second of the day. Thomas didn't like her nearly as much as he had before the Purge.

'Something like that,' Thomas said in an even tone.

'Well, please sit down,' Paige replied, motioning to a chair opposite hers, across the table.

After he was seated Thomas asked, 'So what's this all about?'

Dr Paige held up a finger, looking annoyed. 'Just a moment. Teresa should be here any second.'

On cue, the door opened again and Teresa came bustling

through, offering a few nods of greeting before sitting next to Thomas. She always looked so . . . busy. So preoccupied.

Hi, she said to him, sending as much warmth along with her greeting as she could.

Good to see you, he replied. Truer words had never been spoken. He missed her.

Dr Paige got down to business. 'I want to introduce a couple of new friends who will be helping with some upcoming projects.' She turned towards the two newcomers to her right, the man and the girl he seemed to hover over. 'This is Jorge and Brenda. Jorge is a Berg pilot, a very good one. And Brenda has some training as a nurse, with big plans to become a Psych someday. Isn't that right, Brenda?'

The girl nodded, not showing a hint of shyness or awkwardness. 'Whatever it takes to find a cure,' she said. It seemed like an odd response, but something haunted hid behind her eyes, something that probably explained exactly why she'd answered that way.

'*Hola,*' the man named Jorge said, looking each of them in the eye for a moment. 'I'm excited to work with you.'

'Work with us?' Teresa asked. 'What's going on?'

He'd got Thomas's attention. He was now madly curious.

'We'd like you to help us on an upcoming expedition,' Dr Paige said. 'In a few weeks, Jorge, Brenda and quite a few others will be sent to a place called the Scorch. We're very interested in what we may find inside a nearby city infested with Cranks. Significant research potential.'

'A city infested with Cranks?' Thomas repeated. He had a bad feeling he wasn't hearing the whole truth here.

'Yes,' she said, offering nothing else. 'And we think it will be valuable to have you there. We'd like to test the long-range effectiveness of your implant technology, especially the remote monitoring of your killzone patterns and other measurements. We need to know it can work at long distances. Now, here's what we have planned . . .'

Thomas worked over what she'd just said, tuning her out. Why would they need to know about long-distance monitoring? Was WICKED planning on moving them somewhere? There was more going on here that they weren't telling him, and he had a bad feeling about it. A feeling he'd had for a while but could only now admit to himself. It made him feel sick.

WICKED was never going to stop.

They were never, never going to stop.

55

Thomas walked with Chuck down the long hallway, which seemed to stretch out infinitely before him. That was how everything felt today. Long and never-ending. Really, he was just in a sad mood. The day had finally come.

Chuck was going to be inserted into the Maze.

Thomas had asked for this hour with Chuck to eat a last meal of sorts and talk through things. Their own goodbye. Then Thomas planned to leave Chuck in the hands of the experts and make himself scarce. He didn't think he could handle watching Chuck get his memory erased, see him handled like a corpse, watch him get thrown into the Box like a heap of trash. They'd have their goodbye, and then Thomas could hide in his room until the next morning rolled around.

The cafeteria was quiet during the lull between the breakfast and lunch crowds. After grabbing plates of breakfast leftovers, he and Chuck sat down by one of the few windows that looked out over the Alaskan forest. They'd barely talked since Thomas had retrieved Chuck from his room, and now they both picked at their food. Neither had actually taken a bite yet.

'I might as well get the dumb question out of the way,' Thomas finally said. 'You scared?'

Chuck held up a limp piece of bacon and studied it. 'You're right. Dumb question.'

'I'll take that as a yes, then.'

Chuck chomped on the bacon, his face wincing a little. 'Tastes like klunk.'

'Of course it does. They fried it almost three hours ago. But your one wish for today was to sleep in, so they let you sleep in. Maybe your wish should've been for crisp bacon. Or, you know, a one-way ticket to Denver.'

Chuck gave him a polite smile, the most adult thing he'd ever done.

'Come on, man,' Thomas said. 'Open up here, buddy. Tell me what you're thinking. What you're feeling. I'm worried about you.'

The kid shrugged. 'Do we really have to get all cheesy like this? They're sending me into the Maze and there's nothing I can do about it. I'm going to miss it here, going to miss you guys. But there's no point whining and crying.'

'You'll have to go a while without seeing my beautiful face every day. You better be whining and crying. I'm talking puffy eyes, wet face, snot pouring into your mouth, the whole bit. I don't see that in the next three minutes, I'm gonna be offended.'

'What happens after I get there?' Chuck asked, acting like he hadn't heard a word Thomas just said. 'I mean, this can't go on for ever, right?'

And just like that, all the air drained out of the room.

'Of course not for ever,' Thomas said. 'I hear they're getting close to a full blueprint. And once they have that, the cure's next. I'm sure we'll be reunited before too long.'

Thomas didn't know if he could actually count all the lies

he'd just told on one hand. But what did it matter? Chuck was about to have his memory wiped, and Thomas didn't think it could hurt to get his hopes up a bit.

Chuck was staring at him.

'What?' Thomas asked.

Chuck told him he was full of something, and he didn't use the word *klunk*.

'I am not,' Thomas rebutted. 'Look, man, you're right. We don't need to get all cheesy. We're saying goodbye, but we'll both still be inside this huge complex. And I'll be watching you, rooting for you. Always. I promise.'

'I won't even remember you,' Chuck said. 'So it's really like we're saying bye for ever.'

'No, man, no.' Thomas got up and went to the other side of the table, sat right next to his friend. 'I was just thinking about this recently. There'll be a time, in the near future, when we have a cure and we'll all be living in the same neighbourhood – rich, fat and happy. Everyone will have their memories back, and life'll be sweet. Just look forward to that.'

'If you say so.'

'I say so.'

'Okay, then.' The boy smiled, then looked away, the swell of a tear threatening to spill from his eye. 'Sounds good.'

'You know what?' Thomas said. 'We don't even need to say bye. Byes are too hard. I'll just get up and walk out, like no big deal, and then I'll see you when I see you, okay? No sayonaras necessary.'

Chuck nodded, but when Thomas made the first move to get up, his friend catapulted forwards and pulled him into a hug, squeezing him fiercely with both arms

'I'm gonna miss you,' the boy said through a sob. 'I'm gonna miss you so much.'

Thomas hugged him back, his own tears dropping into Chuck's hair. 'I know, man. I know. I'm going to miss you, too.'

They might've stayed that way for ever, but Dr Paige sent

someone to summon Chuck and she gently escorted him away. His look back right before they left the room just about shattered Thomas's heart.

He sat at the cafeteria table for a long time, imagining Chuck in the Maze. Imagining Chuck being attacked by a Griever. Chuck starving or dying of thirst. He imagined Chuck dying a hundred deaths and no one doing anything to help.

He thought of Newt, of Alby, of Minho.

He thought of Teresa.

Something grew hard deep inside Thomas's chest. For now, he had to go along with whatever WICKED wanted of him. But that wouldn't always be the case.

An idea occurred to him. A ridiculous, ridiculous idea. A plan. Teresa had said once, long ago, that someday they'd be bigger. And now they were.

What if I saved them? he thought.

What if I saved my friends?

56

231.12.11 | 10:46 A.M.

It was only Thomas's second time on a Berg, and the first he
could scarcely remember.

At first he hated it – his stomach bouncing and churning,
waves of nausea filling his mouth with saliva – but when he got
used to it, he kind of liked it. Then he hated it again. Being
inside the large flying beast was exhilarating, unlike anything
else he'd ever experienced. Living in such a ruined world really
made you appreciate something so powerful that even gravity
couldn't keep it down.

Teresa hadn't come, staying back to do her part in testing
the long-range abilities of their implants. Every day they
grew more distant. She buried herself in WICKED and their
mission, and Thomas sometimes hesitated to tell her what
he was thinking. But they needed to have a talk – a big talk.
Soon.

Thomas looked out one of the viewing ports set into the
floor of the Berg. He watched countless landscapes flash by
below him, in complete and utter awe. Despite the devastation

that had been wreaked on his planet, it remained beautiful. Breathtaking. Greens and blues and oranges mixed with lots of pale brown. Of course, this high up, you couldn't see the details. You couldn't see the Cranks and the starvation and the poverty and the terror.

No wonder back before the sun flares, every kid wanted to be an astronaut.

'Hey.'

He looked up and saw Brenda, who'd been busy with Jorge prepping all their supplies for the Crank city expedition. They were also delivering a bunch of equipment to the Scorch for WICKED, for reasons no one shared with Thomas.

'Hey there,' he said back. 'You guys about ready?'

She sat down next to him. 'As ready as we'll ever be. Jorge made me check everything about a hundred times. He likes to be prepared.'

'When are we supposed to get there?' He knew almost nothing. But the land below had already started to look like a desert, various shades of red and orange and yellow taking over the palette. There were almost no signs of life, or that life had ever been there, for that matter.

'I think half an hour or so.' She rubbed her hands together, and her expression looked strained. 'Man, I'm getting nervous. This all sounded like a fun adventure until about ten minutes ago.'

'What's there to be scared about?' Thomas asked. 'A post-apocalyptic city with no government or security, surrounded by a desert and swarming with Cranks. I mean, come on. Don't be a sissy.' He flashed the girl a quick smile to let her know he was joking.

Brenda rolled her eyes.

'Or . . .' he said with exaggerated chagrin, 'it could be scary.'

'You should be nicer to Teresa, you know,' she said after a long beat of them staring down at the wasteland, the hum of the Berg's engines so soothing Thomas suddenly wanted a nap.

'What do you mean?'

'She obviously feels strongly about you. And it just seems like you haven't been that nice to her. Sorry if it's none of my business.'

Thomas thought about it, a topic he usually tried to avoid in his own mind. 'No, it's okay. She's my best friend. We've been together for more than half our lives, and we can talk to each other . . . like no one else can. Without even speaking sometimes. Maybe that's why it seems like I'm not nice.'

Brenda nodded as if that made sense to her. '*Just* friends? After all this time? I've never seen you two holding hands or kissing or anything. You're one slow mover.' She laughed at the last part.

'It's complicated,' Thomas said, surprised at this conversation, the things it was making him think about. 'She means the world to me, and nothing will ever change that. But it's kinda hard to be romantic when you have a dying world outside your home and your friends are stuck inside an experiment.'

Brenda seemed disappointed. 'Yeah, but come on. People *love,* Thomas. Best of times, worst of times. People love. You should make sure she knows how you feel. That's all I'm saying.'

Thomas felt a surge of emotion he didn't understand. He thought of his mom, and his dad, and his friends. And it all just welled up inside him and tears began to leak from his eyes. He didn't know what he needed in life, or what he was meant to accomplish. Friends were what he had, and they were all that mattered. Somehow he had to save them.

Brenda noticed his tears, and her face melted into something so soft and full of kindness that Thomas shook. She pulled him into a hug, and he hugged her back, felt like he was hugging everyone who'd just flashed through his thoughts. They stayed that way, pressed together, until the Berg tilted to the right and started its descent.

They'd arrived at the Scorch.

WICKED had sent armed guards with them, and they spilled down the open ramp first, to the dusty, blistering-hot ground below. When they gave the all clear, Thomas walked down with Brenda and Jorge, all three of them squinting against the blinding brightness of the sun.

'Good glory,' Brenda said. 'Imagine what it was like down here when the flares actually hit.'

'You sure you don't want to come with us, *hermano*?' Jorge asked. 'We're going to have ourselves quite the party.'

He and Brenda both laughed, but Thomas had a hard time finding anything funny about it. This place was terrible.

The Berg had landed surprisingly far from the Crank city, and the technicians Thomas was supposed to work with were gathering their things as if they intended to go in the opposite direction. He saw nothing that way but a wasteland, which made him more than a little nervous. He found himself anxious to head back to Alaska, and hoped the tests they wanted to run didn't take terribly long.

Thomas shielded his eyes and looked towards the city. It appeared to be several miles away. Dirt and rust and shattered glass made up half of it. Ruined skyscrapers reached for the sky like broken fingers. It was hard to believe anyone could live there, even Cranks. Beyond the devastated city, mountains rose. The sun flares might have taken some of its plant life away, but the stone and soil seemed to call out, 'We're still here. What else ya got?'

Thomas tore his eyes away from the scene and saw Brenda staring at her soon-to-be new home.

'You sure about this?' Thomas asked. 'You sure you want to go into that place?' He'd meant it to be a little lighthearted, but he knew how serious it was as it came out of his mouth.

'If we had a cure, a lot of people I love would still be alive,' she said, gazing unwaveringly into the distance. 'People like my mom and dad, people like my brother.'

'I know, I know,' he murmured. 'Believe me, I know.'

'That's why Jorge and I volunteered,' she continued. 'Not just in general, but for this.' She nodded towards the broken city in the distance. 'I have to do my part.'

'Yeah,' he said.

Before he could add something nicer, Jorge yelled that his group needed to get going. He wanted to be in the city well before the sunset.

'Be careful,' Thomas said, trying to communicate with his eyes that he was sorry. That no one else should have to give up their life for this sickness. 'Seriously. Be careful.'

'I will,' she said. 'Hard to believe they're going to bring your friends out here next, huh? Poor guys. Well, see you later, alligator.'

She gave him a feeble wave, then hurried after Jorge.

'Wait, what did you say?' he yelled.

She didn't respond, running farther away.

He stared at her for a long moment, noticed the sands shifting beneath her feet.

'What did you mean?' he whispered.

57

hase Two.

That was all he could get out of the WICKED technicians he'd been assigned to. *Phase Two.* He asked each one of them about what Brenda had said, and those were the only words he got back. Other than things like *Go ask Dr Paige. It's not my place to talk about it. I'm just doing my job.*

But none of that mattered because Thomas knew exactly what was going on. He should have seen it long before Brenda let it slip.

WICKED planned to send the Gladers into this wretched place for another phase of trials. That was the reason they wanted to test the long-range monitoring of his implant technology – so they would know how effectively they'd be able to do it with the others once *they* were there. The lies just stacked up higher and higher. Things were even worse than he'd imagined. Far worse.

If there'd been the tiniest seed of doubt before, it was now gone completely. No matter what it took, Thomas was going into the Maze to save his friends.

The Scorch got nastier with every step.

He walked with the WICKED technicians across the hard, dead land, gripping a towel beneath his chin. He'd wrapped the rest of it around his head to shield himself from the sun, which beat down on them, raining pure heat. The only relief was a breeze, though it covered him in sand as well. They were heading for some kind of underground tunnel where they supposedly needed to run tests and set up equipment. And now Thomas knew what for.

As he and the others trekked across the wasteland, he had plenty of time to think over his budding plan to save his friends. It could happen. It really could. He just needed to convince WICKED of two things – insert him into the Maze, and do it without erasing his memories. For any kind of plan to work, he had to have his mind intact. Only then would he know how to get them out.

There were details to figure out. How, when and where to get weapons. How to shut down the Grievers. Where to go if they *did* somehow escape the WICKED complex. But he had time.

It really could work.

He tried to stay that positive and kept moving through the desert.

One foot in front of the other. Sweating profusely.

On and on they went.

'Here!' the man leading the group eventually yelled out. The others crowded around him as he dropped to his knees, then felt around in the sand. He swept away a thin layer of dirt and revealed a metal hatch with a simple handle on top. It didn't even have a lock to secure it – what were the odds of someone stumbling upon the tunnel entrance out here in the middle of a ruined nowhere?

A woman leaned in and took hold of the handle along with

the man, and they heaved the covering up and open. Thomas stood on the tips of his toes to catch a glimpse over someone's shoulder – a long flight of stairs disappeared into darkness below.

'Believe it or not,' the woman said, shouting over the wind, 'there used to be a prison nearby. This was an escape route built by the cartels. We just adapted it for our purposes. It'll be about another hour's walk down there.'

She didn't say anything else, just began descending the steps. One by one, the group followed, Thomas going down last.

It was a long, surprisingly cool, unsurprisingly creepy descent into the depths and down the endless tunnel that WICKED had commandeered. No one spoke much as they walked and walked and walked, but when they did, it was usually in a whisper that echoed like a ghost's haunting call.

'Almost there,' a man named David announced, spooking Thomas. He'd become accustomed to the quiet, and the sudden voice jarred him from his thoughts.

'Almost where?' Thomas asked, his words bouncing back at him off the walls.

'There's a Flat Trans up ahead that we installed on our last trip here. It's finally ready to be activated.'

'A Flat Trans?' Thomas repeated. Was that how they planned to transport the Gladers to the Scorch?

'Yeah,' David replied. 'Let's hope it works, because that's how we're going to get back home tonight!'

Thomas almost stumbled when he heard that.

'You have no idea how much these things cost,' the man continued. 'Before the Flares, only billionaires could afford them – there were even some governments who only wished they'd had enough money to get one.'

'WICKED's that rich?' Thomas asked.

David laughed. 'They don't need to buy this stuff. They just steal it from billionaires who are too dead to care any more. Or too Cranked past the Gone. Anyway, don't worry, once it's up and running, there's nothing to be scared of. It's a cool way to travel, that's for sure.'

'Here we are,' a woman called back. She shined a light on a tall rectangular structure that looked like a large door to nowhere. Or, more accurately, a doorframe that was missing its actual door. A panel of controls, dark at the moment, was attached to the right side of the device.

David moved forwards to stand next to the woman. 'We've run every test imaginable. All that's left is to turn the sucker on.'

Thomas stepped away from the WICKED staff as they pulled out tools and began doing their jobs. He didn't know any of these people very well, so he felt like a total outsider. He went to the wall of the tunnel, just on the edge of the pool of light, and leaned back against the dirt and stone. He folded his arms, watching the people go about their business.

A humming sound filled the air that made his bones rattle. A green glow lit up the control panel of the Flat Trans. The hum grew louder. He couldn't believe that in a matter of minutes he was going to step through a magical wall of engineering and reappear thousands of miles away. It made him nervous, made him worry he'd end up scattered across the quantum universe, nothing but a galaxy of atoms and molecules that had nothing to do with each other.

A loud buzz made him stand upright; then a shimmering wall of staticky grey filled the space between the rectangular frame of the Flat Trans. It wavered, flashed into and out of existence a few times, then held steady. The soft, continuous pulse of its energy made the skin on Thomas's arms tingle. He was really going to do this. He was really going to walk through that wall of power.

'All signs are steady,' David announced, looking at the display screen on the control panel. 'Sending a test item now.' Then, like a kid standing beside a lake with a skipping stone, he tossed his torch through the Flat Trans. A few seconds later, it popped right back out and he caught it. He laughed. 'Guess we're good.'

'Who wants to go first?' a woman asked. 'Thomas, how about you?' She gave him a teasing smile.

'Actually, yeah.' Not knowing what had come over him, he squared his shoulders and walked straight for the Flat Trans, trying desperately to show no hesitation or fear. He figured if there were any cause for concern, they'd stop him in the few seconds it took to walk from one spot to the other. But no one said a thing. A couple of them let out a whoop. One person clapped.

Thomas stepped right into the shimmering wall of grey.

58

A plane of cold passed over his body, as if he'd stepped into a deep pool of icy water. But then it was over, as quickly as it took to step through any door. Several people waited on the other side, in a room he'd never seen before. Dr Paige was there, as were Teresa and some others he didn't know.

Teresa reached him first, pulling him into the tightest hug he'd ever received.

'Thank God,' she whispered into his ear. Then she said it again in his mind.

He returned the hug, feeling so much relief at her warmth that he trembled as he squeezed. He wanted to tell her about his plan for the Maze, and this reception confirmed for him that he would do it soon. He'd need her help if he had any chance of pulling it off.

'It's okay,' he said back to her. He noticed Dr Paige looking at both of them like a proud parent. 'Nothing bad happened at all. We were totally safe.'

'I know. I know,' she said, but she didn't loosen her hold

on him.

'Hey,' he said as gently as he could. 'What's the matter?'

She finally pulled away from him. 'Nothing. Just . . . having you so far away. Made me nervous.'

'I missed you too.' A lame response, but he hoped she could see how he felt in his eyes. *We need to talk,* he said quickly to her mind. *Soon.*

'The results of your long-distance monitoring were very positive,' Dr Paige said before Thomas could explain anything further. She stepped closer, beaming with a smile that looked forced. 'Things are going very well overall, in fact. We're making progress every day.'

Thomas nodded, his mind racing, thinking, *If you only knew.* He looked at the unfamiliar surroundings – it seemed like a huge dormitory, but nothing like the barracks at WICKED. He saw brick and plaster and wooden doors.

'Where are we?' he asked.

'A new facility outside headquarters,' she replied. 'We've been pulling in volunteers for more research and needed a place to keep them.'

Thomas didn't believe a word of that. Why would they have a Flat Trans linked to the Scorch if this place was meant to house research volunteers? Could it possibly have something to do with Phase Two and the Gladers? Either way, he had to make sure those plans never came to fruition.

'We have a shuttle heading back to the main complex,' Paige said. 'There's a lot of work to do.' She seemed to focus this on Teresa.

'How far is it from here?' Thomas asked.

'Just a few miles by road. Less than two if you cut through the forest.'

He sighed in relief. 'Good. After the Scorch, I really need a walk through air that doesn't want to bake my lungs. You guys go on ahead – I'll meet you there.' His legs ached from walking so much already that day, but he really wanted to be alone. And he needed some time to prepare his speech to Teresa.

'Well . . . we haven't had many Crank sightings lately,' Paige answered, considering. 'But it's dark out. I tell you what. Take a Launcher and I'll let you do it. *And* one of our guards. No, make that two.'

Thomas opened his mouth to argue but didn't bother once he saw her face. It was too much to think she'd let him go alone.

A few minutes later, with two nameless guards assigned to him, he left the building.

'We better get moving,' one of the guards said. To his credit, he and his buddy seemed to respect Thomas's clear wish to be alone, but they'd also been put in charge of his safety. 'Getting late.'

'Is it true that you haven't had many Cranks around lately?' Thomas asked him, turning his back to the new building, facing the woods and darkness.

'Yep. I think the ones around here have either died or wandered into the pits. But being dark and cold and all – I just think we should hustle.'

Thomas liked that the man hadn't taken on the role of tough-guy guard. At least, not yet. And the other one seemed like a mute. 'Okay, sounds good. You guys leading or am I leading?'

'I'll be right behind you.' Mr Talkative held up his Launcher and pointed in the direction of the WICKED complex, somewhere deep in the forest. Thomas had his own Launcher slung across his shoulders with a strap that dug into his neck. 'That way I can see you and scan the forest at the same time. Xavier here will scout out ahead. That sound like a plan?'

Like he had an option. 'Of course. Let's do it.'

Without a word, the man named Xavier stomped through the brush and into the woods. Shivering suddenly from the chill, Thomas followed, the other guard right behind him.

Half an hour passed, the forest silent and dark. Branches loomed over them, a canopy of countless wooden arms and fingers, barely visible in the starless night. The heavy silence hung in the air, broken only by the soft crunch of their footsteps in the fallen leaves. Thomas aimed the beam of his torch out in front him, every once in a while pointing it up and around, terrified he'd see some unworldly creature from a storybook. Yellow eyes, fangs, a ghostly apparition. He was spooked, and wished he'd just taken a ride with Teresa and everyone else.

An owl hooted so loud that Thomas jumped. Then he laughed, and so did the guard behind him.

'An owl?' Thomas said. 'Seriously? I feel like I'm in a horror movie.'

'It's creepy out here,' the man agreed. 'Cranks or no Cranks. Kids had plenty of things to have nightmares about before the Flare ever came around.'

'Yeah.' Thomas searched the branches above him, looking for the owl. Sometimes he forgot that there was an entire animal kingdom out there that didn't know or care about a disease called the Flare. The culprit was nowhere to be seen. Thomas continued walking.

The exercise had warmed him up a little, and his legs had loosened from their stiffness. He was relaxing, just feeling better about the day, when he realized he'd lost sight of Xavier up ahead. The man had made a turn around a huge pine tree, but when Thomas rounded the same tree, he couldn't see the guard.

'Xavier?' he called.

No answer, no sign of him anywhere.

A sudden flurry of footsteps, crashing through the undergrowth, came thundering up behind Thomas. As he whirled around to see what it was, another sound flew through the air. Followed by a squelching, crunching noise.

And then he saw it.

The guard at his back had stopped in his tracks and dropped his weapon. Blood dripped out of his mouth. A long

branch had been jammed into the side of his neck, its end –
drenched in red – coming out the other side. As the man fell to
his knees, Thomas saw who'd done it – the person still gripped
the end of the makeshift spear with both hands, grinning at his
prey, who choked for air.

The attacker looked up, straight at Thomas.

It was Randall.

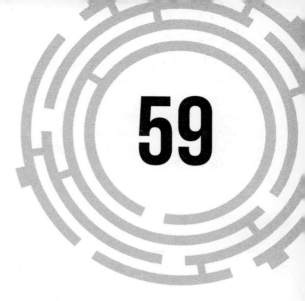

59

Randall didn't look so well.

There he stood, battered and bruised and filthy, wearing several layers of ripped clothing. His face was crusted with dirt, his eyes were wild, and his hair was a mangled mess – the nightmare visage Thomas had worried about. But this was no storybook.

'Randall,' Thomas whispered, as if pleading for the person who used to be Randall to come back. But that man was no more. The Crank standing before him had passed the Gone a long time ago.

Randall said something unintelligible, then wrenched the spear out of the guard's neck, letting the man finally tumble to the ground, the life drained out of him. He lay still, blood pooling on a bed of pine needles.

'Xavier!' Thomas yelled. Still no answer.

Trying not to make any sudden movements, he reached for his Launcher, slowly settled it in both hands, placed his finger on the trigger. Randall stood there looking at the gore on his own weapon as if he was pondering licking it clean. Then he looked back at Thomas.

'Once upon a time,' the Crank said, his words slurred but understandable this time, 'I was a tasty treat. Tasty as can be.'

In a blur of movement, Randall sprinted for the trees, disappearing into the darkness before Thomas could do anything. He aimed the Launcher in that direction, pulled the trigger, heard the charge and the shot. But the grenade hit a tree and exploded in a burst of electricity. When it died out, complete silence enveloped the woods. No sight or sound of the Crank.

Thomas gripped his weapon so hard it hurt his fingers. Holding it out in front of him, he spun in a slow circle, searching the darkness between the trees. He'd dropped his torch and now picked it up, shut it off. He didn't want to be a sitting duck and he didn't want his eyesight to be worthless. Anxious for his eyes to grow accustomed to the dark, he continued turning slowly around and around, finger itching to pull the trigger again.

He couldn't believe Randall was still alive. How had he survived out here? Survival aside, it seemed impossible that the disease itself hadn't killed him yet. The Flare didn't just drive you crazy; eventually it shut your brain down altogether.

He thought of the guards then. A wave of sadness and guilt crashed over him. The men were dead because Thomas needed to take a walk, like some over-privileged spoiled brat. More lives on his hands. How many more would there be?

His foot came down on a branch, broke it. The crack echoed through the night and he froze. His eyes had indeed got used to the darkness, the trees almost seeming to glow, their many branches silhouetted against the sky. Thomas didn't see anything out of the ordinary, but he was certain Randall hadn't gone far – his retreat would have made more noise. The Crank was close, probably following him.

Then Thomas remembered.

Teresa! he called out. *Teresa! Randall attacked us. He killed the guards. I don't know what to do. How can he possib—*

Tom! Her response cut him off. *Where are you? Paige says she'll send someone out. Do you still have your Launcher?*

Yeah.

Just stay there. Don't try to make it back. Someone will be there soon.

Thomas thought he heard a noise to his left, swung his weapon towards it. Saw nothing.

Tom?

Yeah, okay. I'll just keep turning in circles until I puke. Hurry. Keep talking to me.

No, he replied. *I need to stay focused. I know he's close.*

Fine, but call out to me the second something happens.

I will.

The dark forest loomed over him, seeming almost to float, the trees uprooted from the ground, stretching out. His senses started to play tricks on him. He kept seeing something out of the corner of his eye, kept thinking his own breaths were someone else's. Finally he broke.

'Randall!' he yelled. 'They're coming! They know we're here!'

No response. He didn't know why he'd called out – Randall had no more capacity to reason than one of the trees surrounding him. His eyes had shown him past the Gone like no other Crank Thomas had ever seen.

'I miss the tasty treats.'

Thomas sucked in a breath. Randall spoke quietly, yet his words seemed to boom through the air. Thomas swung left, then right, then turned in a complete circle, his weapon held out before him.

'Randall!' he screamed.

Then something hit him, forcing the air from his lungs. It was on top of him, pressing his head and neck in a weird direction, driving pain like nails through his tendons and muscles. To protect himself he collapsed to the ground. He lost his grip on the Launcher. The strap dug into his neck as he reached for whatever had attacked him, and fingers found wet skin and greasy hair.

'Tasty,' Randall's voice whispered directly into his ear.

Thomas screamed, twisting his body, struggling to get out from under the monster pinning him down. An arm slipped around his face, covering his mouth in the crook of an elbow. It smelled of sweat and rot; Thomas gagged. Randall squeezed, cutting off Thomas's air. He managed to get his mouth open, bite down with all the might of his jaws. An acrid, sour taste filled his mouth.

Randall roared, a horrible sound that was far from human. He loosened his grip just enough that Thomas could twist out of the man's hold, throwing elbows wildly, connecting with a couple. The Crank staggered backwards as Thomas struggled to his feet, panic transformed to sheer adrenaline. He grappled for his Launcher, which had flipped all the way onto his back. He grabbed it, slung it around to the front of his body, got it in position.

He almost had it when the Crank charged him, scuttling across the leafy ground like a monstrous spider, leaping at the last second to crash into Thomas's chest. It slammed the hard edge of the Launcher into his sternum, knocking the wind from his lungs again, and he fell to the ground, the Crank on top of him. Randall started pounding on Thomas with both fists like some rampaging gorilla, shrieking with every punch.

Thomas couldn't fight back against the wild creature attacking him. He thought of Chuck and Teresa and Alby and Minho and Newt. If he died now, he'd never have the chance to save them.

He forced himself to relax and focus. He closed his eyes and gathered his strength. As Thomas stilled, the blows had slowed. He took his opportunity. He lashed out with his right hand and grabbed Randall by the ear, twisted, and yanked the Crank's head to the side. Randall lost his balance just enough that

Thomas could thrust his chest out and kick him away. He jumped to his feet, backed up as he fumbled for his Launcher, got it, found the trigger, pressed it.

The static sound of its charge filled the forest as Randall ran at him once again. But a grenade hit the Crank's chest, throwing him to the ground, and tendrils of white heat danced across his body as he convulsed on the ground, shrieking in agony.

Thomas ran to him, held up his Launcher like a club. He slammed it down into the face of the man who'd once been Randall. A sickening crunch cut off the Crank's inhuman yells. Now the thing's body twitched in a different way, as if its internal communication system had shorted out.

Thomas, heaving every breath, lifted his Launcher one more time and brought it down with all the strength left in him.

This time, the Crank went completely still.

Teresa found him kneeling next to the dead body, staring down at it, transfixed. A man he'd once known, a man he'd never really liked. Never liked at all, actually. But no one deserved an ending like that. No one.

She practically had to carry him to the transport. He was as dazed mentally as physically. Spent in every way. He planned to sleep for a week.

Teresa, he said with his mind on the way back to the complex.

Yeah?

After a long pause, he finally said it.

They'll never find a cure.

60

231.12.13 | 6:11 A.M.

Thomas woke up before his alarm went off. He didn't want to wake Teresa before she got a full night's rest, so he forced himself to wait. He inspected his body, gingerly touching each bandaged spot in turn, wincing as he did. Time ticked by at a snail's pace.

He'd given himself a full day to recover, gather his thoughts, and make a precise plan to convince Teresa. And with every passing minute, his resolve had strengthened.

The kicker had come in a conversation he'd overheard in the infirmary yesterday. Something about 'bulb creatures.' Thomas didn't hear much, but he was pretty sure it had something to do with the weird, glowing vats filled with veiny limbs and tumorous growths he and Newt had seen in the R&D lab. Creepy as hell.

Yet more evidence of what he already knew – WICKED would never stop.

Finally his patience ran out.

Are you awake? he asked Teresa.

Only three or four seconds went by.

Yeah, she said. No rebuke for waking her up, which was a good start.

Meet me at breakfast the second the cafeteria opens. Sit close, whispers only. He didn't know how much WICKED could follow their telepathy and he wanted to make sure they didn't overhear this conversation.

Okay. She was a woman of few words this morning – just fine by him.

Awesome. See you soon. He rolled out of bed and limped to the shower.

In the cafeteria, Thomas had found a quiet spot away from the few workers and subjects eating. He picked at his food as he waited for Teresa. He drank three glasses of water. He finally pushed his tray away, folded and unfolded his arms, shifted in his seat. When she showed up, she skipped the food line altogether and came to sit next to him.

What's up? she asked his mind.

'No,' he spoke quietly. 'Just talk normal.'

They sat shoulder to shoulder, Thomas's plate of eggs and bacon resting on the table in front of them. He had to get these plans off his chest. He leaned in close to Teresa and started whispering.

'Keep an open mind, okay? Hear me out, too, before you start arguing.'

She looked up at him, searching for a hint of what he was going to say. She nodded and looked back down at his food.

'Sorry, this is just really important to me. So . . . Look, I'm at the end of my rope, Teresa. The absolute end. The Purge, the lies, the cruelty in the maze. And I've heard enough things over the last few days to figure out that WICKED has plans for an entirely new phase of trials – in the Scorch – and who knows what else. Did you know about any of this?'

Teresa shook her head adamantly, looking genuinely

horrified. 'I mean, I suspected something – and then the expedition to the Scorch, those barracks they built, the Flat Trans. But they haven't shared anything with me.' She paused, shaking her head again. 'Are you sure about what you heard?'

'Totally.'

'Sometimes they really do make it hard to believe in them, don't they?'

Her reaction made Thomas feel like he'd cleared the first hurdle.

'Exactly,' he said. 'I *went* to the Scorch. It's horrible. And I've seen those bulby things they created in R&D. They're like something straight out of a nightmare. It's gotta stop, Teresa. All of this has to *stop*. I mean it.'

She didn't respond at first, her emotions impossible to read. But when she finally spoke, her words had a slight tremor to them.

'What could we do, Tom? WICKED is too big. And whatever they're doing, at least they have some justification for it.'

'The cure?' Thomas scoffed. 'It's never going to happen. I just don't believe in it. After all this time and all this work, they don't even have a preliminary treatment, no trial runs of drugs, nothing. All they do is get more vicious with their Variables, chasing this ridiculous blueprint they're always spouting about.'

'Do you really think they're sending them to the Scorch?' she asked.

'Yes. Don't you?'

She sighed. 'I guess I do.'

'Those are our *friends*, Teresa. Think back to the good times we had together. My God, if nothing else, think of them throwing Chuck into the Scorch, much less to the wolves in that Crank city.'

That seemed to really get her. Her eyes moistened.

'Even so,' she said. 'What could we *possibly* do? The two of us against the mighty empire and all their guards and all their weapons?'

And now it was time to tell her. He gathered his courage and went for it.

'This is the part you need to hear me out on. First, we convince Dr Paige to send us into the Maze. We'll convince her they need to shake things up a bit. But we make sure they send us in with our memories intact. That's the key. We tell them they should let us do some serious analysis from the inside and we can report back. The Psychs would think Christmas had come again – imagine all the Variable possibilities. We can throw all our enthusiasm into it, really convince them we want this. Maybe we even suggest we go in for one month, then come back out. It doesn't matter what we say, we just need to get inserted.'

'And then what?' she asked. At least she hadn't outright rejected the idea.

'We make preparations before we go in. We get keys to one of the weapons rooms, or hide weapons near the Maze exit. We do some research on Grievers, figure out a way to shut them down at the right time. Map out the closest town we can escape to once we get everyone out. Then, once we're in, we'll spend a few days convincing the Gladers what's going to happen, make a plan, and go for it.'

'You make it sound so easy,' she replied. 'For one thing, they'll be observing our every move and listening to everything we say.'

'Then we'll do a lot of whispering. A lot of talking in the dark, avoid beetle blades, whatever. They trust us, and that'll be the biggest thing we have going for us.'

Teresa leaned even closer, found his ear. Her breath warmed his skin. 'You really think we can just go into the Maze and grab the Gladers and march out of there? Without killing a bunch of people? Getting killed ourselves?'

He exhaled. 'I know it's outrageous. But it's worse to sit back and let this continue without trying to stop it.'

She sighed but didn't say anything.

'Teresa, I'm pouring my soul out to you. It's probably Chuck who's finally pushed me over the edge. I love that kid so much. I can't . . . I just can't let WICKED keep hurting him. Not to mention the others. I can't. Please, please say you're with me on this.'

He'd never talked to her this way before. He'd laid it all out there.

She looked at him, her eyes weary. 'You really mean it, don't you?'

'Absolutely. Saying it out loud only makes me feel more sure.'

She was quiet then. Quiet for a very long time.

Finally she stood up. 'Give me twenty-four hours to think about it, okay?' And then she walked away, leaving a very anxious friend behind.

In the end, she only needed about fourteen hours.

Thomas had spent the day making use of his free time. In between his check-ups, tests, and observation time, he scoured his research tablet for any information on Grievers in the files unprotected by passwords. Stopping the creatures would be a huge factor if they were going to escape. There wasn't much, but he did find a schematics copy of its biomechanical make-up embedded in a huge collection of miscellaneous information dated years earlier.

He was in bed, studying the schematics for potential weaknesses, when Teresa called to him telepathically.

Okay, she said. *I'm in.*

He almost jumped out of his bed with excitement. *Really? You're on board?*

For you. For Chuck. For our friends. I'll help you.

Awesome. That's awesome. Now we just need to convince Dr Paige.

Don't worry about her. I actually think she'll love the idea of inserting us in Group A and Aris and Rachel in Group B. Let me

take care of that part.
    Really?
    Really. I'll meet with her first thing tomorrow.

Thomas stood in the observation room, watching a close feed of Newt as he ate his dinner by the big tall pole in the Glade. For some reason, he was alone. Maybe he just needed some time to himself. Maybe Chuck had talked his ear off all day – par for the course. But he sat there, taking his bites, chewing, swallowing, staring off at nothing in particular, deep in thought.

    Thomas thought of Newt's sister, Lizzy, somewhere off in Group B's maze. Wouldn't that be a thing, to save both of them? 'I'm coming for you, Newt,' Thomas whispered, so softly that no one could possibly hear him. 'I'm coming for every last one of you.'

The next day, he got the official word.

    Dr Paige had approved the insertion of the Elites into the Maze Trials.

61

Dr Paige stood at the head of the table, with Thomas and Teresa sitting on one side, Aris and Rachel on the other. A few Psychs and technicians sat farther down, staying mostly quiet. But every once in a while, Dr Paige shot them a glance for confirmation of what she was saying.

The plans for the Elites' insertion had been laid out, and they were going over some final details. Thomas fought to maintain patience, to play along as if he had devoted his heart and soul to the things that were planned for them. But it was his intent – and serious hope – that none of it would ever happen.

'You can look up here,' Dr Paige said, gesturing to a screen on the wall behind her, where a long chart full of information had been projected, 'and see just how many new and unique Variables our Psychs have developed surrounding this insertion. We've taken it far beyond your simple suggestions, Teresa. We see this as a golden opportunity – a catalyst, if you will – to stimulate many killzone patterns that we've never been able to measure before.'

Thomas had been squinting at the display, trying to get a read on any of the individual line items But the words were too small. And then, at a signal from Dr Paige, the screen went blank again.

She continued. 'Even the first twenty-four to forty-eight hours will bring events to the Glade that have never been seen before. Events that will significantly disrupt what has become a routine there and spur many new emotions and thoughts. Subjects arriving on consecutive days, a member of the opposite sex arriving for the first time – we're just really encouraged by the possibilities. So I have to give a lot of credit to Teresa for this idea.' Her smile beamed down on Thomas's friend.

As for him, he didn't care one whit that she was taking all the credit. The plan might have never worked if Thomas had approached them. None of it mattered anyway. As much as he'd once loved Dr Ava Paige, he hoped that soon he'd never have to see her again. Or anyone or anything related to WICKED.

He looked at Aris, and then Rachel, both of whom seemed less than happy. They hadn't spoken much lately, and he and Teresa were still trying to decide whether to bring them in on the plan. Things were complicated enough, with too many risks. But he also couldn't imagine *not* telling them. Either way, he fully intended to save Group B along with his own friends in Group A.

'Thomas?'

He snapped back to attention and realized that Dr Paige – along with everyone else – was staring at him.

'Sorry,' he said, shifting in his seat. 'I kind of spaced out there. Did I miss something?'

She looked back at him sternly. 'I asked if you had an opinion on the memory swipe.'

He felt a prickle of sweat, an uncomfortable warmth. 'What do you mean?'

'It's the one aspect of this insertion that still gives me pause.

Every subject before you has had their memories removed, and it worries me to break the cycle of consistency. I wanted to know your opinion on the matter.'

He pulled himself together, collected his wits. This could be the most important moment of his life. 'I can understand that, but Teresa and I have talked about this a lot.' Including her could only strengthen his argument. 'We think it will just add to the things you're speaking about, all these new opportunities. Having someone on the inside, up front and close, reporting back to you here. That's a perspective we've never had. I see it as the next level in the countless observations I've made over the last couple of years.'

'That's a good point,' Dr Paige replied. 'Is this really that much different?'

He fought for composure. 'But it's not just from that side of things. Even more importantly, think of the analysis you can do on me, on Teresa, on Aris and Rachel. Don't forget that we're subjects, too. Studying our patterns, *with* memories instead of without, inside the Glade and the Maze, is something you've never been able to do before.'

Dr Paige nodded as he spoke, but not in a way that necessarily meant she agreed.

'There are a lot of other ways I think it can be valuable, but those are the most important.' He decided to end it right there instead of rambling on and hoped his last comment would work to make her think there actually was a lot of value left unsaid.

'Well spoken, Thomas,' Dr Paige said. 'You'll be relieved to know that most of us in this room agree with you.' She smiled, almost as if the question had been a test.

Good job, Teresa said to him.

Thanks, he replied. *I've got some serious sweaty armpits going on right now.*

The meeting went on for at least another hour. But in the end, Thomas thought, it couldn't have gone any better. The plans were finalized and approved.

Thomas would go into the maze first. The next day, Teresa would follow. Both of them with their memories intact. Rachel and Aris would follow the same pattern over in the Group B Maze. Thomas had got everything he wanted.

And now there was work to do.

62

231.12.31 | 11:24 P.M.

Finally the time had come.

Thomas had exhausted himself preparing for it.

He knew as much about Grievers as possible, including their weaknesses and power sources. If he combined that with what he knew from building the Maze and how the Griever hatch worked, he felt good about the possibility of facing one down and coming out alive. With Teresa's help, he'd got the codes to a weapons cache very close to the entrance to the Maze, from which they and the Gladers would escape. They'd found an Alaskan town where they could seek asylum, only thirty miles from the WICKED complex. Aris and Rachel did know about the plan, but they wouldn't try anything until Thomas and Teresa came to their maze to get them. Everything had fallen into place. Mainly there was the waiting. Nothing could happen until they were in the Maze and could gather supporters among their old friends.

And that time had finally come.

Thomas sat on his bed, leaning back against the headboard.

Teresa sat in the desk chair, which she'd pulled up next to the bed. She leaned towards him, her face only a couple of feet away. They'd been talking for hours, ever since getting back from dinner. It was the first time they'd done something like this since before the Purge.

'You swear you're not going to chicken out?' Thomas asked. 'And you won't let them change their minds about the Swipe?'

'You just broke our streak, dummy.'

They'd sworn not to talk about the escape plan, at least for one night. And they'd mostly succeeded. Remembering their childhoods, laughing about some of the times they'd had with Newt and everyone else, philosophizing about the world's future. They even talked about space, about science, about history. Weird things like famous conspiracy theories. The big wars. What life had once been like. They talked and talked and talked.

Until Thomas had ruined it and brought them back to reality.

'Yeah, I know,' he said. 'I ran out of stuff.'

'Well, I swear on the life of everyone I've ever loved that I'll be in the Glade, with you, twenty-four hours after you're inserted, just like we drew it up – memories intact. Okay? I promise.'

'Pinky promise?'

She sat back. 'Now hold on. That's some serious stuff right there.'

He held out his pinky. She wrapped her own around it and they shook.

'Phew,' he said. '*Now* I feel better.'

She still hadn't let go of his finger. Their hands had come down to rest on the mattress of the bed. 'Sometimes I forget what a sweet dork you can be. I wish you'd let this side of you come out more.'

'My sweet dork side? I didn't know I had such a thing. But I guess I'll take that as a compliment?'

'*Yes*, you should take it as a compliment.' She let go but moved the chair up until she was right next to him. 'I know I've been a dud for months now.'

'Nah,' Thomas replied, but even he couldn't make it very convincing.

She laughed. 'It's just . . . there's still a part of me that thinks a cure is possible. Don't you feel that way? At least a little?'

'Yeah, of course I do.' He felt a little ashamed at the rebuke. 'But there has to be another way. All I know is that if they have to achieve it by torturing my friends, then it's not right.'

'And things seem like they'll only get worse,' she said.

Thomas suddenly felt a swell of elation. He sat up, swinging his legs over the side of the bed to rest his feet on the floor. He faced her, his left leg pressed against hers.

'It's weird,' he said. 'In a way, I'm excited. I think it's more like relief. I've got so sick of the waiting, the waiting, the waiting. Now it's finally here, past the point of no return. All I can do now is . . . get into the Glade and make something happen. Sound nuts?'

'Nope. I feel the same way.' She smiled, then moved to actually sit next to him on the bed. She pulled him into a hug, resting her head on his shoulder. 'You mean the world to me,' she said.

Everything hit Thomas at once. A surge of emotion filled his chest and burned there like a thousand flames. All the years, all the memories, all the hard times and all the good. He broke into a sob, releasing all of it, his body trembling. She held him tighter, crying herself. And there they sat, for several minutes, letting it all out. Though laden with sadness, it also felt good. Exhilarating. He burned with something closer to joy than he'd ever felt before.

'Tell me that we'll survive this,' he said when he could finally get the words out. 'Tell me that we'll get in there, and get our friends out.'

'We will survive,' she replied. She brought up her hands and held his face, looking into his eyes. 'I promise.'

He nodded, not sure he could say one more thing. They wrapped themselves up in each other's arms and pulled their feet up onto the bed, lying down together. They stayed that way through the night, until morning came and the Maze beckoned.

63

232.1.1 | 9:03 A.M.

'Everything feeling okay?' Dr Paige asked. 'Normal? Strong?'

Thomas sat in a chair in one of the medical rooms, having just finished a medical rundown. Paige had just walked in to see him one last time. She held a steaming cup of coffee or tea.

'Yeah, feels great.' The truth was that he'd never been so nervous. In a matter of hours he'd be with the Gladers. It seemed impossible. 'A little jittery, to be honest.'

'That's why I brought you this.' She handed him the cup.

He took it, sniffed it. It smelled like berries. 'What is it?'

'A special brew of tea I made up just for you. It will calm your nerves a bit.'

'Thanks.' He took a slow, careful sip. 'Man, that's good.' He took another sip, decided to try his hand at acting, throw her off the scent of his plans. 'So, how's everything on your end? You feel good about the plan?'

'You're a part of this now, Thomas. We can't share much information with you any more. For these things to work, we do need a little separation.'

'But I'll be reporting back to you.'

'I know. But like you said previously, we need to remember that you are a subject in all of this. We can taint the results if we say too much.'

He'd guzzled half the tea already, the burn worth the warmth he felt all over. Tingly. Floaty. 'Can't you just drop me one hint? Throw me a bone? Is there some big finale planned for the Maze Trials?' He hoped his naive enthusiasm showed that he didn't have anything malicious planned.

'You know all the details you need to know,' she replied, somewhat curtly.

'You're going to miss me, right?' he asked.

He thought she'd smile, but it never came.

'Don't fight it, Thomas. Everything will be all right in the end.'

'What do you mean?' His head was spinning now.

'It's your incalculable ability to trust others that has always touched me,' she said, looking sadly into his eyes. Her face had started to blur. 'And I'm sorry to have taken advantage of it so many times. I've just always done what needed to be done.' She stood up, but he saw three or four of her now, warping, expanding, retracting.

'What do you . . .' he tried to say. His mouth wouldn't work properly.

'It was me, Thomas. I know you won't remember this, but I want to say the words to you anyway. Explain myself. It was me who infected Chancellor Anderson and his senior staff. They wanted to end things after the Maze Trials. They wanted to give up. And I could never allow that, could I? What we're trying to achieve is much too important.'

'What . . .' he tried again, but it was pointless now. He was already slouching in his chair, unable to sit straight. The cup dropped from his hands and shattered on the floor. He felt as if candy floss had filled his ears.

'You were always my favourite,' Dr Paige said. He sensed her attention move to someone else. 'Let's get him prepped.'

Betrayed.

Thomas lay flat on an operating bed, fading, fading, unable to move, looking up at the odd device that looked like a mask from some demented hell of robotic creatures. The device that would trigger his Swipe mechanism, facilitate memory loss. He could feel his consciousness fading, knew he'd be totally out of it soon. Then they'd lower the mask and the process would begin. His life as he knew it had only minutes, maybe even seconds remaining. The panic was a lightning storm exploding in fiery bursts throughout his body and mind.

Yet he couldn't move.

Soon the memories that haunted him so much, made him so sad, would be gone.

He didn't want them gone. WICKED had tricked him. Of course they'd tricked him. Hadn't he known this was who they were all along? Wasn't that why he'd planned to rebel in the first place? Because these people were nothing but manipulative, single-minded monsters? And Dr Paige had confirmed it all.

If only he could see Teresa one last time. His last words to her – 'See you tomorrow' – they hurt so much. Yes, it was true. They *would* be reunited the next day, but their memories would be gone. He wouldn't even recognize her.

WICKED had played them both to the very end.

Unbearable anguish filled him.

Then the relief of sleep swept in and took him away.

He opened his eyes inside what he knew to be a dream. He lay on a dazzling, unworldly bright-green field, grass swaying in the soft breeze around him. A brilliant blue sky shone above, broken by scattered, fluffy clouds that seemed close enough to touch. Supposedly every person who experienced the Swipe did so in his or her own unique way. And here he was, memories still intact, immersed in beauty.

Once again, panic exploded inside him.

But he couldn't move. Couldn't scream. He tried to call out to Teresa, but she didn't exist here.

A large bubble entered his field of vision from the right, just a few feet away. It jiggled and shimmered with an oily sheen, distorting the world behind it as it floated even closer, coming to a stop directly above him. Inside the bubble, an image appeared, a moving image. A complex, three-dimensional image. Even though his senses clearly told him that the image was inside a bubble, it also seemed to consume him, surround him. The whole of it relaxed him, as if opiate drugs had been pumped into his veins.

He was a boy. Sitting on a couch, his dad beside him, an open book shared between their laps. His dad's lips moved, his eyes lit up with mock drama, reading the story that obviously enraptured the very young version of Thomas. A small spark of joy flashed in his chest. He didn't want it to end. *No*, he thought. *Please don't take this away. I'll do anything. Please don't do this to me.*

The bubble popped.

Tiny drops of liquid sprayed outward, magically hovering in the air, catching light in little winks that made Thomas squint. Confusion made him blink. What had he just seen? Something about his dad. Something about a book. It was fuzzy, but still there. He tried to recall it but stopped when another balloon appeared.

Again, it hovered, colours shimmering across its surface, distorting the clouds beyond. It came to rest directly above him again. A moving image appeared, simultaneously small yet filling his entire world at the same time.

He walked along a street, his hand tiny in his mother's. Leaves blew across the pavement. It was as if he were there. The world had already been devastated by sun flares, and yet little trips outside were okay now. He looked forward to each moment out in the elements, despite the sadness and fear he sensed in his parents' demeanour. Despite the risk of radiation even a few minutes caused. He'd been so happy at times like—

The bubble popped. More drops of liquid hung suspended in the air, joining the others. Dozens of sparkles in the sun. Thomas's confusion increased. He was still aware of the Swipe process, that these memories were being taken from him. But they'd only weakened, not disappeared. Despite the rush of sweet bliss, he raged against it, battled with his mind. He screamed silently, mentally.

More bubbles came.

More popped.

Playing tag. Swimming. Baths. Breakfasts. Dinners. Good times. Bad times. Faces. Emotions. Things Dr Paige had told him. He wanted to cry out when he saw his dad going crazy from the Flare.

That bubble popped.

More of them came, no longer one by one. They flew by in a rush, a sensory overload that numbed his seething mind. Music. Movies. Dancing. Baseball. Food. The kind he loved (pizza, hamburgers, carrots) and the kind he hated (beef stroganoff, squash, peas). Faces in the memories started to blur, the voices to slur. The bubbles came and went so fast he could hardly keep up with them. The residue of their bursts filled the entire sky above him, millions of drops of whatever liquid formed them.

He had forgotten what he'd been so upset about.

A great wind came. A brutal, churning wind. It spun the drops in a grand circle, a cyclone of dew twisting above him. Bubbles popped before they even reached him now, the remnants of their predecessors ripping through them, obliterating them before Thomas could even experience their memories. All of it churned above him, spinning faster and faster. Soon everything blurred together, a writhing tornado of grey mist, devoid of all colour.

Thomas felt as if he were a flower wilting from lack of sun. He'd never felt such confusion, such . . . emptiness. The world spun above him. And he grew ever emptier, his mind being sucked away, lost in the towering twister *stealing* him. Stealing what *made* him *him*.

Gone.

It was all gone.

He closed his eyes. He wept without weeping. A deep blackness consumed his mind and body. Time stretched before him like an endless sea, no horizon ever to come. Nothing ahead, everything left behind.

Hours later, he opened his eyes.

He was awake.

He was standing.

Surrounded by cold darkness and stale, dusty air.

EPILOGUE

WICKED Memorandum, Date 232.1.1, Time 3:12
TO: Leadership Council
FROM: Chancellor Ava Paige
RE: Reasons

I want to briefly thank everyone on the
WICKED staff. It's been ten years, but our
pre-trials are finally over. You've taught
our Elite subjects well, and at this point
we are ready to begin the final days of
the Maze Trials - what we've always known
to be most important.

Thomas and Rachel have been fully prepared.
Everything leading up to this moment,
their insertion into the mazes, would not
have been possible without each and every
one of you. It took a lot of long hours
and meticulous planning and care to get us
where we are today. Thank you for the hard

work you've so tirelessly accomplished over the last decade, and especially over the last two years.

We never knew who the final candidates would be, but today we are happy to celebrate Teresa and Aris and their loyalties to our purpose here. Phase Two is imminent, and I believe our future is brighter than ever.

Again, thank you.

WICKED Memorandum, Date 232.1.1, Time 2:01
TO: All Staff
FROM: Teresa Agnes
RE: A last word

I've just said goodbye to Thomas, and he's
now in the Glade, safe and sound. Tomorrow,
it will be my turn. Dr Paige has asked me
to send a final note to everyone, sharing
my thoughts. I'm more than happy to do so.

I feel good about the plan to leave my and
Aris's memories intact. You need someone
in each group with whom you can communicate
and plan during the phases of the Trials.
Aris and I can also coordinate throughout.

I promise to keep my role a secret. I will
act the part of their true equal to the
best of my abilities, and I will not
interfere with the decisions they make
unless you instruct me to do so.

I've been with WICKED for well over ten
years, the vast majority of my life. I
barely have any memories of my time
before. Most people in the world would
consider me lucky to have lived a life of
comfort — I've had clean clothes, warmth,
safety, food. I'm thankful for what WICKED
has provided. I'm thankful for the friends
I've made, friends who are the finest
people in the world. I'd never do these
things unless I fully believed that one
day they'll understand and thank me. I'm

grateful for what I've learned, for the
growth I've had, for the many experiences
that have shaped who I am. I'm thankful
to be alive.

I also want to make it clear that I
believe in what WICKED is doing.

I plan to write three words on my arm
before entering the Box, hoping that its
simple message will plant a seed in the
Gladers who see it. To remind them, even
subconsciously, what it is we fight for.
It's a phrase I saw on a cold, dark night
long ago, the Crank pits seething behind
me. It's a phrase that I believe with all
my heart, despite the horrors.

I think you know what it is.

ACKNOWLEDGEMENTS

I always repeat myself, for good reason. The following people have made my life what it is, and there's no possible way I could ever repay them or do them justice with a simple thank you. Hopefully, to no one else's offence, I'm only going to list a few to truly show them what they mean to me and my career.

Krista Marino, my editor. This book was tough and we fought a little. And like the best of siblings, we came out of it loving each other more than ever. Side note: she's always right.

Michael Bourret, my agent. It's impossible to describe just how amazing it is to have an agent who also feels like your best friend. Cliché or not, he's the island in the middle of a raging, violent storm.

Lauren Abramo, my international agent. This is the woman you can thank if you read this in a language other than English. It's through her tireless efforts that we're now in over forty languages. Plus, she loves soccer/football, which makes her a perfect human.

Kathy Dunn, my publicist. As you can imagine, life got a little crazy lately. And Kathy is the one who made sure I didn't go insane or get overwhelmed. It's a rare thing when a publicist cares more about you as a person than your success as an author.

Last, and most, my family: Lynette, Wesley, Bryson, Kayla, and Dallin. The last few years taught me to appreciate them on a level I never understood before. I love them more than I could ever describe, no matter how many thesauruses you threw at me.

And you, the reader. I dedicated the book to you. And I meant it. Thank you.

How the Elephant got his Trunk

by Rudyard Kipling

Retold by Anna Milbourne

Illustrated by John Joven

Reading consultant: Alison Kelly

Long ago, elephants
had short noses.

This story tells how
their noses became long.

Baby Elephant
was always asking
questions.

What does Crocodile
eat for dinner?

Elephant went to see
his friend Snake.

Elephant went down
to the river to see
Crocodile.

Crocodile smiled.

"I eat...

ELEPHANTS!"

Crocodile caught
Elephant by the nose.

SNAP!

Crocodile pulled...

Elephant pulled.

Snake wound himself around Elephant and pulled too.

At last, Crocodile
let go.

Elephant's nose had
stretched.

"Don't worry," said
Snake. "It might
be useful."

19

It was! Elephant could squirt water...

brush flies away...

and pick fruit from
high trees.

21

So all the other elephants
went to see Crocodile...

and they got
long noses too!

25

PUZZLES

Puzzle 1

Put the story in order.

A

B

C

D

E

Puzzle 2

Spot five differences between the two pictures.

Puzzle 3

True or False? With his trunk Elephant could...

squirt ink.

brush his hair.

pick fruit.

Answers to puzzles

Puzzle 1

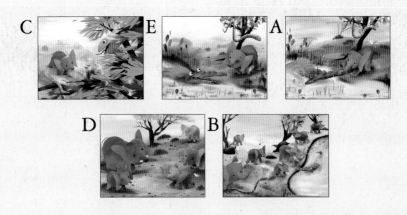

Puzzle 2

Puzzle 3

Elephant could...

...squirt ink.
False
He could
squirt water.

...brush his hair.
False
He could brush
flies away.

...pick fruit.
True

About the story

This story is from the book *Just So Stories* by Rudyard Kipling, which tells how animals came to be the way they are.

Designed by Sam Whibley
Series designer: Russell Punter
Series editor: Lesley Sims

First published in 2015 by Usborne Publishing Ltd., Usborne House, 83-85 Saffron Hill, London EC1N 8RT, England. www.usborne.com
Copyright © 2015 Usborne Publishing Ltd.